Good Gone Bad
A Romantic Suspense Novel

Susan Mills Wilson

Code 3 Publications
Copyright © 2013 Susan Mills Wilson
All rights reserved.
ISBN:10-0991169107
ISBN-13: 978-0-9911691-0-8

To Ron, the love of my life.

CHAPTER ONE

Shrouded in darkness, the man's apartment appeared deserted. Jay Stiles could have sworn he saw lights from at least one window when he drove up. He stepped up to the door to knock. It was unlatched and creaked open into an abyss of blackness. Like stone, a stillness and hush seemed solid, unyielding. It spooked him, but he walked in.

Out of nowhere, someone or something slammed into him, pinning him to the wall. He was put in a headlock, his assailant's hot breath on his neck, his chin forced upwards so that his eyes saw nothing more than a dark ceiling. Something cold and metallic jabbed his jaw. The barrel of a gun.

Then, it was over. He was pushed away. The light switch flicked on. Still stunned, his eyes locked onto ones that were gray and suspicious, but familiar. The man looked like a Marlboro cowboy and reeked of cigarettes from his two pack-a-day habit.

"Jesus, Streaker! Who in the hell were you expecting?"

"Well, it wasn't you."

"Apparently not."

If a person were to ever inquire about Wayne Johnson, all they'd get would be a blank stare. To everyone who knew him, he was simply Streaker. He had dull eyes that were nothing more than slits etched into a face with lines like granite and texture like leather. It was more a consequence of lifestyle than weathered by wind and sun. He kept his eyes cast downward, staring a hole in the dingy carpet.

Jay figured an apology would not come. From their six-year relationship, he knew the former cop was always on edge. Scars from two gunshot wounds and a knife slashing explained why. But Jay didn't know him back then or the details of his brush with death. He made Streaker's acquaintance when he had hired him as a private investigator to unravel a tangle of lies by a potential investor in a real estate deal. His findings saved Jay from a bad deal that would have cost him thousands.

Streaker walked into the center of the room and plopped down in front of the 60-inch flat screen television set that was turned off. He sat cross-legged in faded jeans and bare feet. As he stretched forward, he retrieved his pack of cigarettes, resting on top of a beer can. He tapped one out and lit it.

Once his nerves had settled, Jay made himself comfortable in a plush faux-leather recliner. He drew his leg up so that his ankle rested on his knee, then tapped the side of his Bruno Magli loafers, polished to a high gloss.

"Someone must be after you, Streak," Jay said. "Are you screwing somebody's wife again? Or do you owe somebody money?"

"If it's any of your business, a combination of the two."

"So, that's what that shit was about. Damn, Streak, will you ever learn?"

"Come here to lecture me, Goldie?"

"Quit calling me that."

"Well, your blond hair is so pur-dee, Goldilocks. It drives the women wild, doesn't it?"

Jay gave him a hard stare, but let the remark go unchallenged. The joke was getting old, but if he protested too much, he felt sure the asshole would use the nickname even more.

Streaker watched a smoke ring float up and dissipate into the air. He took the last swallow of stale beer from the can and crushed it with one hand. "What brings you here so late? It's after ten," he said.

"I have a job for you. Serious money. Cash."

"How much?"

"Ten grand."

Streaker gave a low whistle. "No shit. What do I have to do for that?"

"Help me dispose of a body and cover my tracks."

With one brow raised, Streaker said, "You're going to whack someone?"

"I don't have any other choice."

"You always have a choice, Jay."

"Not this time." He shook his head and frowned. "It's the only solution I can think of to make the problem go away. Someone wants to destroy my life, my career. I'll lose everything and I'm not going to let that happen."

"Jay, you ever iced anyone? Trust me, you don't wanna go down that road. And you know damn well, *I* ain't gonna do a murder for hire. You better think long and hard about this."

"Believe me, I have. I know what I'm doing. It'll look like suicide. No one will suspect murder. The guy's life is falling apart. He's involved in a bitter divorce and his girlfriend just left him. Yeah, no one will be surprised if he did himself in. Trust me. I've devised the perfect plan. It'll be quick—and clean, but I need you, man."

CHAPTER TWO

A change of scenery would do him good, Matt Garrison thought when he pulled his Mustang into a designated parking space for guests at the Hyatt where he'd made a reservation. The 250 miles between Savannah and Charlotte would put a distance between his lousy job and a broken heart.

He reached the downtown area of Charlotte at the height of the five o'clock rush hour. After he checked in and carried his luggage up to his room, he showered and changed into clean clothes, a new pair of khakis and a black polo. Thirty minutes later, he found that a leisurely stroll was a welcomed relief from his long, tedious drive via interstate. He walked toward the center of downtown, a place known as The Square where historical statues adorned the four street corners at Tyron and Trade Streets.

A boom of thunder and overhead clouds, pregnant with moisture and about to pop, sent him into a bar called Frankie's Place to seek shelter. The interior mahogany walls were about as dark and dreary as the sky, but the soft jazz from the speakers lightened the ambiance as well as Matt's mood.

One beer later, he met a beautiful woman named Camille. At the time, he had no idea that she would change everything he knew about life, love, and loss.

Before she arrived, he chitchatted with the bartender who seemed bored and talkative with only a handful of customers to serve. The big burly guy introduced himself as Harry as he leaned over the slick glossy counter and wiped up sweat rings left by cold drinks.

He looked up at Matt and said, "So, you drove up for a job interview. From Savannah, huh? Got a buddy down there. Works at a bar on River Street. Know the area?"

"Sure. There are a lot of good bars on River Street. Is it on West River?"

"Hell if I know. He keeps telling me to come down, but you know how it is. Can't get away from this place."

"You should come down. You'd like Savannah."

"Well, maybe someday. I get some vacation next mo...Well, hello," Harry said with a big grin as he looked over Matt's shoulder.

The tall striking blond that had caught Harry's eye broke off any further conversation with Matt. She took a seat at the bar next to him and gave him a cordial smile. Just cordial, not inviting. Matt kept his distance, hoping for some sign from her that made him think he'd have a chance.

She ordered a glass of chardonnay from Harry. A special brand that sounded Italian. No doubt she was there to meet someone. Her purse on the stool beside her was a clue. But she got a phone call and apparently the man, *her man*, was not coming. Matt could tell she was upset. There were no tears, just a volley of angry words that he couldn't help but overhear. She told the caller that their relationship was officially over. She made it clear that this time she would not forgive him; she would not take him back. The poor sap was history.

When she tossed her phone onto the bar, she bumped Matt's arm. She offered an apology. When he introduced himself, she held out her hand and said she was Camille, named for her grandmother on her mother's side. Matt didn't realize he was still holding her hand until she dropped her gaze downward. He jerked his hand away.

Not smooth, Garrison. You big dope.

"So, Matt, you're named after your father, right? You're a junior or maybe you're a third generation Matt. You got Roman numerals after your name?"

"No," he laughed. "I was named for one of the disciples in the Bible."

"As in Matthew, Mark, Luke and John?" He smiled and nodded. "Is that the gospel truth?" Again, he nodded and shared a laugh. "Wow, that's heavy," she said. "Then, I should call you Matthew."

Other than the origin of their names, they divulged little information about each other. He offered to buy her another glass of wine, but she refused. Occasionally, she glanced out the window as though concerned about the impending storm. He didn't give a shit about the weather. His undivided attention was on her.

One minute she was there telling him places to see in Charlotte, and then she was gone. It had happened so fast. She just vanished. It was as if he had only dreamed her up. He closed his eyes and tried to recall every detail about her. He liked the way she twisted a long strand of blond hair around her finger while she talked. Her brown eyes were flirtatious, playful. Her full pouty lips formed a dazzling smile whenever she spoke. When she crossed her shapely legs, she tugged at the hem of her short skirt, but still there was plenty left to see. Her foot would occasionally hit against his shin, but not that he was complaining. He said something, he couldn't remember what, that made her burst into laughter. She placed her hand on his forearm. The touch, although brief, sent a tingle through the center core of his body. If it hadn't been for the storm, she would still be next to him giving him that wonderful, but strange feeling that made him want to freeze time. But before they could progress past first names, she left! *Damn it!*

"Well, what are you waiting for?" Matt snapped out of his trance and looked up. The bartender who had barked the question stared back at him. In response, Matt mumbled something incoherent that only seemed to irritate Harry more. He said, "Go after her!"

From behind the counter, Harry produced a small umbrella that he slapped down on the bar. Matt stared at it. "You heard her," Harry said. "She had to go before the rain started. She has to walk four blocks back to her car. Guess what, buddy? She didn't beat the rain. Right now, she's getting soaked. Be a gentleman, take this, and walk her to her car. Or you could just sit there like a chump." Harry tilted his head toward the door. "Get outta here."

§

Jay reached his destination, but remained behind the wheel of his Porsche. He reflected on Streaker's forewarning: *Once the gun is fired, there's no turning back.*

He scoffed at that. "I know what I'm doing," he said out loud to no one there. Then, why was his heart pounding in his chest? Why were his palms clammy?

The black clouds overhead were like an omen. A storm was as imminent as the dark deed he was about to carry out. If only there was another way. If only. But Morris brought about his own demise, he concluded. He refused to be reasonable. He seemed to enjoy the threats that Jay knew, without a doubt, he would carry out. A lawsuit, a lien against property, and an investigation into fraud and money laundering were just for starters. Only God knew what else. It all depended on how far back the prosecutor was willing to go.

Jay pulled into the parking space closest to the front door of Morris Construction Company. There were no other cars in the lot. The red and white sign with black lettering was more impressive than the building itself. It was a flat-top gray granite structure as unassuming as other businesses Jay had passed along the way. He knew Morris always parked in the back next to an outbuilding that housed building materials. The front door was locked and Jay was sure all employees were gone for the day. He tapped on the glass door and saw Morris peek out from his office window. Seconds later he appeared and turned the deadbolt lock. As Jay entered with a brown paper bag in hand, Morris stared down at it, but didn't inquire about its contents. And Jay did not bother to explain.

A clap of thunder sounded just as Jay strolled in. Morris said to him, "You're just in time. I'd given up on you. I was on my way out."

"Told you I'd come. I've got the check in my pocket." As they walked toward Morris's office, Jay said, "Man, it's going to pour outside. Glad I put the top up on my car."

Morris walked back to his desk and plopped down in his leather chair. He extended his hand, offering the visitor chair to Jay. Without delay, Jay pulled a folded check from his inside coat pocket and slapped it down in front of Morris. When he leaned over to inspect the amount, Jay said to him, "Trust me. It's all there. Full payment. All seventeen invoices."

When Jay handed over a tri-folded sheet of paper, Morris looked up with puzzlement. Jay explained, "This is a statement I want you to sign and date. It just says that I have paid you in full. I know it's silly, but my accountant insisted. So, if you'll oblige."

Morris held it in his hand, read the script, and tossed it down onto the desk. "How do I know the check is good? I'll sign this after the check clears."

"Don't be difficult, Morris. You know I'm good for it."

To Jay's relief, he scratched his signature and date and handed it back. Morris swiveled his chair around when the rain began to pound against the window behind him. A zigzag of lightning flashed white into the room. Thunder roared its anger. Already a bundle of nerves, Jay almost jumped out of his skin, but Morris displayed a calmness that seemed a permanent fixture of his persona.

Jay directed his attention to the paper bag he had carried in. He smiled as he said, "I brought a peace offering. Your favorite brand of scotch."

From the bag, Jay pulled out the bottle. He turned it so Morris could see the label. Morris accepted the gift and set it down on his desk, mumbling his thanks. As if unsure of his next move, Jay silently stared at the man behind the desk. The sound of the storm's fury and the thumping of his own heart rattled him, but he took a deep breath to calm himself. His eyes stayed on Morris as he pulled something from behind his back, beneath his coat. With disbelief, Morris stared at the .38 revolver pointed directly at him. He wheeled his chair backwards and held his hand up like a traffic cop.

"Now wait a minute, Jay. Come on now."

"You've left me no other choice. Now hand over the check or I'll pull the trigger."

With more anger than fear, Morris snatched up the check from the desk and extended his arm out toward Jay. Keeping his distance, he said, "Here, man. Take it. Now put that gun away."

"I'll put the gun away after we walk outside—together. All I asked for is a little more time. I never wanted it to come to this, my friend." He jerked the gun to the right and gestured toward the door. "Shall we? Don't mind a little rain, do you?" Jay added almost as an afterthought, "I told you that you'll get your money. I just need time."

As Morris walked toward the door with the barrel against his back, he said, "Funny thing, Stiles. The money was there. In an escrow account. Your buyers wrote checks to you for the upgrades I contracted to do. The custom cabinet work and all that other shit. All the work was completed. So, what happened to the money, Jay? You stole it, that's what. I'm not *only* going to sue you and put a lien on everyone's property, I'm also reporting you to the Real Estate Commission. There'll be an investigation. An audit. Your license will be revoked, but I guess you won't need it in prison. I know your father. A good man. And because of you, the business he built will be destroyed. You managed to do that in just five years. Congrats, man."

"Give me more time and I'll put the gun away."

"Like I told you, you've got until the end of the week. My lawyer will file the lawsuit on Friday morning if I don't have my money."

"Then, you've left me no choice."

CHAPTER THREE

After Matt left the bar, he spotted the blonde a block ahead of him. Although she had failed to outrun the storm, she took brisk steps in her high heels. Holding the umbrella over his head, he sprinted to catch up. A group of women huddled under a raincoat held high over their heads. They managed to take up the entire span of walkway and slow him down. A few steps off the curb and he managed to maneuver around them. Still, he could not catch up to the blonde. Out of frustration, he yelled out, "Camille!"

She came to a stop and looked in his direction. With her eyes trained on him, she stood very still, already soaked to the skin. The water had molded her short skirt around her thighs and revealed a beige bra beneath a sheer white blouse. Water dripped from the ends of her hair. When he reached her, he held the umbrella over her head. Her smile, more than the cold rain, sent a tingle down his spine. It was crazy, maybe kinky, but he found her even more beautiful in the disarray of bad weather.

"I tried to catch you before the storm hit," he said. "I'll walk you to your car."

"You don't have to do that. I'm fine. Really."

"Which way to your car? Straight ahead?"

With a shrug, she said, "Two blocks straight ahead. It's in the parking garage next to the high-rise condos."

"Let's go." As he held the umbrella up with his left hand, he placed his right arm behind her although he kept it suspended in air, avoiding in direct contact.

She smiled at him when she said, "Thanks for coming to my rescue although you're a little late." She looked down at her soaked clothing. "But it was a nice gesture."

"The least I could do."

"No. The least you could do would be to stay nice and dry in the bar." Again, she gave the throaty laugh that put a smile on his face.

Matt was in no hurry to get to her car. He appreciated that the shelter under the umbrella made their closeness a necessity. They walked in synchronized steps. Her body against his was fluid, soft. The sweet scent of her hair made him almost dizzy with desire. He felt like she was a dream. Too good to be true. He feared that when they reached her car, she would tell him goodbye. Then, the coldness of reality would set in.

The time came too soon. Once they entered the parking garage, he folded up the umbrella. On the cement flooring, their footsteps echoed against the concrete walls. She led him over to a silver Jeep Cherokee and fumbled in her purse for her keys.

His heart plummeted when Camille extended her hand out to shake his. "Thanks, Matthew." Again, there was a little tease in her voice. "I hope the job interview goes well. You might like Charlotte. Not that it's any better than Savannah, but it's a nice place. And we could use more Southern gentlemen who want to keep chivalry alive."

"Camille, maybe we could go somewhere for dinner." When his suggestion was met with a blank stare, he scrambled to add, "Uh, I mean, I heard your dinner plans got cancelled. Just thought maybe you would let me take you somewhere. Your choice. I don't know the city."

She regarded her soaked apparel and shook her head. "I can't go anywhere looking like this. Thanks for the offer, but I think I'll pass. Bye and thanks again."

Deflated and defeated, he took her hand in his. "Goodbye, Camille. It was nice meeting you." On a whim, he did something that surprised even himself. He leaned forward and planted a kiss on her cheek, then turned to leave. He walked by three parked cars before he heard her call his name. As he pivoted around on one foot, he saw that she was coming his way.

"I can't go into a restaurant looking like this, but I have an idea."

He raised his brow, interested in what she had to say.

§

Rain pelted against Jay and Morris the moment they stepped outside. Jay jabbed Morris in the back with the .38 and prodded him forward. When Jay ordered him to stop, Morris spun around with his arms extended out as if to say, *What now?* He appeared more agitated about standing in two inches of water than scared of the gun pointed at his chest.

"You gonna shoot me, Jay? You got your damn check back. What more do you want?"

"I want you to forgive my outstanding debt. That's what I want."

"Not gonna happen. I don't do work for free." Morris ran his hand down his face to wipe away the rain. "Jeez, you're crazy! We're talking over three hundred grand. Are you nuts?"

"Then, give me more time."

"Nope, you've had plenty of time. I file suit on Friday."

"Then, I have to kill you. I won't let you destroy everything I worked for."

"You don't have the balls to kill me."

Jay held the gun with both hands to keep it steady. His heart pounded. To Jay's amazement, Morris looked amused. The stubborn hard-ass was no more swayed by a loaded gun pointed at him than if he'd received a slap on the hand.

Jay pushed the safety off and aimed dead center for Morris chest. Morris stared back, daring him to do it. The gun had six bullets, six tries. All Jay had to do was pull the trigger. When his hands began to tremble, he hesitated, but kept the gun on its target.

Morris gave a smirk. "What are you waiting for, asshole? Like I said, you don't have the guts."

"You are wrong about that."

What happened next was like a blur, like the spinning of a roulette wheel. The cacophony of sound interrupted the drone of rain. Gunfire. Thunder. Car horn. An ambulance screaming its siren. The drop of a body into standing water. Blood that turned the water crimson as it flowed downhill on the sloped lot.

CHAPTER FOUR

I must be dreaming. Any minute now I'll wake up and the blonde will be gone. Until then, I'll let her lead me inside a high-rise building, up eight floors to a condo that she claims her brother owns. If he does, then he's got a crap load of money. She wants to drink wine and order pizza. Does it get any sweeter than this? I think not.

"We're here," Camille said as she stepped forward the minute the elevator doors opened. Matt did not move. "Matt, I said we're here."

He was jolted back by her words. "Oh, right. Sorry." She led the way down the corridor and then stopped at a door marked 803. From her purse, she withdrew a single key. She looked back at Matt and said, "My brother is away on business, so it's just you and me."

Sweet! "You sure he won't mind?"

She turned the doorknob and pushed the door open with her backside while she kept her eyes on him. "No, he won't mind."

They stepped into the foyer and then strolled into the living room. Matt regarded the furnishings of a world he knew only through business associates. He gave a low whistle. "Wow! This is something!"

"Yes, Kyle let me have free reign to do whatever I wanted. Money was no object."

"You did this?"

"Yes, I'm an interior designer. Creations by Camille."

"You're very good at what you do. This is awesome!"

"Thanks," she said. "Make yourself comfortable while I get out of these wet clothes."

Ten minutes later she padded across the plush carpet in bare feet and stood before him. He tried to say something, but his mouth wouldn't work. He just stared.

Omigod! Does she have anything on under that T-shirt?

"Kyle's favorite team."

What did she say?

Camille ran her index finger under the writing on the front of the T-shirt he assumed came from her brother's drawer. "The New York Yankees," she said. "When he lived in Manhattan, he took me to one of their games. It was so exciting to be there in Yankee Stadium. Kyle is a diehard fan."

"Your brother must do very well. I can only imagine what a place like this cost."

"Yes, he's done very well. He's a lawyer, but I wouldn't be a bit surprised if he went into politics. The guy definitely has opinions. So passionate about his views." She tilted her head back and laughed. "But we have this rule. We don't talk politics. We have better things to discuss, like how I can spend more of his money." She regarded the room. "This is a work in progress. I have more ideas."

Camille eased down onto the soft-as-butter leather sofa. She drew her leg up under her and draped her arm over the back of the sofa. With her other hand, she brushed a lock of hair off her cheek. It landed in a swirl on her shoulder. Matt sat next to her, but kept a respectable distance. He watched as she shifted to get more comfortable. The quick peek of silk panties did not escape his notice. She followed through with her suggestion of pizza. She picked up her cell phone to order for delivery. Although it had been hours since he had eaten, Matt hadn't thought about food since he met Camille.

"It should be here in twenty minutes," she said as she ended the call. "Why don't we open a bottle of wine?"

Before he could respond, she stood up and walked over to the bar. Behind the bar and over a black granite counter was a wine rack of dark wood that spanned the width of the room. Below it, wine glasses hung down from their bases.

"Matt, come help decide which one."

He figured there were at least a hundred bottles from which to choose, apparently sorted by types, and perhaps by vintage and cost as well. Reds were in one section and whites in another. Champagnes occupied the top. Camille decided on a bottle of Merlot imported from Italy. He'd never heard of the label, but to him it looked expensive. While he took the wine opener and twisted the corkscrew down, he said to her, "You seem to be very trusting."

"What do you mean?"

He pulled the cork out and filled two glasses that she set out for him. "I mean, I'm a total stranger and yet you invited me up to be alone with you."

"You're not a serial killer or rapist, are you?"

"No, but—"

She cut him off, saying, "I was thinking the same about you. *I* could be someone dangerous." He laughed at that. "No, I'm serious. I could be a femme fatale that could snap your neck in seconds. You don't know."

"You're certainly beautiful enough to qualify, but I doubt you could overpower me."

Camille took the wineglass from his grasp, clamped her hand around his wrist and pulled him away from the bar. She positioned him facing her, but standing off center, to her right.

"What are you doing? You don't have to prove anything," he said.

"Scared, Garrison? Afraid a girl might take you down?"

He saw the tease in her voice and decided to play along. With one hand flat on his shirt front, one on his arm, she kicked the back of her leg against the back of his knee while using her upper body strength for leverage and pushing him backwards. Matt's feet flew up and he tumbled to the floor, but took her down with him, locking his arms around her to soften their landing. Camille broke free of his hold. Side by side on their backs, they broke into laughter.

Camille rolled over to face him. She threaded a section of hair away from her cheek and spoke through a smile, "You fell on purpose. I know you did."

Only inches separated them. "Yeah, but I like the outcome, don't you?"

She bit down on her lower lip and smiled. He felt an urge to pull her closer and kiss her, but he didn't want to risk it too soon. There would be the perfect time later. Before he could talk himself into doing it anyway, her phone rang. Camille jumped to her feet and left him on the floor, exhaling an exasperated breath. It was the concierge downstairs saying their pizza had arrived.

Her sweet scent lingered until it was replaced by the aroma of tomato sauce and pepperoni. When it occurred to him that he should pay the delivery guy, he rushed over to her side. He gave a big tip and carried the box to the kitchen counter.

Camille set plates, napkins, and forks on a small table in the breakfast area. It offered a great view of the downtown buildings. Through the beads of rain that dotted the window, they could see an awakening of lights as darkness closed in. Camille claimed that if not for the storm, they could see the football stadium where the Carolina Panthers play. In the gray soupy mess, visibility was impossible.

Camille held up a slice of pizza and looked over at Matt. "Let me see if I've got this right. You drove up from Savannah for a job interview. You love your work, but you detest your boss. Someone recommended you for this position in Charlotte and you thought this might be your ticket out of hell. Right?"

He laughed and took a sip of wine. "I don't think I explained it quite like that, but yeah, I guess that's the short of it. Charlotte looks promising." His eyes locked on her, hoping she'd understand the implied meaning of his words.

She smiled back at him. "Yes. It has a lot to offer."

Amen to that.

"If I was the guy doing the interview, I'd hire you on the spot."

He laughed. "Is that so?"

"Yeah. I'd go with my gut feeling. And you know what my gut says about you?"

"What's that?"

"That you're hard-working, conscientious and good with people."

"And you know all that about me?" Matt raised one brow as he took a sip of wine. "Okay, then, what profession am I in? As far as I remember, I haven't said."

16

Camille took another bite of pizza and studied his face with squinted eyes. "Architect. You're an architect."

His eyes widened with an incredulous stare. "Damn, you're good."

"So, I'm right?"

"No, but I did study to be an architect. I'm a construction supervisor. I'm blue collar, not white."

She shrugged. "I was so close." The room seemed to lighten. Camille looked past Matt to the sliding glass doors that led out to the patio. She had a big smile when she said, "The rain has stopped. Come on, Matt. Let's go out on the patio and smell the clean fresh air. Don't you just love the way everything smells after a spring rain?"

CHAPTER FIVE

The smell of gunpowder and the sight of Morris's lifeless body were hard evidence of the cruel deed, but Jay felt like he was having an out-of-body experience. A river of blood flowed downhill, across the lot and into a creek. More blood than he had ever seen. The gravel under Morris's head turned scarlet in an instant. A section of his scalp was blown open, but stayed attached to the head. Pieces of brain were scattered about, landing on gravel and bare ground. Shocked by what he saw, Jay could not bring himself to look away. In disgust, he picked up the gun he had dropped to the ground and flung it as far as he could. His legs became shaky. A wave of dizziness caused him to bend over and brace his hands on his knees.

Out of nowhere headlights bounced across the lot and blinded him. When did the sky turn black? Jay wondered. It was daylight when he and Morris stepped out. A pickup truck skidded to a halt in the slick gravel. A figure bounced out and sprinted toward him. The man jabbered away in rapid-fire Spanish. The man was Manny Sanchez, a guy he knew who could use a few extra bucks and also be trusted to keep his trap shut. At least, he hoped so. When Streaker said they needed an extra hand, Jay recruited his hardworking construction foreman from the warehouse project. Speaking of Streaker, he wondered what had happened to him. Then Jay saw him, his long legs coursing across the lot from the corner of the building toward him.

As he approached, Jay walked backwards away from him. He turned to face the shrubbery that lined the back of the building. He almost tumbled forward when his foot tripped over the landscaping stones along the edge. He doubled over and vomited until there was nothing left to puke. The dry heaves came next. Beads of sweat formed on his forehead. He remained bent at the waist, his back to the two men who he knew were watching him with disgust. Suddenly, a hand grabbed his coat collar and yanked him upright, spinning him around. He was only inches from Streaker's face. He saw fire in his eyes.

"This is all on you, Goldie," Streaker said through clenched teeth. "Goddamn you! Nothing comes back to me, you hear? This is your deal! Your mess! Yeah, I'll clean it up, but I'm warning you. If you get caught, my name better not come up. If it does, then you and your little girlfriend will be dead. Understand?"

"Give me a minute, Streaker. I don't feel so good. It happened so fast."

"C'mon on, you pussy. Pull yourself together. There's no time to fall apart. This is what you wanted, isn't it? He's dead!"

"Let's go over the plan."

Streaker laughed like the devil himself. "It's simple, Goldie. A three-part plan. Step One: Kill the son of a bitch. Step Two: Dispose of the body. Step Three: Make it look like suicide. I've got it covered, dude. I do clean-up detail, remember? My specialty."

"What about the blood?"

"By morning, there won't be a trace. See it going downstream? The perfect storm," he said. "Now, let's get the body in the bag and loaded into my truck. Manny will drive it out and I'll drive Morris's truck. You, Goldie—well, you go somewhere and establish an alibi. Maybe a stiff drink will help you calm down."

§

Camille bounced over to the French doors leading out to the terrace with the enthusiasm of a little girl allowed to go out and play. She flung the doors wide and looked back at Matt with a big smile, too alluring for him to stay put. He picked up their unfinished wine and followed her outside. Indeed the rain had stopped although the air was still a fine mist. While he looked on with amusement, she stomped in every rain puddle she saw in the uneven pavers. She even used her toe to kick up water at him and then giggled.

She weaved her way between the potted plants and trees, around the wrought iron furniture with padded cushions, and over to the Jacuzzi. She stripped the vinyl cover off and looked at him with a mischievous smile. When she put her hand on her hip, the long T-shirt inched up, showing more leg.

"Wanna join me?"

Before he could process the question, she jumped in the Jacuzzi and settled into a seat molded into the fiberglass lining. She pushed a button on the side to make the water swirl around her. White foam up to her neck made it impossible for him to see below the surface. When she zeroed in on the glasses in his hand, he handed over the one with the lipstick print.

"Thanks," she said and then took a sip. "You should come in, Matt. The water feels so good."

"I don't want to get my clothes all wet. I'm fine watching you."

"You could strip," she said.

"Don't think so."

"Don't worry, I won't look." She laughed. "Yes, I will. This may shock you, but I've posed nude before."

"Are you serious?"

"Yes, for my neighbor, Tyler. He's a very talented artist. There wasn't anything perverted about it. I held a sheet in front and he painted my backside. It turned out to be a beautiful painting."

"I'd love to see it sometime," he said and meant it.

"Well, it's hanging in my boyfriend's townhouse. I'm going to demand it back."

He noted that it was the second time she had used the word boyfriend in the present tense. As he took a sip of wine, he looked over the rim of the glass to make eye contact with her. He offered a smile when he said, "You're very different from the girls I know in Savannah."

She laughed. "How's that?"

"I don't know, just different. Spontaneous."

"Is that a complaint?"

"Absolutely not. I'm just saying—"

"We only get one life. Might as well enjoy it." After another sip of wine, she said, "I'll just be in here another minute. I thought it would feel good on my aching foot. I sprained my ankle over a month ago and high heels don't help much. My doctor told me to stop wearing them, but I won't. Of course, the dang shoes are what caused me to fall in the first place."

While she enjoyed the whirlpool, Matt wandered over to the metal railing that bordered the terrace. Water dripped from the rails onto the brick pavers that lined the terrace. As he leaned forward, he saw that visibility had cleared enough for him to see a section of the stadium. He imagined on game day how the roar of the crowd could be heard from where he stood. Down below he saw little traffic and few pedestrians. The storm had kept people inside. With darkness looming, headlights were on as were the squares of light that peeked out from random windows where he could see empty desks and computers asleep.

He was so busy enjoying the view, he missed Camille's exit from the Jacuzzi. When he turned around, she stood hugging her chest while beads of water ran down her arms and legs.

"Let's go back inside. I'm getting goose bumps," she said through chattering teeth.

While she went into the bedroom to change, he reflected on how fast she did everything. Wine, pizza, Jacuzzi-dip, hell, even a little self-defense move that took him down—happily. Bam, bam, bam. Now what? he wondered. From the wine bottle they had left on the table, he poured the remaining contents, reasoning it shouldn't go to waste. As she reappeared, he held two glasses in mid-air and couldn't help his stare.

She returned wearing one of her brother's dress shirts. Since she had skipped buttoning the first three buttons, the opening fell open across her chest, exposing the swells of her breasts. If that wasn't enough to cause an electrical shock to his heart and a stirring down yonder, his eyes got a nice long drink of her sexy long legs. Her wet hair was combed straight back, tight to her scalp as if daring him to muss. Since she had applied pink lipstick, her lips looked even more vulnerable, more kissable, than when they were laying on the floor face-to-face. He had wanted desperately to kiss her at that very moment, but he was afraid of her reaction. If he had to guess, he figured she had no idea how irresistible she was, or did she? Was she just a tease? he wondered. While he stared stupefied, she led him over to the sofa where they plopped down side by side. He managed not to spill any wine and handed a glass to her.

She tapped her glass against his and said, "To life. Enjoy to the fullest."

He noted that she swallowed a pill with her wine. *Holy crap, does she do drugs?* He cleared his throat and asked, "What was that? What did you just take?"

"Vitamin D. When I went to the doctor about the foot thing, he said I was Vitamin D deficient, and suggested I take a supplement twice a day with meals. And since I forgot earlier, I guess it's okay to take it now with wine. Why not?"

In the next fifteen minutes of conversation, he thought he understood why she lived life as if to experience as much as possible as soon as possible. Her father died in his late twenties when she was a small girl. A car accident, she explained. "He was reckless. Speeding as usual and ran off the road. Died instantly. Left my mom alone with two kids. I was four, and Kyle was six. The insurance paid for the funeral, nothing else."

He swallowed hard when he noted the tears pooling in her eyes. He placed his hand over hers. When she raised her chin and shook her hair back, her demeanor changed. Her dark eyes were again playful. "So, I grew up poor. Sometimes went to bed hungry. Now, everything is okay." Her eyes regarded the room. "Just look at how well my brother has done. And I've managed to do okay myself." She turned her glass up for the last swallow. *She even drinks fast.*

"I live in the moment, Matt, which reminds me. Tomorrow I have to deal with breaking up with my boyfriend."

Matt found out that her relationship with the dude went much deeper than he thought. She told him they had been together almost a year. He had begged her to move in with him, but she refused. The breakup would not be as simple as he hoped. Apparently, she had been down that road before. Three times, to be exact and each time, she took him back.

"This time is different," she promised. "I've had it. Tired of his crap."

"Do you still love him?"

Instead of answering his question, she stood up. "I think I'll see if my clothes are dry. It's getting late, and you have a job interview tomorrow. Besides, my brother is flying in tonight. I don't think he expects to have company when he gets in."

"Camille, are you going to answer me?"

"Sorry. What was the question?"

"Do you still love him?"

"I guess a part of me will always love him."

She dressed hurriedly and then insisted they should leave. He followed her out with a sinking feeling.

This is it? We're done?

In the elevator, through the lobby, and into the parking garage, they said nothing. Something was different. *She* was different. He stood next to an aloof, quiet individual. Gone was the spontaneous, lively woman that had kept him entertained and enticed for the evening. The silence strangled what should have been an opportunity for future plans, a goodnight and not a goodbye.

At her car, his heart sank when he looked down to see her extended hand.

"Matt, it was a pleasure. I had fun."

He took her hand and said, "Me, too."

"Good luck with the interview. If the guy has any sense, he'll hire you. If you get the job, we'll celebrate. Pizza on me, okay? You have my card."

"Sure."

With her keys in her hand, she faced the car door. If only he had not asked the question about her boyfriend, he lamented. Like a shift in the wind, it seemed to change the direction of the night. At least, he could hold the door open for her so she could climb in behind the wheel. Maybe she would allow him to kiss her, he thought.

As he stood behind her, he watched as she leaned forward, pressing her forehead against the doorframe. He heard what sounded like a moan. Slowly she turned around. He grew alarmed when he saw that the color had drained from her face. Her eyes closed, and she fell against him.

"Matt, I don't feel so good. That's why I was in a hurry to leave. Something's wrong."

CHAPTER SIX

As if God had turned the faucet off, the rain stopped. It was just in time for the men to begin the chore of removing the corpse from the crime scene. It took all three to maneuver Morris's body into a heavy-duty plastic bag and into the bed of Streaker's truck. Manny pulled a canvas tarp back to reveal two shovels, a pick ax and a kerosene lantern. Once the bag was added, Streaker yanked the tarp over all the goodies and threaded rope through holes in the lining of the bed.

Jay offered little assistance. Although the color had returned to his face, he was still unsteady on his feet. His heart pounded when sirens screeched in the distance. He became paralyzed with fear as they grew closer.

"We gotta get outta here!" He tugged on Streaker's sleeve. "Someone saw us!" With eyes wide with panic, he scoured their surroundings. He was in a part of town deserted after dark. The adjacent businesses were shut tight for the night. From the back of the building where they stood, even the street was not visible. Jay considered all this and still said, "Streaker! They're coming!"

Streaker grimaced and shook his head. "Relax, Goldie. No one's coming. Fire trucks, not cops."

The sirens wailed, getting closer. The area flashed red as two trucks whizzed by, sounding their horns. The smell of smoke scented the air, but no one saw the source of the emergency.

"Probably a lightning strike, guys. No problem." Streaker pulled a pack of cigarettes from his pocket and tapped one out. He cupped his hand around the end as his lighter ignited a flame. After he exhaled a cloud of smoke, he said, "Okay, boys, let's get a move on."

"You've got the directions to the wetlands?" Jay asked. "No one will look for a body there. I guarantee it. In fact, it's off limits to everything."

"Got it, Goldie. You've already told me five times. Relax, dude." Streaker turned to Manny and tapped his arm. "We better get going. Just follow me out."

As the men started to make their way to their perspective vehicles, a sound shrilled. They stopped in their tracks and listened. Rock music. It came from the pickup, under the canvas.

"Morris's cell phone," Jay said as he lifted the canvas.

Streaker clamped his hand over Jay's arm. "What are you doing?"

"See who it is, that's all."

"Morris won't be taking any more calls, Jay. Ever."

§

Matt paced the floor at the foot of the bed where Camille lay. When she collapsed against him in the parking garage, he didn't know what to do, or where to take her. Emergency room? Back to her brother's condo? Drive her home? He didn't choose any of those options.

While she leaned into him like a ragdoll, he walked her to his hotel room, two blocks down College Street. He got some strange looks in the lobby, but so what? All he cared about was helping Camille. From the elevator to his door, he carried her in his arms. As soon as they entered the room and he set her down, she made a dash for the bathroom where she proceeded to vomit in the toilet. Finally, she emerged and complained about the room spinning. Then, before he could process what she was doing, she stripped down to her beige bikini panties and matching lacy bra. Face forward, she fell across the bed. Matt rolled her over and removed her high heels. Then, he called Dr. Scott Garrison, resident in Emergency Services at Medical University of South Carolina Hospital in Charleston. Fortunately for him, his brother took his call.

"Slow down, bro," Scott said as Matt tried to explain his emergency. "Take your time. You said this girl you're with mixed wine and codeine, right?"

"Yes. I saw her take it, but she told me it was a Vitamin D tablet. On the way to the hotel, I tried to get her to explain what was going on. I finally figured out that she thought she was taking Vitamin D, but she took the codeine by mistake. She said something earlier about a sprained ankle, so maybe it was for that. I'm freaking out, man. She's out cold on my hotel bed and I don't know what to do. Help!"

"Didn't you say she already regurgitated?"

"Yeah, as soon as we got in, she rushed to the bathroom and puked her guts out."

"That's good! Now, look at the bottle and tell me how many grams and how much alcohol she's consumed."

"Hang on." Matt rummaged through her purse and found a pill case, but no prescription bottle. "Bad news. She has this little fancy pill box with different pills in it. Everything mixed together, but no bottle. Shit! She had two glasses of wine with dinner and one at the bar earlier."

"You said she was taking codeine for a sprained ankle, so the narcotic should be a low dosage. I think she just needs to sleep it off, Matt, but if her breathing or her pulse changes or anything looks different, call 911."

Matt looked down at Camille as she hugged the pillow to her chest. With her eyes closed, she looked like a person in heavy sleep. With relief, he ran his fingers through his hair.

"Thanks, Scott. I think you're right."

"She should be okay, unless I'm wrong."

"Unless you're wrong? Now that sounds encouraging."

§

The place Jay suggested as perfect for the disposal of a body was like trying to walk while dragging a concrete block. Streaker and Manny trudged through the muck far away from the street. Their boots sank into the wet spongy soil that formed the bank of a creek. While Streaker carried a flashlight and kerosene lamp, Manny followed behind with the pick ax and shovels balanced on his shoulder. They found the area Jay mentioned, the highest elevation in the wetlands where water never pooled. But after thirty minutes of digging, the hole slowly filled with water. A second try in a different spot was no better. With each stroke and removal of earth, water seeped in.

Finally, Streaker surrendered to Mother Earth. He tossed the shovel down and removed his work gloves. "It's no use, Manny. We're losing time here. Got any ideas?"

Manny speared the dirt with his shovel. He rested his chin on his gloved hand that gripped the handle. "Yes. I know a hole already dug. All we have to do is put the body in and throw in enough dirt to cover it. Tomorrow morning tons of dirt will be dumped on top and nobody will ever know it's there."

"What are you talking about?"

"Where I work. The warehouse renovation. A ditch has been dug and a pipeline has been set in it. Tomorrow a crew is going to fill it in with dirt."

"I don't know, man."

"It's fine. We wedge the body under the pipe and put dirt around. No one will notice it. I'm in charge, so I'll make sure no one sees. And if they do, who's going to the cops? Not my guys. They're undocumented, just like me. I think Mr. Jay will be okay with this plan."

"No! We *don't* tell Mr. Jay," Streaker said. "Besides Jay and I decided on no phone contact."

"Okay," Manny agreed with a shrug. "Fine with me."

"Then, let's get busy. We still need to get to Morris's place before light." Streaker looked up at the sky and said, "The next part's easy. Manny, you like boating, don't you?"

CHAPTER SEVEN

Jay emptied the shot of bourbon in one swallow, so strong it burned the back of his throat. Still, he asked the bartender for another. He was annoyed by the incessant chatter, the meaningless chit-chat and laughter all around him. And he hated the music blasting from speakers. How was a person supposed to think with that racket? Jay was not in a party mood. He didn't even feel like flirting back at the two women eyeing him from the corner of the bar.

Yeah, he was glad that the deed was done. Morris was dead, but there was no sense of relief. What if they got caught? What if *he* got caught? He couldn't do time. Besides looking awful in an orange jumpsuit, he would be terrified every minute of every hour. Hard timers liked pretty boys like him.

As fast as his car would take him, he left Streaker and Manny to deal with the body and drove to his townhouse for a change of dry clothes. His suit, tie, and shirt were splattered with blood. He put everything in a garbage bag that he tossed into a dumpster miles from his home. Finally, he could pretend to be normal and blend in with the crowd at the bar. No one would suspect what he'd done. When they looked his way, they would see a successful businessman, not someone who had just committed a crime that carried a life sentence, or worse—*death!* North Carolina still had the death penalty, didn't they? He couldn't remember.

Sitting at the bar with his back to the door, he suddenly felt a hand on his shoulder. It made him jump. Inches from his ear, a voice said, "There you are."

Jay relaxed when he saw the familiar face. "Ernie, glad to see you."

"Sorry it took so long to get here. I was having a good ol' time spending your money at Lulu's." Before he took the stool to the left of Jay, Ernie dug in his pants pocket for something and then tossed it down on the counter. "Your credit card and a receipt. Don't be surprised when you see the amount. I bought a couple of drinks for this hot babe I met. It was worth it, though. I got her number." He proudly unfolded a cocktail napkin and held it up. "Ashley. Very cute. Had on skin tight jeans and a little top with a great view."

Ernie got the attention of the bartender in a tight T-shirt with the bar's name and logo printed across the front. His eyes stayed on her breasts as he said, "Sweetheart, I'll have whatever beer you have on tap." She didn't move until he made eye contact and smiled. Once she stepped away, he swiveled on his stool, one elbow on the bar and eyes trained on Jay. "I might have a buyer for that piece of land you've been trying to sell," he said. "There's this guy in the moving and storage business. He needs a new location to put a building with about 12,000 square footage. Wants it near the interstate."

"Great. Can you set up a meeting?"

"Already have. Unless the time isn't convenient for you."

"Any time is convenient for me."

Ernie let out a hearty laugh. "That's what I thought." The bartender set his beer down on a napkin. "Thanks, sweetheart." He turned his attention back to Jay and tapped his arm. "Now aren't you glad you made me your sales director? Told you I could do it. I just needed some time."

Why in the hell didn't you find a buyer sooner, Jay thought. If he had, then the disposal of Morris would not have been necessary. Jay wanted to grab the guy by the collar and scream at him, but he resisted the urge. After all, Ernie didn't know shit about his troubles, only that he was anxious to sell.

"This calls for a toast," Jay said as he clinked his shot glass against Ernie's mug.

§

Step Two was complete. The body was buried. However, Streaker worried that in the dark, he and Manny may have failed to conceal every inch of the black plastic bag that contained the corpse. They wedged it in sideways because the concrete pipe was too heavy to lift or move. After they pushed dirt back into the hole, Manny stood on top to pack it down tight.

Now to Step Three.

Streaker was delighted to find that Morris's Toyota Tundra had a built-in GPS. Although he had gotten directions from Jay, he found Morris's lake home address programmed into the system. He motioned for Manny to follow in his truck. Since he just met Manny, he wasn't sure of the Mexican's driving skills. If he wrecked his prized Ford F150, then there would be hell to pay, he vowed.

Almost an hour into the drive, they pulled off the main highway onto a gravel road that wound around overgrown trees and bushes. As they bounced along the bumpy road, their headlights shot beams of light over all the dense growth. Gravel kicked up under their tires as it hit the undercarriage. At the dead-end, they found the one-story house. The front faced out toward the shoreline with a dock that harbored two boats: a twenty-foot, V-hull cruiser and a small fishing boat. Streaker parked the car where he was sure Morris did, under a carport and next to a boat trailer. An oil spot on the concrete floor left no doubt. Careful not to leave prints, Streaker kept on the Latex gloves he slipped on before he drove off in Morris's truck. He told Manny to wait outside while he used the key on Morris's keychain to unlock the back door. Just as Jay said, there was no alarm. He took off his boots, covered with surgical shoe covers, and entered the house in stocking feet. Just inside, he found a pair of sneakers, one size too large, but manageable to walk in. After he slipped them on, he meandered around the kitchen and then into the den where he found what he needed. On a wet bar, he found an empty glass with a few drops of scotch left in. Under the counter was an opened bottle, half full. Perfect! He slipped both items into a plastic bag.

In the hall closet, he found a vacuum cleaner and extra bags. He'd run the thing over the seats and floorboard of Morris's truck to remove any trace evidence. Once done, he planned to replace the used bag with a new one and take the used one with him to toss out somewhere down the road. The damn canister-style Hoover was big and clunky, but he managed to haul it outside.

Once that was done, he went back inside the house. A light switched on in various rooms was intended to make it look as though Morris had been at home. Streaker found a bottle of pain killers in the medicine cabinet. A narcotic. Hot damn! He emptied the contents into his hand, wrapped them in tissue and stashed them away in his pocket. He left the empty prescription bottle on its side beside the sink.

In the laundry room, Streaker found the boat key on a hook. Beside it, he found Morris's lightweight jacket and ball cap, which he put on in case he was seen. Anyone watching would assume it was Morris out in his boat.

As Streaker stepped outside, he motioned for Manny to join him. Streaker hitched his chin to indicate the dock. "I'll take the cruiser out to the main channel. You follow in the little outboard. You *do* know how to operate the thing, right?"

"Yes, yes. I told you. I had a fishing boat like it. Well, maybe not exactly like it. Mine was smaller, but still—."

The men walked out onto the dock where the dense moist air picked up the clunking sound of their boots against the wood. Before they stepped into their assigned vessels, Streaker handed a pair of latex gloves and shoe covers to Manny. Intentionally, Streaker walked down to the dock on the bare spots where no grass grew in order to leave prints of Morris's sneakers. He ordered Manny to walk on the graveled path so there would not be a second set of prints.

Once they boarded the cruiser and small boat, they started their engines. At first, the outboard motor sputtered and gave Manny some trouble, but at last it whirred to life. For Streaker, it was just a sweet turn of the ignition for the inboard/outboard to purr and churn through the water.

On a moonless night, they squinted in the darkness as they guided the boats out of the cove and into open water. The lake was under the jurisdiction of the Charlotte-Mecklenburg Police, but as far as Streaker knew they never patrolled at night.

However, he didn't want to leave anything to chance. He made sure the required navigational running lights were operational.

In the main channel, the cruiser sliced through the smooth water with the ease of a skater on ice. Tomorrow, it would be churned up by the wakes of motorboats when the anchored cruiser was discovered with its occupant missing. They would find the empty liquor bottle and glass tumbler that Streaker set down near the stern. Maybe they'd find the cap and jacket that he slipped under the water. Later, after they traced the boat to Morris and went to his home, they would find the empty prescription bottle. They could only draw two conclusions from their findings. While drugged and intoxicated, Nick Morris either jumped off his boat to commit suicide or he accidentally fell overboard.

Satisfied at the placement of the boat, Streaker waved Manny over. He had made circles around the bigger boat making the water choppy and more difficult to come alongside.

"I hope you drove my truck better than you steer that damn boat," Streaker yelled at Manny in his third attempt. At last, the fishing boat bobbed against the side of the cruiser. While Manny wrapped his hand over the transoms of both boats to keep them close together, Streaker stretched his leg over to board the smaller one. Despite the undulate motion, he maintained his balance and kicked away from the cruiser. He sat down on the bench seat facing out the bow. "Think you know your way back?" he asked Manny.

"Yes, I just make my way toward the light on the shore. The dock is to the right of that."

"Great! Step Three was a piece of cake, right, Manny?"

"Yes. Now we're home free. Well, almost home free. We still have to get back to the truck and back into town. Then I will relax."

"Why did you agree to this deal, Manny?"

Manny kept his grip on the handle of the outboard and rested the other arm on his knee. He shrugged at Streaker's question. "I need the extra money. Mr. Jay won't let any of us work overtime at the construction site until the new boss is hired. My little sister needs surgery. It cost a lot, more than I have."

"So, how come you speak English so good? You weren't born here, were you?"

"No. My mama worked for a rich lady, and I did gardening for her. She gave me lessons every day. Miss Lola said if I wanted to make it in America, I had to speak fluent English. But Americans think I don't understand them half the time and I don't bother to tell them that my English is good. I keep my mouth shut."

"Why? You seem like a smart guy."

"That's why I keep my mouth shut. You would be surprised at what I learn from people when they don't know I understand them. Amazing. Sometimes it is a game."

Streaker laughed. "You're slick. You wanna be like a fly on the wall."

"You Americans with all your little sayings." Manny rolled his eyes.

Streaker started to get out his pack of cigarettes, but then realized he couldn't. Smoking would leave a trace of his presence. He said to Manny, "I think you're smarter than Stiles. Maybe you could own his company some day."

"That will never happen. As you Americans say, I stay under the radar. I'm afraid that one day Immigration will send me back. Maybe my whole family will be rounded up, except of course, my little sister. She was born here, but if we go, who will care for her?"

Once the boat was tied up at the dock, Manny and Streaker headed for the Ford truck. Streaker stopped and remembered his boots left at the back door. Whew! That was close, he thought. It would have been a stupid blunder to leave them. He made a 180-degree turn to retrieve them and slipped them on. He tucked Morris's shoes in the crook of his arm and gave Manny the green light to make their departure. Once they reached the bridge, he planned to stop midway and throw the sneakers into the lake. Damn shame too. They were nice, even if they were too big.

Before they climbed inside the cab of his truck, Streaker paused. "Wait a minute," he said. "This calls for a celebration. We got 'er done, didn't we?" He stood on tiptoes and leaned over the bed of the pickup. After he grabbed the side handle on a cooler, he pulled it closer. "Want a beer, pal?" He opened the lid and grabbed two cans of Bud Light, tossing one to Manny.

As they drove out, Streaker put the high beams on. "This place is darker than dark. I don't know why anyone wants to live out in the sticks anyway. 'Course the lake and the boat are a plus, but it's so isolated. I like being in the middle of the action. Know what I mean?"

He turned on the main road, which wasn't any brighter than the graveled one. It was four o'clock in the morning. The storm had left the air heavy with mist. A white vapor swirled around the beams of the headlights like a mystical apparition, he thought. An eerie forewarning? Nah. Voodoo, hoodoo, superstitious rubbish. He shook off any bad feelings he had and took another sip of beer.

He reached over and tapped Manny on the chest with the back of his hand. "We're home free now, dude. This is all behind us."

In a matter of minutes, he would find out how wrong he was.

CHAPTER EIGHT

It took a minute or two for Camille to realize where she was. A hotel room. *Damn!* The sunlight was a golden stripe through the curtain opening. She rubbed the sleep from her eyes. When she turned on her side, she saw the wrinkled impression in the sheet where someone had slept.

"Good morning." She heard a voice coming from the end of the bed. It belonged to Matt Garrison who was busy tucking his shirttail into his dress pants. As he zipped up, he smiled at her. "How are you feeling?"

"Better." Suddenly aware that she was only in her bra and panties, she bit down on her lower lip. "How drunk was I?"

"Don't worry. Nothing happened. You just slept."

Covering her face with her hands, she said, "I'm so embarrassed."

Matt walked around to stand at her side of the bed. He smiled down at her. "Don't be. It's okay. It was a mistake. You took the wrong pill, that's all. I called my brother and he said you'd be alright."

"Your brother?"

"Yeah. He's a doctor. I was worried about you."

"That's sweet."

"You might feel better if you shower." Matt reached inside his suitcase and pulled out an orange T-shirt. He held it up for her to see. "You can put this on. It's from Wild Wings Café, a place near the Straw Market in Charleston." He tossed it to her. "I called room service. They're bringing breakfast and a toothbrush for you."

"Great." As she sat up, she grabbed for the shirt and inspected the print on the back. It made her laugh. "Perfect." She read the message out loud. "Beer. It's not just for breakfast anymore."

"Thought you'd get a kick out of that."

§

Streaker gained consciousness when he heard the whir of a saw. Every part of his body hurt. He couldn't move. When his eyesight came into focus, he saw that a branch from a tree had fallen onto the hood of his truck and now poked through a hole in the windshield. People were around him, telling him to hang on. What the hell?

In full gear, a firefighter stood beside the truck and peered at him through the side window. A paramedic was next to him as if waiting to go into action. On the other side, the firefighter with the saw cut away the top of the truck cab while another used a crowbar to pull back the metal as though opening a can of sardines. The firefighter closest to Streaker looked on, yammering about how the airbag had failed to deploy. Streaker wanted to tell him to shut the fuck up.

His left leg throbbed with pain. He rubbed his hand over it and realized why it hurt like hell. A deep gash bloodied his jeans right above his boot. He became aware that the steering column was twisted and bent. Luckily, it missed his male package. Thank God for that. But still he was trapped, unable to slide out from under it.

He turned his head slowly to the right and hoped Manny had fared better than he. The passenger seat was empty. No Manny. The door was wide open. He wondered if the accident had thrown him out.

"Sir, we'll have you out in a few minutes," the airbag-obsessed firefighter said as he leaned in closer to Streaker. "Just stay still. Try not to move."

Streaker cursed in pain. He looked up at the firefighter and said, "My friend. Where is he?"

"Who, sir?"

"The guy in the truck with me. Where is he?"

"There wasn't anybody in here but you."

Holy shit!

And if things couldn't get worse, a deputy sheriff walked over and sniffed the beer that had spilled onto the floorboard on impact. The deputy elbowed the firefighter out of the way in order to scoop up a beer can from the passenger seat. With a scowl on his ruddy face, he said to Streaker, "How many of these have you had?"

"One. Just one."

"Then how do you explain two cans, Mr. Johnson?" Between his fat fingers, he held the vehicle registration card. He waved it for Streaker to see.

"Look, I'm in pain, Officer. Give me a break. The beer had nothing to do with the wreck, I swear to God."

The deputy closed the passenger door. Since the window was busted out, he poked his head through the opening. "You sure about that?"

"It wasn't beer. It was a deer."

The whir of the saw prevented him from hearing Streaker's answer. He cupped his hand around his ear and said, "Whaddya say?"

Streaker mustered enough strength to shout out, "I said it wasn't beer! It was a deer!"

The deputy chuckled. As he hooked his thumb over his belt, he said, "Not beer, but a deer, huh?"

"Damn straight. A deer. I swerved to miss it. Trying to save Bambi and look where it got me."

When the firefighter went back to cutting the truck frame, the deputy stepped back. He waved over two deputies who showed up to help with traffic. Leaving their patrol cars parked on the side of the road with lights flashing, they made their way over to the wreck. Streaker looked out the rearview mirror that dangled precariously sideways and gulped. The trio walked around the back of the truck and then to where the paramedic stood on the driver's side.

The paramedic charged with treating Streaker's leg wound was at a disadvantage since he was still trapped in the car. He asked Streaker to lift his leg if at all possible. When he did, the paramedic started cutting away his jeans. A discovery on the exposed flesh prompted him to say, "Did you know you have another deep gash on the thigh? See the blood? We just need to cut away the whole pants leg."

"Hey, now wait a minute! Is that really necessary?"

Streaker's protest had no effect. The paramedic ripped the denims into two parts with very sharp scissors. All of Streaker's hairy leg was exposed. The paramedic felt a lump of something in the pocket, so before he could cut there, he had to remove the item.

It looked like an ordinary wad of tissue. Streaker had forgotten it, but when his memory kicked in, he cursed under his breath. He tried to snatch it away, but the paramedic was spreading apart the folds. The deputy leaned in to have a better look.

"Gimme that," Streaker snapped.

"Pills," the paramedic said. He turned his head to address the deputy. "A narcotic. This is Oxycontin."

"Let's not make a big deal out of this," Streaker said. "I'm a little embarrassed. It's not Oxycontin. It's Viagra. So, let's just keep this quiet between us guys."

"That's not Viagra!" the deputy yelled. "I take that and it's a little blue pill."

"Well, would you believe Cialis?"

The paramedic again turned to the deputy. "I'm sure this is Oxycontin."

The deputy removed his aviator sunglasses to peer sternly at Streaker. "Looks like this is our lucky day. You must be the person selling narcotics in this part of the county. We've been looking for you."

"Not me, Officer. I swear."

"If it is, we'll find out soon enough. Possession of a controlled substance looks suspicious. If nothing else, we can still charge you with having an open container while operating a motor vehicle. Maybe high on drugs, or at least, alcohol. We're gonna do a breathalyzer as soon as you're outta there. Let me see your license, cowboy."

"Okay, okay. I can explain. See, it's like this. I was digging a hole to plant a tree and I hurt my back. The pills belong to my Aunt Betty. She gave them to me. I just didn't want to say anything 'cause I didn't want to get her in any trouble. If you don't believe me, you'll see the shovels in the back."

"Maybe you bought them from this so-called Aunt Betty."

Streaker gave a smirk and said, "No, maybe I was selling them to her. 'Course if you want, I'll sell 'em to you instead, or maybe I'll just let you have 'em if you promise to go away. I'm in pain, Officer. I could actually use one of those pills right now."

"Now we're going to charge you with intent to sell and bribing an officer of the law."

Streaker's eyes went wide. "I was joking! A joke! It's called sarcasm!"

"Unfortunately for you, I don't have a sense of humor. The Aunt Betty thing is a bullshit story, cowboy. I don't want any more lies when I ask my next two questions. So, be careful how you answer."

"What is it, Deputy?"

"How come there's an empty gun holster in your glove compartment and do you have a license to carry a concealed weapon?"

Oh, shit!

CHAPTER NINE

Breakfast delivered by room service was a nice treat, Camille thought. Matt had ordered Belgian waffles with fresh blueberries, whipped butter, and maple syrup. With wet hair combed straight back and dressed in Matt's T-shirt, she took a seat at a small table next to a window overlooking the plaza below. Flowers and trees, lush and vibrant from the previous evening's rain, lined its perimeter.

Matt sat down across from her. While Camille chewed a bite of waffle, she regarded his dapper appearance with appreciative eyes. His white dress shirt was open at the collar. A gray suit jacket and tie were laid out on the bed.

"You look nice, Matt."

"Thanks. So do you," he said as he looked at her and smiled.

"Oh, please. I just got out of the shower."

"And you're still pretty."

Crazy, but she imagined running her fingers through his short dark hair. Maybe she did that last night; she couldn't remember. While she fixated on him, he kept his stare on the view of the plaza.

"You must find something amusing," she said. "You haven't stopped smiling since you've been staring out the window."

Her words jolted him back. As if she could read his private thoughts, he looked embarrassed. "I was thinking about your butterfly tattoo," he explained with a sheepish grin. To make him nervous, she prolonged her silent stare. He diverted his eyes down and scratched his cheek. "I like it. I saw it while you were sleeping. Just a peek. I mean, I'm not obsessed with your butt or anything. I'm not a pervert. It's there, so I looked." He exhaled an exasperated breath. "Maybe I should just shut up."

She laughed. "I'm glad you like it." She stirred her coffee, letting the spoon noisily tap the side of the cup. "I got it on a whim. Girls gone wild. Myrtle Beach. My friend and I thought a tattoo would look cool with our bikinis. What about you? Got any?"

"Nope. No tattoos. No body piercings." Matt glanced at his watch, took a sip of coffee, and stood up. "I've got to get moving, but you can stay as long as you like. At least until the maid shows up."

He disappeared into the bathroom and came out minutes later with his toothbrush and toothpaste that he stashed in his bags. Then, he picked up his tie and walked over to the bureau mirror. As he looped it around his turned-up collar, he glanced over at Camille. "I wish we had more time together."

"Me too. What about after your job interview? I could give you a tour of the city."

"I wish I could, but I have to get back. I'm meeting with an owner late this afternoon. We're going over a punch list for a project I just completed."

After Matt zipped up his overnight bag, he walked over to Camille. She rose from her seat to stand only inches from him. He took both her hands in his.

"I guess this is goodbye," he said with finality, but reluctance, she noted.

"Thanks for taking care of me, Matt."

She put her arms around him for a farewell hug. After her hand landed on his chest, she pressed her lips lightly on his cheek. Her eyes locked with his as he wrapped his hand around hers. Just from his smile, a sensation shot through her like a bullet. She felt a flush rise to her cheeks. Her stomach did a flip-flop. Her heart beat faster.

Damn! What is happening to me?

"You are so beautiful," he said. His lips touched hers only long enough for her to blink.

She could only stare back at him and attempt to reign in the arousal she felt. This is crazy, she thought. Matt pulled her tighter, closer, and gave her the kind of kiss that counted. The passion and heat it created left her breathless. But he didn't stop there. She felt his lips on her neck, her chest. Wherever he touched her, she felt his heat, his scent. As he threaded his fingers through her damp hair, he pressed his forehead against hers. She heard his long exasperated breath. With his hands on her shoulders, he pushed her back, looked into her eyes, and then stroked her cheek with the backside of his fingers.

"I better stop now before I go down a path of no return," he said.

She smiled back at him. He seemed at a loss, so she gave him a little urging by stroking his chest.

"Camille, I want to see you again."

"I would like that."

He smiled his pleasure. "You have this effect on me. I can't explain it."

"Well, *you* make my butterfly flutter."

Through a smile, he said, "I have to go now. I'll call you. We'll work something out."

As he started to reach for his bag, she wrapped her fingers around his arm. "Don't go. Blow the guy off. Tell him you have to reschedule. Tell him you have car trouble."

He shook his head. "I can't do that. I'll call you. If you break up with that guy maybe we can get together. Savannah's not that far."

"What do you mean *if*? I told you, Matt. It's over between us. This time I'm not taking him back."

Matt pressed his fingertips into his closed eyes and shook his head. "Camille, I've just come out of a similar relationship. She said the same thing you're saying. But guess what? She went back to the jerk. Broke my heart. I can't go through that again."

"That won't happen. What can I say to convince you?"

With his hands on his hips, Matt stared out the window. His silence kept Camille waiting, but at last, he turned to face her. "I'm coming back on Saturday for a trade show at the convention center. It's not something I'm thrilled about, but I'm required to make an appearance since the company has already paid the fee. So, here's the deal. You have until then to end it with that guy and if you still want to see me, then I'll be at the same bar where we met. Saturday night around seven. If you don't show, then I'll know you decided to stay with him."

"I'll be there. Will you call me when you get back to Savannah?"

"I prefer that we don't have contact until you end it with that guy. I don't want to get too invested before I know for sure that it's over for you."

"Damn, Matt, I said I'd be there. Don't you trust me at my word?"

Her tight lips were meant to show her displeasure, but he stayed firm. "Sorry, Camille. I didn't mean it that way. I'm just safeguarding my heart."

She managed a smile and came into his arms for a final kiss. "I understand. It's fine. Really. There's no question about whether or not I'll show up—I have to." When he raised his brow, she explained, "I have to return your shirt."

He grinned back at her. Although loaded down with his bag and suit jacket, he managed to draw her into his arms for a final kiss. After he left, Camille pressed her back against the door. She put her hands on her cheeks and realized that the smile on her face would linger all day. Almost as permanent as the tattoo.

§

It was business as usual for Jay. Nothing could appear out of the ordinary. He stopped at Caribou Coffee for his usual double espresso, bought a morning paper at the newsstand, and greeted his administrative assistant with the same cheery greeting he always gave her.

"Good morning, Amber. How are you?"

"Same as always. Underpaid and overworked."

"That's nice."

Whatever she mumbled, he didn't know and he didn't care. He picked up some files she had set out for him and scanned the tabs on each.

"I need that Agreement to Purchase contract on the industrial property," he said. "Ernie thinks he's found a buyer. We might have to change a few things before we present it."

"Do you want me to email it to you as an attachment or print it out?"

"Just print it for now. I'll mark up a hard copy."

"Okay," she said. "Don't forget you have an appointment at ten."

He took his eyes off the files to look up at her. "I do?"

"Yes. The interview."

"That's this morning?"

"Yes, don't you remember? The guy is coming up from Savannah."

"Oh, that guy. Yeah, I forgot it was today. Refresh my memory. What's his name?"

"Matthew Garrison."

"Well, call me when he gets here. In the meantime, I'm going to be holed up in my office looking at some reports. No interruptions unless it's an emergency."

An emergency found him as soon as he entered his office and answered his cell phone.

"Streaker! I told you no phone contact. I'll meet you at lunchtime like we planned."

"Well, I only get one phone call, and you're it."

"What are you talking about?"

"Right now I'm getting patched up at the hospital. Then, they're going to take me to the intake facility downtown."

Jay's heart pounded. "What are you talking about?"

"I've been arrested, Goldie! I'm handcuffed to the damn bed in the emergency room. They're taking me to the county jail in Charlotte. I need a fucking lawyer!"

"You're charged with murder?"

"No, no, no! I'm charged with possession of a controlled substance with intent to sell and having an open container while driving. And the cherry on top of this fucking sundae is the pile of scrap metal that was once my truck. I ran off the road to avoid hitting a goddamn deer. A tree got in the way. If my insurance doesn't pay, then you are!"

"What about Manny?"

"I wish the hell I knew. He's missing. Flew the coop. Are you getting the picture, Goldie?"

"No, the picture is a little fuzzy. Tell me how this happened."

"You're killing me, Goldie. You're killing me. Just get me a damn lawyer, will ya? I'll fill you in on all the nitty-gritty later."

"This didn't go down exactly as we planned."

"Ya think?" Streaker screamed into the phone.

CHAPTER TEN

The crisis with Streaker was in damage control, but it looked like no real harm was done. Jay sighed with relief. Jim Lawrence, the lawyer Jay had contacted, called from his plush office across the street from the county courthouse. He informed Jay that Streaker was being processed. He would be released after appearing before the magistrate, and a court date would be set for the charges filed. According to Lawrence, Streaker had no prior record, unbelievable to Jay, but hey, that was a good thing. He figured they dodged a bullet.

Jay made the lawyer repeat what he had just said, thought he had heard wrong or had a bad phone connection. Lawrence said, "This guy was hailed as a hero at one point in his career."

"Streaker? I mean, Wayne Johnson," Jay said. "What are you talking about?"

"I made a call to a cop friend of mine, see if he knew the guy. He said when Johnson was an officer, he was part of a Special Task Force. Involved in an undercover operation, something about taking down a prostitution ring. There was a shootout and Johnson took two shots in the back protecting another officer, a woman named Samantha Delaney, or something like that. She was the target, and he blew his cover and risked his life to save her. It was a secret operation, so his heroism was kept on the down-low. Anyway, Johnson recovered and transferred to the drug unit, again going undercover. After a few years, he was forced out, but my friend wouldn't give details why. You know the special bond between these guys. He wasn't about to rat him out. I just got the feeling Johnson did something illegal or unethical. If so, I guess the hero image kept him from getting charges filed. Just walked away quietly with his pension intact."

"Interesting," Jay said. "I asked him about his scars one time, but he just shrugged it off, and never did explain. Now I know. Fucking Streaker was a hero. I'll be damned."

"Just thought you'd want to know. I need to get my notes together before we face the magistrate. I'll argue to have the charges dropped—bring up the hero-cop thing, but don't think that will fly. He'll get out on bond, no doubt."

"Thanks, Jim. Call me after he's released."

A crisis averted, Jay thought as he hung up the phone. But minutes later, another met him head on.

§

Right after he hung up with the lawyer, Jay was summoned by Amber. She wanted him to come to her desk. Something urgent, or so she said. From her tone and her secrecy, he figured it was bad news. Jay left his office to walk up the corridor to the reception area where Amber awaited his arrival.

As usual, he figured she'd be all business. They had a strictly professional relationship. He was the boss and she, the subordinate. Secretly, he imagined her as the naughty librarian. Her auburn hair was usually tied back in a ponytail. She downplayed her beauty and femininity in pants suits or straight skirts with sensible low heels. Her only accessories were either a strand of pearls or gold locket. Her tortoise-framed glasses made her look bookish. He fantasized about watching her remove her glasses, then the band from her ponytail, unbuttoning her blouse to show cleavage, and last of all, jacking up her skirt to flaunt shapely legs. Underneath the professional persona, there was a wildcat waiting to be unleashed. Maybe someday he'd find out.

"What is it, Amber?" Jay's tone showed his annoyance.

"Your lady friend, Camille, has erroneously sent me an email that I think she meant to send to her friend. It starts off with a greeting to Alex. Apparently she and I are alphabetically listed in her Outlook Contacts box."

"So?"

Amber removed her glasses, planted both palms on the desktop, and glared at Jay. "I think you will be interested in what she has to say. It's about you, Jay. She says it's over. That she will not consider taking you back. In fact, she met someone else at the bar where you were supposed to meet her. They hit it off. She's crazy about him. He's from out of town, but he's coming back on Saturday, and they're hooking up."

"What guy?"

"She doesn't say. No name, just that unlike you, he's tall, dark, and handsome." Amber smiled when she added, "She says you have that California surfer look, but this guy looks like a cute rugby player, strong and muscular."

"Let me see that."

Jay cornered the desk to view her computer screen. He read the text and stepped away. Although he knew Amber waited for some reaction from him, he ignored her. With hands on his hips, he kept his eyes focused on the window as if the parking lot offered a view worth seeing. Finally, he turned to find her eyes still locked on him. He walked to the side of her desk and lashed out at her trash can. Like a punter, he kicked it as hard as he could as he yelled out, "Fuck!"

"I'm sorry, Jay. I thought you should know."

With hands in his pockets, he turned his attention back to Amber. "That explains why she won't take my calls." In an instant, his hurt look turned into something more menacing. "Print it out for me. I won't let her leave me for some fucking jock. It won't happen, I promise you. I'll make damn sure of it. Maybe I should deal with this guy personally. Is there any way we can find out who this dude is?"

"Jay, be reasonable."

"Okay, okay. I'll work on a plan, and I might need your help, Amber." Before he turned to leave, he said, "Thanks for showing it to me. You did the right thing. Call the florist and send Camille some flowers, whatever you think, and use the same wording as the last note." He paused to reflect and added, "If he slept with her, I'll kill 'im."

§

49

As Camille got out of her car, the morning sun reflected off the frame shop's front window directly into her eyes. She hopped up onto the curb and walked inside. Although no one stood behind the front counter, a bell over the door announced her entrance. A smiling woman appeared from the back room. Hoop earrings, twice the size of shower curtain rings, dangled and got lost in ropy strands of dark hair. Colorful glass beads hung around her neck and blended well with her mustard-colored top and crinkled gauze full skirt. Her makeup was heavy, but effective at disguising her forty-something years. Her bright red lips slid into a thin smile, acknowledging Camille's arrival.

"Girlfriend, do I have a surprise for you." Alexandria Middleton of Middleton Frame Shop made statements with gusto, bubbling up like champagne. Although Camille showed no interest, Alex was about to pop. She tilted her head to the side to indicate an arrangement of cut flowers in a crystal vase. "They came for you, Cam. About ten minutes ago. The delivery guy was pounding on your office door. I told Cutie Pie to leave them with me." She wrapped her fingers around a yellow rose to inhale the sweet fragrance. "Aren't they gorgeous?"

"If you like them, then keep them, Alex. They're yours."

Alex shot her an incredulous look. "You haven't even read the card." She unpinned the miniature envelope that matched the pink tulips and handed it over to Camille.

Camille frowned. "I know what it says. It says he's sorry and he loves me."

Alex slipped on reading glasses and peeled open the envelope. "Wow! I knew Jay was romantic, but I didn't know he was a poet. How sweet."

Camille squinted with suspicion and snatched the card from Alex. "Let me see that. Three words, that's it. Poet, my ass."

"Well, I made you look, didn't I? To be honest, I don't know what the card says. Can't read his scribbling. Is it even written in English?"

"It says, 'Forgive me. Jay.' Apology flowers. How pathetic is that?"

With her head cocked to one side, Alex said, "Let me guess. He stood you up—again."

"Didn't you get my email this morning?"

"What email?"

"That's strange. I was sure I sent it. Well, anyway I'll tell you about it over lunch. Are you free to go with me around one?"

"Sure, that works." As Camille started out the door, Alex called her back. "I almost forgot. Butt Crack came by this morning. He'll fix your roof leak on Thursday."

"It's not nice that you call him that. I think I'll tell him."

"Well, he shouldn't moon me every time he squats down to repair something."

"Thursday, huh? That's just great. It rained hard last night. Bet I find a big puddle in front of the bookcase. Good thing I moved everything out of the way. Be glad you're on the ground floor, Alex. If it wasn't so much work, I'd move my business."

"Then, you wouldn't have me to offer advice. Your love life would suffer." Alex gave her a quick wink. "Hey, come back. You forgot your flowers."

"Like I said, you can have them."

§

Camille climbed the rickety wooden staircase that led up to her office. A small sign to the right of the door identified her interior design business: *Creations by Camille.* She paused in the open doorway to take in the familiar surroundings, but her thoughts were on what she didn't see, rather than what she did see. Years ago, when she first determined to start her own business, she dreamed of a contemporary space with a sitting area, workroom, and storage closet. But what she wanted and what she got were worlds apart. Freight-damaged furnishings bought at an auction were crammed into the 12 by16 foot space. Miscellaneous items that didn't fit into the closet or shelves occupied the corners. Bolts of fabric leaned into the wall and threatened to tumble over. Next to them, binders of wallpaper samples were stacked three deep. If her clients saw her office interior compared to their beautiful homes, she was afraid they would never sign her on as their decorator.

One day things will be different, she thought. Yeah, she'd have a nice office and showroom where she could be proud to bring clients. In recent months, business had been good, but after paying suppliers, operating expenses, insurance and taxes, there was not a lot left. Not enough to find a better location or to purchase new furnishings.

She hoped her new client, Mrs. Larsen, would be the ticket out of the low-rent district. The sweet elderly lady wanted a complete makeover of her living quarters. They'd start with the bedroom and then move forward to the living room. She didn't limit Camille to a budget, which really got her creative juices flowing. She spent the morning picking out top-of-the line fabric swatches, matching them up with carpet samples, and pulling out furniture catalogs.

As she was deep in thought and work, her telephone shrilled. She picked it up and saw Jay's name in the display, but did not answer the call. As it continued to ring, she set it back on the table and went back to work.

§

Work demands were put on hold while Alex and Camille had lunch on the patio of their favorite restaurant. It was the perfect setting to get away from the workday grind. The fingers of a spring breeze combed through their hair and flapped the edges of the white linen tablecloth. Reluctant to go back to their businesses, the ladies ordered a second glass of wine.

With a playful smile, Alex said, "Alfredo is growing a beard. Did you notice?"

Camille looked over the top of her glass at the waiter. "Hmm. I didn't notice. His name is Mike, not Alfredo."

"He likes that I call him that. It sounds exotic. Sexy." Alex stared at his derriere in tight black trousers as he set plates down at another table. She held the glass with her palm splayed out across the base of the glass goblet in a way that made Camille think that Alex wanted to grab his ass. She smiled when she said, "I think I approve."

"Of what?" Camille asked.

"His beard. That's what we were talking about."

"You know he's too young for you, right?"

"I know." Alex shrugged as she took a sip of wine. "I can window shop, can't I?"

"So, you really didn't get the email I sent?" Alex shook her head. "I could have sworn I hit *send*. Anyway, I'm dying to tell you what happened last night when I was waiting for Jay at the bar. You won't believe it."

Alex leaned forward. "Dish it out, girl. Can't wait to hear."

After Camille finished a recap of her evening with Matt Garrison, she leaned back and said, "There you have it. I broke up with Jay over the phone and met someone new the next minute. Crazy, huh?"

"More than crazy. Insane."

"I wouldn't go that far."

"Damn, girl, if you dump Jay Stiles, the most eligible bachelor in town, for some hunky guy you just met, then you've lost your mind. Jay loves you. You don't even know this new guy that just breezed into town."

"I know enough to know that he's sweet and that there was a strong attraction."

"Women had a strong attraction to Ted Bundy before he murdered them! You don't know this guy. You said he doesn't want you to call him before your rendezvous on Saturday. That means he's probably married. He doesn't want you to call because *his wife* might answer!"

"I don't think so, Alex. Look, Jay and I had a wonderful ten months together. It was like a fairy tale. I felt like a princess, but everything changed about two months ago. He says he's dealing with a crisis at work. Once it's resolved, we'll go back to the way it was, but I've run out of patience. Lately I've seen more of my neighbor Tyler than I have of Jay."

"So, he stood you up last night because of work, and you're pissed. Well, la-de-da. Big deal. He works his butt off so he can make enough money to spoil you rotten. I'm glad I'm responsible for you two hooking up."

"That's not true. I met him at the Designer Showhouse. I was an exhibitor."

"Well, don't forget I gave him the ticket to go. Saved him fifteen dollars on the entrance fee, and then he turned around and spent thousands." She laughed as she took another sip of wine.

"Oh, you mean because he asked me to duplicate everything he saw in my display for his bedroom. His purchase was so large, I almost peed my pants." She chuckled with the memory. "But our relationship was strictly business. Well, maybe that's not entirely true."

Alex smiled as she recalled juicy details. "When you got his room all ready for him to see, y'all just had to try out the bed."

Camille felt heat to her cheeks when she realized Mike overheard Alex's remark. "Keep your voice down," she said. When Mike reached over to refill their water glasses, Camille said to him, "I think we're done here. Can you bring us the check, please?" When he nodded and walked away, Camille said, "Did you see his grin? He heard what you said, Alex." She finished the last of her wine. "So, we made love before we ever dated. So what?"

"I just think it's amusing, that's all."

After Camille signed the credit card receipt and placed it back in the binder for Mike, she said, "We better go. I'm working on a project for a new client. I have an appointment with her on Thursday and I've got a lot to do."

"Camille, you know if it wasn't for Jay, you would've given up on your business. You told me so. He sent you a whole slew of referrals, enough to keep you busy and pay the bills. This guy you met—yeah, he might be nice, but is he worth dumping Jay? Are you sure you know what you're doing?"

"No, but I have five days to figure it out."

"Then, think long and hard before you give up what you have."

CHAPTER ELEVEN

The lawyer called Jay around four o'clock to tell him that Streaker was being released. Anywhere Jay suggested, Lawrence would drop him off. They agreed to meet at Francoise's. From there, Jay would give Streaker a ride home since his truck had been towed away to the scrap heap.

When Jay took two steps down into the bar area, he chuckled when he spotted Streaker sitting across from the lawyer. The cowboy PI looked uncomfortable in the swanky French restaurant drinking beer out of a glass, of all things, but it was the perfect ambiance for Mister Charge-big-bucks-by-the-hour and the reason it was chosen. Jay signed some legal paperwork that made him responsible for services rendered and handed over a check for four billable hours just for today's little episode. The greedy fat fingers of the lawyer folded the personal check in half before he slipped it inside his Louis Vuitton briefcase. Then, Lawrence finished his Cosmopolitan and bid the gentlemen goodbye.

Jay dropped the cordial smile as soon as the lawyer was out the door. He took a sip of his gin and tonic and directed his attention at Streaker, although he'd rather flirt with the cute little server with the nice smile.

"Start at the beginning, Streaker. Tell me what went right and what went wrong. Don't leave anything out."

Over the course of an hour, Streaker told him how everything had gone according to the plan except for the burial site, but he wouldn't reveal where he and Manny left the body. It was better that he didn't know, he explained. Less incriminating that way. Jay nodded his agreement.

Streaker ended his half truthful/half bullshit monologue by saying, "If it wasn't for me stealing those stupid pills and swerving to miss the deer, we'd be sitting pretty."

"Don't forget drinking while driving, my friend. That was stupid."

"Yeah, well, Manny and I deserved a little celebration after we completed the mission. Don't forget we did all the heavy lifting while you set your ass on some bar stool drinking a martini. Right now, my leg hurts like hell. I've got battle wounds, my friend, so quit your bitching."

"You did what I hired you to do, Streak, so don't give me any of your shit. Here's the deal. They're going to be searching the lake for about a week and then when a body doesn't surface, they might look at some other possibilities. If they ever connect the dots with the empty pill bottle you left for them to discover and what you were carrying in your pocket, then it's over for you. The disappearance of Manny is another problem. What if they catch him somewhere and he talks?"

"I think he took off because he's illegal. Doesn't want to get turned over to Immigration. My guess is that he's holed up somewhere. I'm not that worried about him talking."

"You know what pisses me off, Streaker? You seemed more upset about your precious truck than anything else."

"I loved that truck! I can't work without it, dude. What do you suggest I do for wheels?"

"I'll let you drive the company truck until your insurance comes through. Manny won't be using it until he shows up."

"No, I think you should reimburse me for a rental. I can't do surveillance in a vehicle with a company sign painted on the door."

"There's no sign. It's a plain white pickup."

Streaker started to say something else, but the server was back. He smiled up at her. "Sweetheart, I'll have another beer, please. Put it on his tab," he added with a wink.

"I'm not paying for a rental," Jay said. "That will just leave another connection between you and me."

"Screw you, Goldie."

"We have to play it safe."

Streaker chuckled and said, "I think that train has already left the station, my friend."

§

After they finished their drinks, Jay drove Streaker to the warehouse construction site where Manny had parked the company truck. While there, Jay wanted to make sure the ditch with the water pipe had been covered up to his satisfaction. Next week, concrete trucks would come in to start on a masonry wall and an open ditch would hinder their movement.

For some reason, Streaker insisted on going with Jay to inspect the work. It didn't make sense to Jay especially since the dude kept complaining about his damn injured leg, but he shrugged and led the way. He wouldn't let the cowboy smoke in his Porsche, but as soon as he stepped out of the car, Streaker lit a cigarette. Jay fanned the smoke away in disgust.

"Smoking will kill you, you know."

"I'm gonna die someway, so it might as well be something I enjoy, Goldie."

With his hands on his hips, Jay looked down at the ground. It had been broken up with a backhoe and a frontend loader. Carolina red clay, great for making bricks but too hard for digging holes, was dumped over the entire pipeline. Riddled with mud and rocks it was packed tight with the help of shovels and lots of manpower. Although Manny was not there to oversee the work, it was completed to Jay's satisfaction. At his side, Streaker seemed to switch from nervous worry to a sigh of relief. Strange, but to Jay, it looked like he made the sign of the cross while staring down at the ground. What was that about? Jay wondered.

Jay said, "I'll go inside the construction trailer and get the keys for the truck. Be right back."

"Gimme the keys to your car first. It's time for the six o'clock news report on the radio, and I wanna see if they've started searching for Morris's body."

Jay tossed them to him as he walked away. "Let me know what they're reporting."

Once inside the trailer, it angered Jay that the keys were not on the hook near the door, where they should be. He had to rummage through all the crap on the desk before he found them.

As he was locking up, he heard the familiar sound of his car's startup. Then, he heard the engine being revved up as it remained in neutral. The turbo engine screamed with super-charged horsepower, chomping at the bit to be released to the road. He turned around to see Streaker behind the wheel. Jay watched in horror as Streaker floored the gas pedal and scratched off, tires squealing where rubber met asphalt and leaving a cloud of dirt. The scene almost made Jay fall backwards down the wooden steps of the trailer. He pulled his cell phone from his pocket and called Streaker.

"That's not funny, Streaker. Now bring my car back!"

"I'm not trying to be funny, Goldie. You owe me some wheels for my inconvenience. I saw your company truck. It looks like crap. I like this better. See ya."

"Streaker, get your ass back here right now!"

CHAPTER TWELVE

In a hurry, Samantha Delano walked right past the silver Porsche parked outside the police station. She twirled around when the driver got out and gave a wolf whistle. With her hands over her mouth, she burst out laughing.

"I know this dang car is not yours, Streaker. How in the world?"

While he rested his backside against the car, he grinned at her and tipped his hat. "Good evening, Officer." He jerked his head to indicate the Porsche. "It belongs to a buddy of mine. He's letting me borrow it. It's a 911 Carrera. This baby will do 60 in less than five seconds, can get up to 175 on the track. Check out the interior, Sam. Even the steering wheel has leather, and look at that console, will ya? It's got a touch screen, and I have no idea what all it can do. Technology out the wazoo. She's a beauty, ain't she? Hop in. I'll take you for a little spin."

She shook her head. "I don't know about that. I was going home and—"

"Ah, come on, girl. It'll be fun. Your husband's not in town, is he?"

"No, but—"

"No buts about it." He indicated the passenger side with a tilt of his chin. "Get in. We'll go back to your place. Catch up on all the news."

"I should have known." She raised her chin in defiance and started to walk away.

He blocked her passage and put his hand on her arm. "Known what?"

"That you just came around to get information from me."

"No, honey, that's not it at all. I missed you, baby. I suddenly got a hankering for your country-style steak and mashed potatoes. You're the best cook ever."

"How come I'm not getting all gooey inside with all that sweet talk?"

"You've missed me, baby. Y'know you have. That asshole you married doesn't even appreciate what he's got. Stays on the road all week and comes home so you can do his laundry. Why are you still married to the bum anyway?"

"It's a marriage of convenience. We both conveniently forget we're married. It's the only way it works."

"Remember when we use to work vice together? After a bust, we'd go down to that little diner and eat good ol' Southern food. They had the best fried chicken and banana pudding. I miss those days."

"Yeah, well I wish you were still in the department. It's not the same without you. One stupid mistake and they show you the door."

Streaker smiled. "They don't take kindly to anyone who gets high off the evidence. But, hey, it all worked out for the best." He patted the roof of the Porsche. "Ain't it a beauty? The motor sounds sweet. I'd love to take it out on the road and run it wide open. Of course with the way my luck's going, I'd get caught. C'mon, baby, let's go to your place."

"I can't ride with you, Streaker. I've got my car, but I'll make you a deal. If you go to the store and buy the stuff we need, I'll cook that dinner you want, but with one condition."

"Name it."

"That we skip dessert. I've put on five pounds. Look at these hips."

"I'm seeing them and I'm liking what I see. You're fine just the way you are. Honey, I'm gonna have *you* for dessert. That way we'll both burn off calories."

"You have a way with words, Streak. I'll go get my car and I'll meet you back at the house. Oh, and while you're at it, pick up a bottle of wine. You know what I like."

§

Once Streaker arrived at Samantha's house with two bags of groceries, she instructed him to pull the car into the garage and close the automatic door. "No need to give the nosey neighbors anything to talk about," she explained.

She changed into a pair of the shortest shorts he'd ever seen. He liked that they showed not only her shapely legs, but a little butt cheek too. She pulled her copper hair back into a messy ponytail that swung back and forth as she walked around. While she stood in front of the stove, he sat at the kitchen table to smoke and enjoy a glass of wine. He'd prefer a beer, but she didn't have any. He assumed her no-good husband took all they had with him. He knew the guy worked for a freight carrier and drove up and down the East Coast. Why a good-looking woman like Samantha married his sorry ass, he'd never know. Streaker wasn't the marrying kind, but he came close a few times. Now he just liked to have lady friends with benefits. Samantha seemed perfectly fine with that arrangement.

Samantha excelled in the kitchen as well as the bedroom. In his opinion, only his grandmother could fix a meal as tasty as hers. As usual, he wolfed down his food like a field hand, a habit he picked up as a patrol officer. He waited for Samantha to finish eating her meal before he got down to business. In order for her not to suspect a thing, he decided to ease into the conversation real slow.

After he lit his after-dinner smoke, he leaned forward, one elbow up on the table while his opposite hand gripped the wineglass across the opening. As a ploy, he swirled the red wine around, keeping his eyes cast down and not on her. He said, "So, I hear some dude is missing up on the lake. Did you hear anything about it?"

"Just what I heard on the radio. They have rescue boats with sonar and the fire department has their divers out there. That's all I know."

"Do they know what happened?"

"No, not really. Or if they know, they're not saying. They haven't released the name yet, pending notification of next of kin. Why the interest?"

"Just curious." He took a sip of wine and crushed out his cigarette in the ashtray she provided. He hesitated, but then said, "Sam."

"Yes?" She placed her hand on his arm. "Is something wrong, Streak?"

"I got busted today."

"What?" she shrieked.

"It's not that bad so don't get all worked up." He strained to give the semblance of a smile. "It's just possession of a controlled substance with intent to sell and—"

"And what?" By her scowl, he could tell that Samantha was pissed.

"And having an open container. I got a lawyer who says I'll probably just have to pay a fine and get a suspended sentence. He'll get the intent to sell taken off, because that's just bullshit, cops jerking my chain. I may have to go to a treatment center though, which is a complete waste of time."

"I thought you kicked your pot habit. Now you're taking drugs?"

"No, baby. They weren't mine. I just got caught with them." His eyes locked with hers. "I might be in some trouble, Sam."

"What kind of trouble?"

"It's like this. The police kept pushing me, asking all kinds of questions. Man, they just wouldn't let up. They've been looking for some dude selling drugs in that area, and they thought I was their guy. I couldn't tell them the truth, so I finally blurted out that I got them off the street. Then, they wanted to know the dealer's name. They kept pressing and pressing and my leg was killing me. I wanted outta there so bad. They wouldn't even let me take my pain medicine that I got in the emergency room."

"Emergency room? You got hurt?"

He shrugged. "Just a couple of cuts on my leg that had to be stitched up and a bruise here and there. I wrecked trying to avoid hitting a damn deer. My poor truck, it's totaled. That's why I borrowed my friend's car. Anyway, when the cops kept pushing me for a name, I blurted out Slick. It was the first name that popped into my head. I just made it up. Then they wanted me to pick him out of a group of photos they showed me. If it wasn't so serious, it might be funny."

"What's that?"

"There really is a dealer named Slick and of all the mug shots to pick, I picked his." He gave a nervous laugh. "It was a no-brainer. I pointed to the guy with the shaved head. Get it? Slick."

Samantha put her elbows up on the table and covered her face with her hands. She shook her head back and forth and moaned.

"What is it, Sam? You're scaring me."

"I hate to break it to you, Streak, but Slick is a big-time coke dealer. He's the baddest of the bad, and if he knows you fingered him, he'll kill you."

"You don't have to sugar coat it, darlin'. Is there anything you can do to help me out?"

"The best advice I can give you is to contact your lawyer, go back to the police, and retract your statement."

"I don't think I can do that. If they knew where I got those damn pills, I might go to prison for life. Why didn't I just flush them? I shudda done that. Shit!"

Her silent stare was not what he wanted or needed. He knew he had disappointed her, once again.

In a voice that lacked conviction, she said, "I'll see what I can do, Streak. I don't even want to know what you did to get so jammed up, so don't go making any kind of a confession to me, okay? I want to keep thinking you're that sweet guy that always kept me safe on the streets."

He thought he saw a tear in her eye. He hadn't been sweet in so long he didn't know how that felt. She should have learned that by now.

Later in bed, she whispered in his ear that his lovemaking technique made her wanting more, if she just wasn't so damn tired. She said she had missed their intimacy. How long had it been? Neither could remember. She told him no man could satisfy her the way he could. She liked to be on top while he lay on his back and watched her arousal build. While she straddled him, she rode him like a bronco, up and down until she worked herself into a frenzy and screamed in ecstasy. Streaker figured her loser of a husband was lousy in the sack or maybe unappreciative of his wife's skills in the bedroom. She certainly got him worked up. In fact, she aroused him too much. It was always over too soon, but he liked to hold her in his arms afterwards, especially at times like this when his world seemed turned upside down. It felt good just to have her close.

If he had it to do over again, he would have told Jay to find another dude to do clean-up detail. Even if he managed to get off Slick's radar, there was always the possibility that Jay or Manny would give him up to the police. He would have to make it perfectly clear to Jay what would happen to him or his girlfriend if he ever did. From now on, it would be about survival, like an animal in the wild. Jay Stiles was a weaker prey. Figuratively, he could be devoured, eaten alive, his bones picked clean, but not Streaker. He knew he was indestructible because he always managed to stay one step ahead of danger. The time he got shot and the time he got cut up, he survived because he was too pissed off to die. He fought off death as hard as he fought off any adversary.

§

When Amber first heard the name of the missing man, her heart missed a beat. While she applied her makeup, she listened to the television reporter give details of the search that had expanded to a larger area of Lake Norman. For the third day, rescue boats equipped with sonar sliced through the choppy waters. According to the report, Nick Morris's boat was found adrift in the widest expanse of the lake where the depth was between eighty and one hundred feet. Helicopters were called in for an aerial search. Divers from the Charlotte Fire Department and Charlotte-Mecklenburg Police had no success in locating the body. A foot search, including SAR dogs, was added with the possibility that the body could be lodged between trees along the banks. A reporter at the command center handed the microphone to a family member, Morris's twenty-year- old daughter. Through her tears, she stated that the family and friends were still optimistic that he would be found. However, she didn't use the word "alive." Amber assumed that the search and rescue had changed to a recovery operation.

Her heart ached for the family. She knew Morris as a good man with sleepy eyes and a slow smile. Never had she seen him upset or rattled, even when he and Jay argued over a project, or more recently, money. She knew Jay's company had been delinquent in payment; she had taken Nick's calls. The day before Nick went missing; however, Jay told her it was settled. He had paid in full.

When Amber arrived at the office, Jay was already there. She crept up behind him while he stood bent over the shredder, feeding something small and rectangular into its metal teeth. When she told him good morning, he jumped a foot and looked irritated, as if she had caught him in front of a urinal.

"Don't sneak up on me like that," he barked.

"Sorry," she said. "Let me start over. Good morning."

"Good morning." His voice did not match her chipper tone. "Amber, I need the portfolio on the warehouse development. I may have a tenant for the corner space. Not the 2,000 square foot unit, but the other."

"The 1,800 square footage?"

"Yeah, that one."

Before he could get away, she said, "Jay, did you watch the news this morning? They had another story about Nick. Have you heard any more details than what they're reporting?"

"I only know what you know."

"I can't believe he would kill himself." She was surprised when he walked back to face her. His cold stare made her uncomfortable. She licked her lips and added, "I mean, it doesn't sound like something he would do. There must be another explanation."

"Well, it makes sense to me. He was going through a bitter divorce, and his girlfriend just walked out on him. That's reason enough."

"That's where you're wrong. Things were turning around."

"What do you mean?"

"He'd reached a divorce settlement that he was happy with. At least, his wife didn't end up with everything like he feared. And the girlfriend situation was looking up."

"How do you know all this?"

She shrugged. "We talked while he was waiting to get in to see you. Suicide doesn't make sense. He'd just put down a deposit on an engagement ring. He was going to take his girlfriend to Hawaii to propose." She noted how Jay looked like he'd accidentally swallowed the winning lottery ticket. "Jay, are you okay? Jay?"

"I heard you," he barked. "I'm fine. I'll need that portfolio soon, and later today we need to get together and discuss the Carson strategy."

"The what?"

"You know, to get Camille back. Like I said before, I'll need your help."

"I don't think that's in my job description." She meant it as a joke, thought it might make him smile. The look he shot her let her know that it fell flat.

"There's no damn way I'll ever let her leave me," he said as he walked away.

CHAPTER THIRTEEN

Two days had passed since Streaker sat in the interview room at police headquarters. He remembered the flash of recognition on the detective's face when he blurted out a name he made up. Every drug dealer had a street name. How in the hell could he know that some dude actually used Slick? If the police brought this Slick guy down for questioning and showed him Streaker's mug shot and said his name, then he was toast. No one liked a snitch. And the worse snitch was a liar snitch. The big black man with the shaved head would come looking for him. Teach him a lesson. It was just a matter of time. So far there was no sign of trouble.

Confident that he was in the clear, he didn't bother to scan his surroundings when he walked out of his apartment building and got into Jay's Porsche. He laughed when he thought about all the silly voice messages Jay left demanding his car back. Of course, the fancy man in his fancy suits was not going to be caught around town in the crappy pickup truck that he tried to dump on him. He'd heard that Jay rented a black Audi A-6 with a sunroof. More his style.

It wasn't until Streaker was blocks away from his apartment that he noticed that a 1974 gold metallic Cadillac Eldorado seemed to be on the same course as he. Just in case he was being followed, Streaker circled the block. So did the Caddy. Next test was to run the stoplight. The car stayed behind, did not stop for the light. Tires screamed. A horn blasted. The Cadillac came close to colliding with a Honda Civic that had the green light.

Streaker floored the accelerator. Up to fifty, then sixty, then seventy. If he wasn't in the city, he'd take the sleek baby up to a hundred. Almost as good as sex, the lightning speed of the manual downshift and sweet whine of the engine made Streaker smile with gratification. The sports car hugged the road and took the sharp turns better than the Cadillac. Because the Porsche was like a wildcat released from its cage, Streaker had to reign in its full fury by letting up on the gas.

Was it the dude named Slick behind the wheel of the Cadillac? Had to be. The drug dealer would know his turf blindfolded, but he wouldn't know the whole city like Streaker. In his business, a clean get-away was a necessity. He knew side streets. He knew alleys. He knew abandoned lots and boarded up buildings. He could hide a car for days.

At a higher speed than was safe, Streaker made a sudden turn onto a one-way street, going the wrong way and forcing on-coming traffic to hit the ditch. He tore through a yard leaving tire tracks across the grass, scraped the low chassis of the Porsche when he jumped the curb, and then floored the gas pedal as he steered onto the one-way street that ran parallel in the opposite direction. The Caddy followed, knocking over a garbage can and pushing it for fifty yards on its front-end.

Streaker headed to a nearby shopping center, down a back alley to its loading docks. He parked between two tractor-trailers backed up to the platform as they unloaded their freight. It was the perfect hiding place for the small car. The tense, yet almost orgasmic experience, made Streaker crave a smoke. He pulled out his pack of cigarettes and sat tight.

As he had hoped, the Caddy drove across the parking lot in front of the building, hitting every speed bump along the way. It cruised around the parking lot, but saw no sign of the silver Porsche. Streaker waited until he felt it was safe to venture out. Most people did not realize that there were two exits. Streaker knew that a trucker on a tight schedule could squeeze between the end of the building and an oak tree to get back on the main road without having to deal with speed bumps and the stoplight. He took the short-cut and had no trouble maneuvering the sports car between the building and the tree.

He pulled his cell phone from his pocket. Another missed call from Jay. He laughed. There were four rings before the number he called was picked up.

"Sammy. Hey, baby. I need to see you."

§

Samantha slid into a booth in the back corner of The Comet Café. As she removed her sunglasses, she peered across the table at Streaker. The scowl on her face made him divert his eyes down to scan the menu. His leg did a nervous up-and-down motion under the table.

"I don't have much time, Streak. I had to make up some lame excuse just to be here. What's on your mind?"

"I'll get right to the point. This dude named Slick. How bad is he anyway?"

Just as she started to answer, the server appeared ready to take their order. Samantha ordered a salad, making mention of the five pounds she had put on recently. Streaker winked at the bubbly blonde and told her he wasn't watching his weight at all. He decided on the daily special of chicken and dumplings. It couldn't top his grandmother's, but he ordered it anyway.

When the server walked away, Samantha said, "If you can take your eyes off her ass for one minute, I'll answer your question." Streaker directed his attention back to her. She rolled her eyes and let out an exasperated breath. "Anyway, back to Slick. He just got released after serving two years. I talked to a narc officer who knows him. He thinks some of his pals kept the business going while he was in, but he hasn't pinned down where they keep their supply. They did bring Slick in for questioning about selling Oxy to you. Of course, he denied it and they let him go. Then, his probation officer got on his case. You might remember him. Mosely. The guy with the beak nose and beady little eyes. Ring a bell?" Streaker nodded. "Well, I talked with him and he said Slick is pissed big time that some asshole—that's you—is trying to burn him on something he didn't do. Says if he gets a parole violation and goes back in, then he will wipe the streets with your ass."

"Ouch." Streaker squinted both eyes as if in pain. "He and one of his homeboys gave me a run for my money this morning. They know where I live. Guess I better think about staying somewhere else for awhile and changing rides. Throw him off my scent."

"You should leave town, Streak."

"Nah. I've got a couple of jobs to do. They pay good money. Plus I want to keep my eye on someone in case he starts feeling a moment of weakness. He could make more trouble than Slick if I don't keep him in line."

She shook her head. "I don't even want to know. You promised me that you were going to keep your nose clean. But I swear every time I see you, Streak, you're in some scrape. Thank God we never—"

"Got hitched? That was your decision, not mine."

"We would be terrible together. You know that."

He shrugged and wanted a cigarette so bad he couldn't stand it. He took his pensive thoughts to the view out the window. But the silence dragged out long enough. He engaged Samantha with an intense eye-lock and let a twisted smile crack through. "I never killed anyone who didn't need killing."

"Did I say anything about you killing anyone? Streak, you're one of the good guys. The problem is you don't seem to remember that."

§

It took Jay by surprise that Streaker actually answered his call. Prepared for it to go to voicemail, he was so flabbergasted to hear Streaker's voice that he almost dropped his cell phone. He stammered around and then said, "Finally! It's about fucking time!"

"Whaddaya want, Goldie?"

"You know what I want! My car!"

"Okay. We'll do a trade. The rental for your Porsche. I'm having trouble getting a check from the insurance company for my truck. And I gotta have wheels."

"Deal! Where can we meet?"

"Go to the top level of the parking deck connected to the medical office park near the hospital. That's where I'll be."

"That's a crazy place to meet. What about the park across the street?"

"I have something to show you up there. I think it's perfect."

In the six years Jay had known Streaker, he had learned that you don't argue with the cowboy. It was his way or the highway, even if he was the client with the money. They had conducted business in bars, strip clubs, a skybox at Bank of America Stadium, and a car wash. Never had Streaker been allowed to come to Jay's glass and steel office building in Southeast Charlotte near the affluent Myers Park area. Their hook-ups were chosen at random and only for an exchange of cash and names, photos and documents. Over time, Jay discovered that sometimes the only means of completing a business transaction with a reluctant seller, or buyer, was a sealed envelope that contained items that the seller/buyer would rather remain in the unopened parcel. The power of persuasion, Jay called it.

Jay found the Porsche parked in the far corner in the last chance at shade for the afternoon. He gritted his teeth when he parked the Audi. The Porsche's top was down with Streaker's feet stuck out the side. The steel toes of his Western boots went up and down to the beat of country-rock music that blasted from the stereo speakers.

"Oh, Jay. Howdy, bro." Streaker sat up, threw his legs over the door to hop out, and landed his feet solid on the pavement.

With hands in his pockets, Jay strolled over to the driver's side of his car and bent down to sniff. He reeled back with fire in his eyes. "I knew it! You smoked in my car! Damn you, Streaker. The ashtray—full of butts! Fuck! Now I have to get the car detailed. Get rid of your stink."

"Ah, you hurt my feelings." Streaker stuck out his bottom lip and pretended to be wounded by the rant.

"Oh, forget it. We've got more important things to discuss."

Streaker backed against the Porsche and sat on the trunk. "Like what?"

"Like Manny. Where in the hell is Manny? Wonder if he's been picked up somewhere. What if he's telling them everything that happened?"

Streaker shook his head. "Don't think so. We're cool."

"No, we're not. A cop came to see me today. They called off the search at the lake. Now they want to talk to the last people to see Morris alive, and they know I saw him before he went missing. They have a record of my phone call around two that afternoon. I called to tell Morris I was bringing a check over later."

"So? Did you tell the cops that?"

"Yes, of course. They knew I owed him money. Who told them that? They knew the exact amount. So, I showed them the paper I had Morris sign. Says, *Paid in full*."

"Then no problem. You're good."

"I think they might be looking at other possibilities since no body was found."

"What kind of questions did they ask, Goldie?"

"What time I saw him. What kind of mood was he in? Did he seem upset?"

"The boat in the water and the booze is solid. They'll go down that road. They don't investigate murder based on a feeling or a hunch. They have to have probable cause. There's no forensic, no body, no witness, no known enemies. They ain't got nothing, so relax."

"I wish I could. This whole thing is eating me up. Making me crazy."

Streaker drew out a cigarette and cupped his hand around the tip to light it. He raised his chin to exhale. "How were you when the cops came?"

"I think I did okay. I was cooperative. Showed concern. Answered their questions. I don't think they suspected anything."

"Then relax, Goldie. You're making too much of this. They would've taken you in if they had something."

Jay put his hands in his pockets and paced back and forth. "Things didn't go down like they were supposed to," he said. "That's what's tearing me up. I thought about calling my lawyer. Seeing what he thinks."

Streaker's face became stone. He dropped his smoke and ground it out with his boot. With his chest puffed out, he bumped up against Jay as he tried to back away. He grabbed Jay by the collar with both hands.

"You don't do that! You stay quiet, y'hear?" Streaker released his grip, giving Jay a chance to step back. "I was afraid you'd go pussy on me. That's why I brought you up here."

"What are you talking about?"

Streaker grabbed him by the arm and pulled him to the edge of the deck. With his hand in his back, he shoved Jay against the concrete ledge and forced him to look out at the street below. He pointed straight ahead.

"You see that building there? That's where your girlfriend lives. First floor. She parks her Jeep Cherokee on the other side. That's her window. The third one. Next to the freaky artist dude. I like that I can see right into her bedroom. Do you know sometimes she forgets to close the blinds? 'Course I don't mind." Streaker paused, then said with a chuckle, "Why there she is, right there. Sweet! Look at those gorgeous legs under that T-shirt."

"You stay away from her!"

"I will, as long as you keep your mouth shut. If I hear that you're talking to anyone about what happened, then she's mine. Y'know, I kinda have a thing for tall blondes with long legs and a nice ass. Her tits aren't all that great, but they'll do. I'll run my hands through her long hair, and then slide them down over her breasts, and then between her legs. Nice and slow-like. Get the picture?"

"You do anything to her, and I'll kill you!"

"Told you, Goldie. She's safe as long as you keep your trap shut. Are we clear?"

CHAPTER FOURTEEN

Camille walked around her apartment in Matt's T-shirt. Not only was it comfortable, but it reminded her of him. She had a mental snapshot of his handsome face, sweet smile, and tender brown eyes. She couldn't wait to see him again. She was tempted to send him an email to the address printed on his business card, but she decided to honor his request that they not have contact until they met.

Just two more days.

She padded across the bedroom carpet, cell phone in her hand. With her foot propped up on the low window sill, she stared out at the Charlotte Medical Building and parking garage across the street. She preferred the view out the front of her apartment, a park with plenty of trees and flowers. While she stood there, she dialed Jay's number. He answered on the first ring.

"Hi, baby. You got my note and flowers? Pink roses. Your favorite. See? I remembered."

"You have no right coming into my apartment while I'm gone."

"Sweetie, I pay half your rent. Kinda makes it mine. Besides, I had to leave a note because you won't take my calls. I'm trying to tell you how sorry I am. Couldn't help it. It was an emergency. You know how business is. I'd been there if I could."

"I don't want to argue, Jay. Forget it. I called because I want to meet with you. You have some items that I want back." Tyler's portrait of her in the nude came to mind.

"Jesus, Camille, you make it sound like we're done. When are you going to forgive me? You know I love you."

In the background, she heard a car start up and an engine revved up. Tires squeal. "Where are you, Jay?"

"Outside my office."

She didn't believe him, but why would he lie? She said, "When can we meet?"

"How about Friday night? We'll go to that new restaurant in Piedmont Row. I hear it's very good."

"I don't mean a date. Just a meeting."

"We can meet over a plate of food, can't we? I have many business meetings that way. Is Friday okay?"

She exhaled an exasperated breath. "Okay. Fine. It's not a date, Jay. It's a meeting. I want to make sure you understand that."

"Sure, baby. Whatever you say."

§

There was a tradition at Stiles Enterprises. A signed contract was celebrated with champagne in the conference room. But it had been awhile since the last cork was popped. Ernie did the honors while it bubbled over onto his hands and then the carpet. It was apparent to all that he had no problem tooting his own horn. Earlier that day, he closed the deal on the industrial property. For anyone who wanted to look, he held up the check for $538,000, the down payment. There were six around the table that brought their glasses together for the official toast. Jay noted that Amber was missing.

He excused himself and caught her before she got out the door. With her purse over her shoulder, she turned when he called out to her. "Amber, you're leaving? Come celebrate with us. You helped put the deal together. Come take some of the credit."

As she looked up at Jay, she hooked a section of her long chestnut hair behind her ear. Today she did not wear the ponytail or glasses or a business suit. She wore a wrap dress that hugged her shapely figure. All day long Jay found it downright distracting.

"I have to go," she said to him. "Some friends and I are meeting for dinner. Girls night out."

Despite what she said, he put his arm around her shoulders in an effort to steer her toward the celebration. His arm dropped off when she turned away.

"I better not. I don't want to drink champagne and then drive."

He made sure that she saw his frown. "Just one drink."

"No, Jay. I've gotta go. Look, I'm glad it worked out. I know you've had a lot on your mind lately, especially with the Camille situation."

"Thanks for your help with that. Everything is all set. There's no way she'll leave me after what I have planned."

"It's a lot of money to keep a girl."

He shrugged in dismissal. "I called in a few favors."

"I hope she takes you back. You know why?"

"Why?"

"So you'll be in a better mood. You've been a pill to work for this week." She smiled and playfully slapped his arm with the back of her fingers.

"Sorry about that. You're right, I've had a lot on my mind, but things are looking up."

§

At last, Friday evening arrived and Camille could have closure with Jay. She'd demand to have the portrait back, along with some racy photos that Tyler had taken of her. She could finally move on with her life, which she hoped included Matt Garrison.

Fifteen minutes before Jay was due to pick her up for dinner, a man in a dark suit appeared at her door. He said he was there on behalf of Jay, and he would take her to him. He led her out to an awaiting stretch limousine. Its black paint and tinted windows glistened under the sinking sun. Its ominous presence made her hesitate, but the driver held the door for her and smiled. She wondered what Jay was up to.

The driver passed the street where she thought he should have turned for the restaurant. At first, she was not concerned, thinking Jay had another place in mind. But when he drove west on Billy Graham Parkway away from town, she became suspicious. She knocked on the glass partition to get the driver's attention. In the rearview mirror, she saw his dark eyes and heavy brows. He switched on a speaker and asked if he could be of assistance.

"Uh, where are you taking me?"

"I am taking you to Mr. Stiles. We're almost there, miss."

He pulled into a private airstrip, onto the tarmac, and stopped alongside a small airplane that looked to hold about eight passengers. After the driver assisted her out of the car, she stared up at the Cessna in disbelief.

At first she was too stunned to speak, but then she blurted out, "What the hell is this?"

She turned to the driver, but he had slipped away. She saw him seated back behind the steering wheel. Before she could say anything, he floored the accelerator and sped away. Panic-stricken and confused, she didn't know what to do. She stood motionless on the tarmac, debating her next move. From the corner of her eye, she saw a figure emerge from the back side of the plane. Tall and handsome in tan cargo pants and a knit polo, he gave her a dimpled smile and extended his hand.

"Welcome, Camille. Pete Campbell. I will be your captain. I promise a safe, comfortable trip."

"Am I supposed to go somewhere with you? Where's Jay?"

"Jay has planned a surprise for you. He will be waiting for you when we land. The flight should take about an hour."

He made a gesture as though to lead the way up the steps, but she stood frozen and shrugged her shoulder in resistance. Clutching her purse close to her chest, she said, "I have to be somewhere tomorrow, so I'm not stepping on that plane unless you tell me you can bring me back *tonight*."

"Of course. You can return whenever you wish."

"Promise?"

He smiled and dipped his head slightly in what she understood to be an affirmative response. He extended his arm out toward the plane. Obediently, she followed him into the belly of the plane and was taken aback by the plush interior. It had soft leather chairs that swiveled around from their positions at the window to form a seating area. Each seat had an attached tray that included a cup holder that folded down to the side when not in use. In the rear of the plane, a dozen pink roses rested across a wet bar. A card was pinned to the ribbon that kept it bundled together.

"I'll give you a few minutes and let you know when you need to fasten your seat belt," Captain Pete said before he went upfront to the cockpit. Suddenly the door closed. It was too late to make a getaway, so Camille sank down into the softness of leather.

She noticed there was a box under the roses. Once opened, she folded back the pink tissue and found a one-piece bathing suit. It was from her favorite boutique where she and Jay often went when he wanted to treat her to something new. When they shopped there, she tried on clothes while he charmed the sales clerks outside the dressing room. She assumed that the same ladies helped with his selection. She had to admit she loved it.

A bathing suit in all probability meant the ocean. The time frame fit in with the distance from Charlotte. It wasn't long until she knew her guess was correct. She saw the Atlantic Ocean out the window. The pilot instructed her to fasten her seatbelt as they made a slow descent. The landing was bumpy as the tires hit asphalt, but came to a smooth stop. A limo suddenly pulled alongside.

Camille thanked the pilot for the flight and reminded him of his promise, to which he only smiled and nodded.

CHAPTER FIFTEEN

Camille stepped off the plane and walked over to the awaiting limo. The driver looked like a nightclub bouncer in a dark suit stretched tight over his barrel chest. He held the door open for her. The limo rolled away from the plane to a destination still undisclosed.

Fifteen minutes later, Camille caught a glimpse of the Atlantic Ocean out the front windshield. From the remnants of a sun that had already set, the sky carried its slate-blue color onto the calm water. Looking out at the horizon, she couldn't tell the defining line between sky and sea since they seemed to blend into one. It had never occurred to her that her day would end with her staring out at ocean water, many miles away from home.

The driver made a right turn onto the road that ran parallel to the beach. They headed south for what seemed like a mile and then turned left into the driveway of a beachfront home. The upscale two-story structure was a gray clapboard with white trim and accents of bright flowers in hanging baskets.

To protect it from storm surge, the house was built up on sturdy wooden posts. The open space below was used for parking. From the porch that extended the full length of the exterior, a staircase led down to the driveway. Still seated in the car, Camille looked out the window to see Jay scurrying down the steps to meet her. He was dressed in a blue knit shirt that carried the same bright hue as his smiling eyes. The breeze blew his blond locks onto his forehead in unruly fashion. His tanned face sported a wide grin, indicating his happiness to see her, and perhaps relief that she had played along with the mystery voyage.

The driver offered his hand to assist her out of the vehicle. Then he stepped aside so Jay could gather her in his arms. She stayed rigid in his hold.

"Hi, Camille. I hope you like your surprise. I wanted to do something special."

"I can't stay, Jay. I have to be back in Charlotte. I have plans."

He stepped away to slap a roll of bills into the palm of the driver and relieve him of the gift box and flowers that he pulled from the back seat. Jay then walked back to Camille. He hitched his chin to indicate a van parked beside his Porsche.

"I hired a caterer to fix dinner for us. I thought we could dine on the deck overlooking the ocean."

"You certainly went to a lot of trouble."

He did not address the irritation in her tone, but said with a smile, "Let's go upstairs, honey, so I can set this box down and put your flowers in water."

With her arms crossed, she remained with her feet firmly planted in the sandy soil. He exhaled an exasperated breath, but then his eyes went soft. He said, "Camille, I *did* go to a lot of trouble. And you are worth every bit of it. Am I worth one night? Just one night. That's all I'm asking."

"You have a few hours and then I want to get back on that plane."

His response was a smile, but enough assurance to get her up the steps to go inside. As an interior designer, it took something spectacular to gain her approval, but the décor in the great room did just that. The sitting area had a high cathedral ceiling and a massive stone fireplace. The two sofas met at a ninety-degree angle and were accented with a plethora of throw pillows. The walls were adorned with seascape oil paintings, serene and beautiful. The floor-to-ceiling window looked out over the ocean, bringing an abundance of light into the room. French doors led out to the deck, partially open to admit the sound of the surf and the ocean breeze. The salty scent fused with the smell of crab, scallops, and shrimp being prepared in the kitchen.

Jay said, "Let's go out on the deck and have a glass of wine before dinner."

When he tried to take her hand, she pulled it away. He gave her a perplexed look, which prompted her to say, "Jay, this is all very nice, but I'm not big on surprises. I have plans for tomorrow, and I have to get back to Charlotte."

Although his expression showed disappointment, he nodded. "Whatever you say."

"I told you it was supposed to be a meeting. Not a date, remember?"

"Camille, please."

She conceded and followed him outside. In silence, she stared out at the ocean where waves curled and spilled surf onto a beach narrowed by high tide. The view alone was worth the unforeseen trip. It was a tranquil setting that contrasted with the battle waged inside her head.

This was the old Jay, the sweet romantic guy she had loved and adored, not the aloof, workaholic he had become in recent months. Although her focus was on the view straight ahead, she sensed his presence even in his silent stance. Tomorrow it would be Matt at her side to start a new chapter in her life. If only she could close this one. But Jay was not making it easy.

§

Their meal was a five-course affair, and by the time it was over, Camille felt tipsy from the wine. The sky had turned black. It was then that Jay told her she couldn't fly back that night. The pilot was not yet licensed to fly by instrument.

"It would have been nice for you to tell me that sooner, Jay. Then, first thing in the morning. I have to get back," she said. "You can have the master bedroom and I'll take one of the other four bedrooms. Who owns this place?"

"Emerson Kirsch."

"That rich guy with the trophy wife?"

Jay chuckled. "Yes, that one."

"I remember them from the party at their house, or should I say their estate? That's a more accurate term. Beautiful place." Camille scanned the room and added, "I assume Jennifer did the decorating. She has exquisite taste."

"Yes," he said softly.

He reached across the table and took her hand in his. His thumb rubbed across in a sensual way that made clear his intent. The flame from the hurricane globe danced across his face. She was mesmerized by his eyes. She remembered their first meeting when she had turned suddenly to find his baby blues fixed on her, making her blush. The bluest eyes she had ever seen. There had been no mistaking their meaning then, or now. His gaze alone seduced her in ways that sent an awakening in the most sensual areas of her body. She was angry at herself for feeling it now.

§

After their dinner and once the caterers had left, Camille and Jay wandered back inside and got comfortable on the sofa. His cargo shorts made it possible for his bare thigh to rub against her knee. She quickly moved away to put some distance between them.

She cleared her throat and said, "Jay, I need to say some things." He gave her a questioning look. She went on to say, "We've been drifting apart the last few months." He tried to take her hand, but she pulled it away. "Don't. You know it's true. Your work has taken over your life, and I feel like you have no time for me. I think we should admit that it's not working."

He placed his finger under her chin and forced her to look directly into his eyes. "I feel terrible, baby," he said. "I've treated you so badly, and I'm so sorry. You are the most important thing in the world to me and I want to make it up to you. I promise—I mean, I swear—that things will be different from now on. You are going to be my top priority. I won't be working as hard as I have. I want to make more time for us. Camille, I love you so much. It would kill me to lose you."

"It's too late, Jay."

"You're wrong. I haven't been the man you deserve, but I can start now, Camille. Give me another chance. Please."

"Jay, I wish that—"

He cut her off, saying, "Camille, I thought I wouldn't have to tell you this, but I guess I do. The reason I've been so distracted lately is a situation with my father. I had to spend a lot of time trying to find a way to get him out of a tough spot."

"What are you talking about?"

"It's like this—he borrowed some money from the wrong people, and they were threatening him. I had to come up with the funds, deal with some scary bastards to get them to go away, quit threatening him. They're not nice people, honey."

"That doesn't sound like your father."

"Are you saying I'm lying?"

"No, it's just that he's such a fine, upstanding man, I never would have thought—"

"Yeah, well, it shocked me too. So, you see, honey, I've had a lot going on and I wanted to spare you. The crisis is over now. I've negotiated a deal, and they're out of his life for good."

"You should have told me, Jay. I would have understood."

He took her hand. "I didn't want to burden you, sweetie. It was a nightmare. So sorry I neglected you. It won't happen again, I promise."

"Still, I think we need a break. Maybe it will do us both some good if—"

She stopped when she noticed him drawing something from his pocket. A small velvet box rested in his open palm. He gazed down at it and said, "I got this for you."

"No, don't."

She tried to stop him from opening it, but he did anyway. A large square diamond winked back at her. The lamplight made it sparkle. The platinum band was adorned with smaller diamonds. It was undoubtedly the most beautiful ring she had ever seen.

"I want you as my wife. I swear to you that I will be the kind of husband you deserve. The thought of losing you made me wake up, baby. I've changed. You know how much I love you, Camille. I've always made that clear."

"Wow," she said as she fixated on the ring. "Jay, I don't—"

"Remember how good it was in the beginning? How happy we were? It only changed when I got so stressed out—work and the situation with my dad. It's going to be different now. No more problems."

"Jay, I don't know if we can ever get back to what we had. You're right. It was great, but now—"

He cut her off. "Just think about it. Okay? Give me that?"

"Jay, this doesn't change.....Where are you going?"

Her eyes followed him as he slipped away down the hallway. He returned moments later, holding a long white tube of paper. Rolled up and held in place with a rubber band, it reminded her of some of Tyler's sketches.

He smiled and removed the band while she looked on. He unrolled the pages of thick paper and held it up for her to see. Between his hands, he held her dream. It had been her dream for the last six years and there it was. Hers for the taking. Jay played his trump card.

CHAPTER SIXTEEN

Jay laughed because Camille was too dumbfounded to speak. In her hands, she held the validation of her dream, what she had worked so hard for, but feared she'd never achieve.

"It's what you've always wanted, honey. Your very own office designed to your specifications. No more rented space. I remembered how you described it, so I had it sketched in the way I thought you would want it. I might have got it wrong, but the building is in the early stages of renovation so you can customize it however you want. It's the corner space. A prime location."

Jay was giving her the space free of charge in one of the old warehouses he had recently purchased. Once renovated, it would be prime real estate. In her head, she did the math. He would lose out on thousands of dollars in a leasing agreement. She didn't know the rate per square foot, but she knew the space was around 1,500 square feet.

She shook her head and covered her mouth. "Jay, I don't know what to say."

"Say you'll marry me. We'll be partners in marriage and partners in business. You can finally get out of that dump you rent. I just want to make you happy, Camille. That's all that is important to me."

"Wow! I didn't know you understood how important a new office is to me. I didn't know you were listening to my ramblings."

He smiled. "Yes, I listened."

She leaned over to kiss him. It was supposed to be a simple gesture of gratitude, but an innocent kiss can turn significantly different in seconds. His arms went around her, his body pressed into hers. She felt his heat, his breath on her neck.

"Jay, don't. It confuses me."

"Is there someone else, Camille?"

"No, of course not."

"You sure?"

She hesitated, but finally said, "Yes."

"Then prove it."

Before she knew it, he was carrying her to the bedroom where he set her down on the bed. He seemed to take pleasure in prolonging his salacious gaze at her supine position, making clear his ravenous longing for her. He undressed her, saying nothing. A slow methodical process. Then, he stretched out over her. He tore out of his own clothes to come inside her. When he thrust deeper, she wrapped her legs around his hips and moaned. Her fingertips dug into his back.

Afterwards, she covered her face with her hands. "Wow! I couldn't help my screams. It just felt so good."

"No problem. At first, I thought I was hurting you."

"No. Anything but. It was fantastic."

He kissed the side of her head. "I love you, baby. Marry me, Camille. Please say yes."

"Please don't rush me."

§

No matter how hard she tried, Camille could not sleep. For awhile she listened to the sound of the breakers as they rolled up on the beach. She was glad Jay left the French doors cracked. Not only was the sound of the surf soothing, but so was the gentle cool breeze that brushed against her like light kisses on her bare skin. As Jay slept on his side, she heard his even breaths. If she got up, he would never know, she decided. After she pulled back the sheet, she eased off of the bed. She pulled Jay's polo shirt over her head and then tiptoed out of the room. She stepped outside onto the deck and sat down in a padded chair, her knees pulled up and her arms hugging her legs tight.

Life was a quandary, she proclaimed. Jay asked her to make one of the most important decisions of her life. But if she was to move forward with him, she would need to look back on her past. The fears that haunted her never seemed to go away. Could Jay wipe them out for good? Could Jay make her feel safe?

Her daddy had promised her that he would, but he didn't. Unlike Jay, Daddy played hard more than he worked hard. He didn't give them much before he died, but left them flat broke after he was gone.

Known for driving well above the speed limit on the back roads of the county, Cade Carson took a curve too fast, overcorrected, and hit a tree head-on. He died instantly from massive head injuries. Camille remembered standing in the kitchen in her pink nightgown with her older brother Kyle at her side. They both stared in confusion at their mother when the policeman brought the news. Mama screamed and collapsed into the officer's arms. Although she was only six at the time, the scene was permanently etched in Camille's mind.

The meager life insurance provided just enough money for a proper burial. The men from the race track where her daddy worked as a mechanic took up a collection that covered another month's rent. The neighbors brought food that lasted a few weeks. After that, they were on their own.

For a short time, they moved back with their grandparents while Mama looked for work. Unskilled and with no experience, she felt lucky to get a job as a cashier at a supermarket. As soon as she earned enough money, they moved into a tiny apartment where they stayed until they missed two month's rent. From there, they rented a cheaper place in a seedy section of town where they stayed locked in as much as possible. Camille remembered that her mama slept with a pistol under her pillow.

A year later, Mama got a job as a bank teller, and Camille believed their life would be better. Mama told Camille that if she worked very hard, the managers would promote her to the head teller position, and then maybe, customer service manager. Soon there would be enough money to move to a better neighborhood. With her goal within reach, Mama went to work early, stayed late, and worked harder than anyone. After all she had done, the promotion went to a pretty redhead that the bank manager took a fancy to. And so it began, a vicious cycle of making ends meet but never getting ahead. But Mama stayed loyal to the bank, even trained managers and loan officers for their new jobs while still doing hers. Then, the bank merged with a larger bank and she was laid off. After twenty-five years, Camille's mother was given a severance package that lasted only six weeks.

Mama was never the same after that, Camille lamented. Although still trim and attractive, she was reduced to a grim, joyless woman. Cade Carson was the love of her life and the bank had been her safety net. To Camille, it seemed a curtain was drawn over her mother's physical presence. Her children were shut out. It was the reason Camille made a vow that two things would never happen to her: growing old alone or having financial worries. She would make damn sure of it.

§

By morning, Camille had made her decision. During their breakfast on the deck with its great view of the ocean, she announced her decision. Yes, she would marry him. No, she did not need to fly back to Charlotte. She'd stay the entire weekend with him, and they'd celebrate their engagement. Jay was so happy he reached across the table to kiss her square on the mouth.

He stroked her cheek and said, "I'm curious, baby. What made you say yes?"

"With you, I'll always have financial security. And you love me. Two things I need. But I'll tell you this, Jay Stiles, if you ever break my heart, I'll make you pay. I'll make you pay big time. If that sounds harsh, then, I'm sorry, but —"

"I like a woman that's drives a hard bargain. I find it a complete turn-on. In fact, it makes me want to have you right here, right now."

She thought he was joking until she noted the look in his eyes. He got up and pulled her close enough to discard his knit shirt that she wore to cover her nakedness. With the shirt now laying at her feet, she wore nothing but the diamond ring he had placed on her finger. Camille slipped behind some potted plants, careful to stay hidden from public view. She was not surprised when Jay gently pushed her down onto a lounge-chair and stretched out over her. They made love with the sound of the ocean waves, children at play, and seagulls squawking as they flew above them.

§

That night Jay took Camille to a restaurant in Murrells Inlet. Originally it had been a small fishing village. Now it was where tourists came by day to go deep-sea fishing, to boat, or to buy fresh seafood. In the evening, they returned to enjoy the local seafood dishes in a variety of restaurants that lined both sides of the narrow street. Beginning at five o'clock, people showed up sunburned and freshly showered in sandals and shorts to put their names on the waiting list for first available seating.

Jay asked the hostess for a table outside where they could hear music from the band next door and enjoy the view of the inlet. Boats with their catch of the day cut through the brackish water between the stalks of saw grass that punched through the black marshy bank. The breeze blew the fusion of salty air and seafood fried to a golden brown. Across the inlet, cottages could be seen in a row facing out almost in a reverent tribute to Mother Ocean.

Camille's thoughts drifted to Matt. He would be at the bar now. Seven o'clock. How long would he wait? Thirty minutes? An hour? No more for sure. If she excused herself from the table to call him what would she say? She would sound more than capricious; she would sound crazy. Instead of breaking up with the man, which she swore to Matt she would do, she was now engaged to marry him! Matt would not offer his congratulations; that was certain. He would think that everything she had said to him was a lie.

"Camille, are you okay?"

Jay's voice brought a halt to her pensive thoughts. She smiled as she held the wineglass to her lips. "Yes, I'm fine. I just remembered that I don't have my charger with me and my cell phone is dead. If I needed to make a call, I couldn't. Not with my phone anyway."

"Who would you call?"

"No one," she said softly.

"Then what's the problem? Aren't you happy, baby?"

"Yes, of course. Why wouldn't I be? I'm marrying a very handsome man who loves me."

But she didn't say *a man whom I love*. Couldn't. Not sure she did.

Matt Garrison.

Jay Stiles.

It wasn't complicated; it was simple. She had a choice to make, and she chose Jay. He was a sure thing. She knew where she stood with him, what to expect. That was not something she could say about Matt Garrison. He was the unknown.

Jay tapped his glass against hers and said, "I propose a toast. To you and me, baby. Forever."

CHAPTER SEVENTEEN

Sunday afternoon on their way home, Jay got a call. Streaker. It made Jay think there was a problem. If he took the call, Camille would be able to hear everything said; therefore, before Streaker could say a word, Jay said he would call him back. He pulled into the parking lot of a fast-food restaurant. While Camille went inside to buy a drink, he leaned against the trunk of the car and dialed Streaker's number.

"Whatever you have to say, Streaker, couldn't it wait until I got back in town? I'm with my girl now."

"Sorry to inconvenience you, dude, but no, it can't wait. Bad news. Morris's death is being investigated as a possible homicide."

The blood drained from Jay's face. He couldn't find his voice, but then he whispered, "Shit!"

"Yeah, that's right, Goldie. A big pile of shit. My source says that the secretary at Morris's company has been on the cops's butts to drop the suicide theory and to look at the possibility of murder. She finally squeezed their nuts hard enough to make them look into it. And since no corpse has surfaced in the lake, they're taking it as a serious possibility." Through his phone, Jay heard a siren and the honking of a car horn, followed by the sound of Streaker's boots against pavement. "I'm walking back to my car," he explained. "Just left Samantha, my former partner. If it'll give you any comfort, she said that they're looking at the ex-wife and her boyfriend. The Lassiter woman hates her guts. She's pointing her finger at her."

"The Lassiter woman?"

"Morris's secretary. She said Morris got into a confrontation with the ex-missus and her new guy at a restaurant. The men exchanged a few punches in the parking lot and the dude threatened to kill Morris. Good news for you, Goldie. You're further down the list. 'Course you may be totally in the clear."

"I have a good alibi if they conclude that something happened that night. Credit card charges in two bars that puts me nowhere near the scene." Jay moved away from his car and walked toward the edge of the parking lot where he stared out at a gas station. The afternoon sun brought heat to his back. He felt a bead of sweat roll down from his neck beneath his knit shirt. "Streaker, I'm still concerned about Manny. Shouldn't we be doing something to find him? What if he talks?"

"I'll put my nose to the ground and see if I can sniff him out. He could be just about anywhere. Hell, maybe he's back in Mexico drinking beer on the beach with his fellow hombres."

"Let me know if you find out anything. I might ask around at the jobsite and see if any of his buddies know anything about his whereabouts." Jay spun around on his heel and saw Camille coming out the glass door with a cup in her hand. "Gotta go. Camille is coming."

"Give her a kiss from me." Streaker laughed. "Remember what I said, Goldie. Nothing comes back to me or your sweet thing will make my acquaintance real fast."

"Go to hell!" He shoved the phone into his pocket and smiled at Camille.

She brought her cup to his lips. "Want a sip?" As he pushed the cup away, he shook his head. "Who were you telling to go to hell?"

"Oh, just some guy I do business with. He can be a real pain in the ass sometimes." Jay brought her into his arms and kissed the top of her head. "Forget about him. Let's get back on the road."

Two hours later they reached Charlotte. Jay drove by the jewelry store where he had purchased Camille's engagement ring. Due to his current cash flow problem, he had opened a line of credit. The purchase was made on an installment plan, and he realized they would be married a long time before the ring was paid in full. He dipped his head to indicate the store. "That's where you need to get the ring sized, honey. The sooner the better. I don't like you wearing it loose. It might slip off."

"Okay, Jay. I'll go tomorrow. It's a beautiful ring. Wait 'til Alex sees it! She will flip out. She's been wanting us to get married. As pushy as she is, I wouldn't be surprised if she'll want to take charge of the wedding plans."

Jay only half listened to Camille. His eyes fixed on the rearview mirror that showed an older model Cadillac that seemed to be glued to his rear bumper. As if the big black dude with a shaved head and dark glasses could hear him, he yelled, "Get off my ass! If I'm too slow for you, then go around me!"

Camille looked back over her shoulder. "Why is he following so close?"

The words were just out of her mouth when the car tapped the back of the Porsche. Camille let out a little scream. Jay looked in the rearview mirror and then at her. "Are you okay, baby?"

"Yes. What's going on? Why did he do that?"

"I have no idea, but I'm sick and tired of people messing with my car. We're turning at the next street and getting away from that asshole."

But before Jay could turn onto a side street, the long sleek sedan rolled up beside them like a golden chariot. In the left lane, the driver kept his focus on the street ahead, never turning to gaze at Jay. However, he brought his right hand up. For a panicky moment, Jay thought it held a gun, but the hand was only extended out to give a one-figure salute. The middle finger remained in Jay's sight until the Cadillac passed by.

"Streaker," Jay mumbled to himself.

"What?"

Jay looked over at Camille and forced a smile. "Nothing, honey. It just occurred to me that the dude might have been a friend of that guy I was speaking with earlier on the phone. I think he was playing a joke on me. Trying to get me riled up." Jay faked a laugh and rolled his eyes. "What a dipshit." For a time, he got lost in his private thoughts and then reached over to place his hand on her knee. "Camille, if anyone ever bothers you, tell me, okay?"

"What do you mean?"

"I mean, if you see anyone following you or trying to creep you out, I want to know about it."

She stared back at him, then said, "Okay, but who would want to harm me? I've got no enemies, Jay."

"Just promise you'll tell me."

§

Camille's neighbor, Tyler, was the first person to hear the news about her engagement. As he leaned against the door jamb, he rubbed sleep from his eyes, pressing his palms flat into his eye sockets.

To most folks, he looked like a member of a rock band. But he wasn't musical. He was an artist who dabbled in everything from charcoal to oils.

His appearance reflected his creative style. Five silver hoops in the left ear, one diamond stud in the right, and tattoos galore down both arms. His yellow hair, in bad need of a cut, stuck out all over like wet straw. He wore polyester shorts with a drawstring that hung loosely on his thin frame. His ragged T-shirt had a silkscreen design of the Grateful Dead. She remembered it from their first meeting over three years ago.

"Sorry to wake you," she said to him. "I forgot about your crazy hours."

As she held out her hand, he gazed at the ring, but said nothing. She found it odd, because Tyler *never* stayed silent. He might mumble incoherently, but he always had an opinion. Never one to mince words, he was known to be brutally honest.

She pulled her hand away from his hold and said, "Well? Aren't you going to say congratulations?"

"So, he went and pulled this shit, huh? Is it for real or just for show?"

"The ring?"

"No, Cammie, the proposal. He's not the marrying kind. I thought you were going to break up with him—you told me you were. What happened?"

Her eyes widened. She spit out her words to show her displeasure. "He loves me!"

"So?"

"So, he wants to marry me. Jeez, Tyler, what is with you? Why can't you be happy for me?"

He scratched his cheek that hadn't seen a razor in days. "Okay. I'll be happy for you. I guess you're going to move into that big-ass townhouse. Well, that's the end of our friendship. He won't let me come over, you know. He looks at me like I have fleas."

"You're crazy. Jay likes you. He liked your painting, didn't he? We'll still see each other."

Tyler rubbed his hand over his face, then made eye contact with Camille. "Okay. I have to say this."

When he hesitated, she said, "Say what?"

"He has a spy. He's watching you, Camille."

"What are you talking about?"

"This cowboy-looking dude. He came around recently asking if you live here. I didn't tell him, but he knew. I saw him another time. He was watching your apartment from the parking deck across the street. With binoculars, Cammie. Your boyfriend is the jealous type, and he wants to make sure you're not two-timing him."

"That is ridiculous! Stay off the weed, Tyler. It's doing funny things to your brain."

"Go ahead and laugh if you want, but it's the truth. Jay told me once that if I ever touched you, he'd cut off my dick. He also told me that I did not have his permission to paint you nude again. Like I *need* his permission."

"You don't know Jay like I do, Tyler. He loves me to pieces. He'd do anything for me."

"I hope you're right, Camille. I hope you're right."

"As far as the stalker guy goes, Jay told me to tell him if anybody creeped me out, so I'll tell him. You're wrong to think this guy has anything to do with Jay. He would never do such a thing."

"Whatever you say, girl."

CHAPTER EIGHTEEN

Camille felt she owed Matt an apology and an explanation. He deserved to know the truth; otherwise, he might think she was one of the shallow women who liked to play games with men. That type liked to toy with a man's heart like a cat plays with a mouse before it goes in for the kill. She didn't want to be one of those; hence, she wrote a two-page explanation to take away some of the sting, some of the humiliation he must have felt when she didn't show. Of course, there was always the chance Alex was right. He could have been looking only for a one-night stand. And as she had warned, he could have a significant other back in Savannah, but she didn't think so. She saw the way he looked at her. It was sincere, heartfelt. Camille read through the letter one last time before she folded it up and stuck it in an envelope to mail.

What would his reaction be when he read it? Hurt? Understanding? Anger? Rage? If she were in his place, what would she think? That Camille Carson was a crazy woman that didn't know what she wanted. She crumpled up the two pages of rambling shit and tossed them into the trash can. Instead, she dialed his number and was relieved that her call went straight to voicemail. She didn't want him to answer and she sure as hell didn't know what she'd say if he did. Her message was brief, but to the point.

"Matt, it's Camille. I'm sorry I stood you up. I hope you didn't wait long. There's a new development in my life, I mean, I guess you could say it's taken a different direction. Anyway, what I'm trying to say is I can't see you. I think you're a terrific guy and if circumstances were different, I'd want you in my life, but it's just not possible. Not now. I'm sorry, Matt. Well, I better go. Bye."

She meant to sound nonchalant, casual, but her voice was tinged with emotion. Her eyes began to pool with tears, but the deed was done. She didn't feel right about being in limbo with Matt, better to make a clean break. She owed him an explanation, even if it was lame and stupid. After a deep breath and a sip of wine, she felt recovered sufficiently to make another call.

This time she called Alexandria. It was no surprise that her friend was overjoyed with her engagement news. Not a detail was omitted as she told her about the whole unexpected weekend trip to the coast.

When Camille finished, Alex said, "So, the deciding factor was when Jay showed you plans for a new office?"

"No, Alex." Her succinct reply let her irritation show. "How shallow do you think I am? I'm not marrying Jay because he can give me a fancy office. You're missing the point. What matters is that Jay knew how important the new office was to me. He knew that was my dream, and he wants to fulfill it. He *gets* me, Alex. That's the thing. Besides, with Jay I never have to worry about financial security. I'm set for life."

"Do you love him?"

"What do you think?" Camille exhaled an exasperated breath and added, "Look, Jay promised me that we can go back to the way we were. He understands he messed up. He should have told me about his father's financial problem. Now that it's resolved, Jay says I'll take priority over everything, including his business. Sometime you have to get a man's attention by threatening to end it."

"I'm happy for you, Cammie. You deserve it, girl. I can't believe you were going to throw away your relationship with Jay for some guy you met in a bar. Don't you know Jay's the real deal?"

"Yes, I know," she said softly. "He won't ever disappoint me, will he, Alex?"

"How can you even ask me that?"

CHAPTER NINETEEN

Jay and Camille had been engaged for four weeks and so far he had managed to maneuver around any specific plans. She pressed him, trying to pin him down to an exact date, but he was able to put her off.

He said to her, "Let's get through the renovation project on your office first, and then we can concentrate on the wedding. Is that okay with you, sweetheart?"

She agreed.

On a drive back into the city after a meeting in Raleigh, he had plenty of time to think about Camille, the investigation of Morris's death, the still-missing Manny, and Streaker's threats. Maybe he worried too much. Nothing bad had happened. The police had not come around again, there was no word of Manny flapping his gums, and Streaker was too content driving around in his new replacement truck to badger him with threats.

For once, Jay was thankful that his overpaid accountant was an idiot with no guts to do oversight. It allowed him to get the money back in the escrow account without drawing attention. He wrote out a new check to replace the one he snatched back from Morris before he died. His debt was now paid in full. No threats of a lawsuit. Finally, he could breathe a sigh of relief.

Stuck in traffic, Jay turned the A/C at full blast. His tie was discarded and tossed into the back seat. He had unbuttoned the top button of his dress shirt but still tugged to loosen the starchy collar that felt too tight around his neck. His sleeves were rolled up, but he continued to smolder when the sun's rays honed in on the driver's side window. A quick glance at the car clock told him he was already ten minutes late. He'd promised Camille that he would take her to the job site to see her new office, yet only the interior framing, electrical wiring, and plumbing had been dealt with so far.

When he arrived at his office, he found that she had helped herself to his desk. He flung his suit jacket into a chair. She looked up as her fingers flew across the keyboard of her laptop. Slowly she closed its lid and stood up, relenting the desk to its rightful owner.

She planted a kiss on his cheek, but that wasn't enough for Jay. He pulled her into his arms, lifted her up and set her down on the desktop. While she leaned back, he stretched over her and slipped his hand underneath her skirt. After a prolonged kiss that required her coming up for air, she placed her hands on his chest and pushed him away.

"Shouldn't we be going?" she asked. "I'm dying to see my new office."

Before he spoke, he took time to enjoy her awkward descent from the desktop with her legs spread apart. "First, let me show you the plans," he said.

From a drawing board, Jay retrieved a fat roll of prints. The cumbersome thick paper crackled as it unrolled. As he swept his hand over the thick stack, he pressed the sheets flat across the top of his desk. His index finger landed on the left bottom corner. He smiled down at Camille. "Your office. Right there. A prime spot. You'll love it. Although it can be seen from the street, the entrance will be inside the atrium area. That will give you more security."

"Who will be my neighbors?"

He beamed as he replied, "The other tenants that have signed leases so far are a book store, coffee bar, gift shop, and a café that will have indoor and outdoor dining on the patio out back. Upstairs, we've leased one side to a law firm and the other side to an engineering consulting group. Only four more retail spaces to lease and we have some good prospects for those."

"It looks great, Jay. Let's go see it."

"You act like a kid on Christmas morning."

"For me, it *is* Christmas morning. I've waited a long time for this day."

Since Jay didn't want to get the car dusty or drive over a nail on the mud-rutted construction site, he parallel parked on the street. With his hand in Camille's, he led the way to the construction trailer located in the back. They scaled the wooden steps leading inside, but before he opened the door, he said, "We have to follow policy, honey. You have to sign a form waiving the company liable from any injury and we also have to get hard hats."

He held the flimsy aluminum door open for her. "We'll get the project manager to take us inside."

The cramped trailer was filled with tables, folding chairs and filing cabinets. An air conditioner chattered noisily in the corner window. Although there seemed to be some sense of order to the confined space, equipment and blueprints were scattered about on two large work tables. The project manager had his back to them as he talked on the phone. Camille tuned out what seemed to be a heated discussion of no concern to her. Besides, she was fascinated by photographs displayed on a cork bulletin board taken of the warehouse before the renovation began and as it progressed. It was obvious to her that the original building had sat dormant for years, which in her opinion, made the restoration project even more ambitious and demanding than she had imagined.

The project manager finally hung up and swiveled around on his metal desk chair to face them. As soon as Camille locked eyes with him she felt the heat come to her cheeks. Her heart began to race. As their eyes met, she gaped at him in disbelief. Jay's lips were moving, and she was certain he was making some sort of introduction, but she needed none.

The man who extended his hand to her for an official handshake was Matt Garrison. She felt her hand go limp in his when Jay said, "Matt, I'd like you to meet my fiancé, Camille Carson."

CHAPTER TWENTY

Matt Garrison's eyes stayed engaged with Camille's. If he was as panicked as she, he hid it well. Although his lips were unsmiling, he maintained a cordial persona.

"Glad to meet you," he said to her. "You'll need to sign a waiver form. While you're doing that, I'll find a hard hat for you."

Jay excused himself to take a call and told them to go on ahead without him. She was left alone with Matt.

"Watch your step," he said as he held the door for her on the way out of the trailer. He stayed a few feet ahead as they traversed a makeshift walkway of two by fours that coursed over muddy, broken ground to the back entrance of the building. In her high heels, Camille took brisk steps just to keep up. While Matt wedged his hard hat between his arm and waistline, she struggled to keep hers from sliding forward over her forehead.

"Will you please stop for a minute!"

"I thought you wanted to see your office space, Miss Carson." Matt stared down at the hand she placed on his arm.

"I need to adjust this hat."

He snatched it from her. "I'll do it."

While she looked on, she said, "Matt, thanks for not saying anything."

He stopped adjusting the inside band to look up at her. "What would I say? 'Oh, Jay, no need for an introduction. We've already met. Your fiancé was passed out in my hotel bed the night before my job interview with you.'"

"I had every intention of meeting you that night. I didn't mean to stand you up, Matt. Things happened that were out of my control."

"Yeah, I see. Instead of breaking up, you got engaged. Congratulations, by the way."

"I called you later."

"Yeah, I got your message."

His annoyance lay exposed to her like a wound, and his words had the sting of an antiseptic. A frown appeared on his face that hadn't seen a razor in a day or two. His appearance was a stark contrast from the morning he kissed her goodbye at the hotel. She had been mesmerized by his dapper appearance in a gray suit and silk tie. Now, he was dressed in faded jeans and a sweat-stained T-shirt. But despite his ragged look, his anger, and the awkward circumstance of their reunion, she still found herself drawn to him.

She started to speak, but he walked off before she could get the first word out. She had no choice but to follow him into the building. Beyond the wood framing, she noted that it was nothing but an empty shell of bricks reminiscent of an era long past. Scaffolding was set up along the rear wall. In the main corridor, a drop cloth covered the wooden floor. The original naked light bulbs encaged in wire provided the only illumination, but fortunately her office space had a large window overlooking the street. Shafts of bright sunlight streaked across the scratched, dingy floor.

"Here it is," Matt said. "This is your little corner. Of course, it will look different once we finish."

Matt avoided her gaze, instead chose to stare up at the ceiling as if inspecting it for repairs.

"Please let me explain, Matt. I am so sorry. I never meant to hurt you."

"No apology needed. You made your choice. He's in, and I'm out."

She frowned and shook her head. "It's not that simple. I was taken away. Out of state. I couldn't have come even if I wanted to."

"You were kidnapped?"

"No." She dropped her head. What was the point? Nothing she could say would make it right, she decided. She was engaged to Jay and that was that. She didn't realize she had a smile until she saw Matt's puzzled stare.

She explained, "I was just thinking about our night together. It never occurred to me that your job interview was with Jay. It's so weird! Who would have thought? Small world, huh?"

His response was a hard stare. He looked past her at the person coming up behind her. Jay put his hands on her shoulders and kissed the back of her head. "What do you think, honey?"

"I- I love it, Jay. I can't wait to see the completed project."

He wrapped his arms around her for another kiss, this time on her lips. Matt scratched his brow with his thumb and looked away.

Jay released his hold on Camille. He turned to Matt to ask, "Are we on schedule?"

"Yes, so far. There's a little problem with getting the sheetrock delivery, but hopefully that will just put us a day or two behind. We'll finish the interior framing tomorrow."

Camille stepped away from Jay. She squatted down in her heels to inspect a dark spot in the flooring. She noted that it was damaged with deep holes and an ugly grease stain.

Her hair fell over her shoulder as she looked up. "What about this?"

Jay squatted down at her side and rubbed his hand over the surface. "This was a mill that manufactured yarn and on that spot was a large piece of machinery," he explained. "It was bolted to the floor, and oil and grime stained the floor over time. Matt and I have talked about it and the only choices we have is to tear it out and add new flooring or we can repair the holes and put down carpet."

As she brought her hands to her knees, she stood up. "I prefer a wood floor, Jay. I thought we already discussed it."

"Yeah, you're right. I forgot. Then that's the way we'll go." He turned to Matt and smiled. "We have our answer now."

Matt nodded. He glanced at his watch. "If that's all, Jay, I need to get back to take care of some details."

"Sure. Thanks, Matt. We'll talk later."

Camille watched him walk away with no parting words. What would he say anyway? "It was nice to meet you, Miss Carson." No way. Her eyes stayed on him while Jay's attention was diverted to the examination of the exterior brick wall. As Matt made his way to the rear door, she studied his broad shoulders and muscular arms. It made her think of that special night when he swept her up in his arms and carried her inside his hotel room.

On their way out, Jay turned to Camille and said, "So, what did you think of my guy?"

"What?"

"Garrison. Did you get the impression he really knows his stuff?"

"Yes, I guess. We didn't talk much."

"I was lucky to get him. He's a fucking genius when it comes to renovations. He's already come up with some ideas that will save money and will actually work better. Madison wanted to hire him, but I offered more money. I told him I needed an answer right away. Didn't want Madison to come back with a counter offer."

"How did you happen to hear about Matt?"

"At a trade show. I was just shooting the breeze with some guy. I was telling him my idea of renovating two old buildings downtown and he told me if I ever did that, I should hire Garrison to do the work. Did you know he has a degree in architecture?" She shook her head, feeling guilty for her lie. "Yeah. He did construction all through college to earn money and was hired by an architecture firm when he graduated, but decided he liked hands-on work better. Anyway, he's a real craftsman."

Outside in the bright sun, Jay slipped on his Ray-Ban sunglasses and continued, "Garrison played a little hardball with me. He talked me into hiring his buddy Danny as an assistant. My cash flow is a little tight, but I agreed. What the hell? This is the future. Renovation. Garrison did a lot of similar projects in Savannah."

"Yes, I know."

"You do? I thought you two didn't talk."

She swallowed hard, took a deep breath, and said, "Well, he did tell me that much."

§

Danny Townsend heard a strange sound coming from the back of the building. A pounding that grew louder as he got closer. Someone was up to no-good. Everyone had left the jobsite except him, so whoever was making a god-awful commotion and destroying property would have some explaining to do. He brought a scrap of lumber up to his shoulder. It was the only thing handy he could find to defend himself. But as soon as he saw the familiar figure, he slung his weapon off to the side.

"Matt! I thought you left! The trailer's locked up, didn't see your truck. What the hell are you doing?"

With a mighty grunt, Matt brought the sledge hammer down at his side. "What does it look like?" he said, "I'm taking out the wall." Danny looked on as Matt blotted sweat from his forehead with the sleeve of his T-shirt.

"Why? The guys are scheduled to do that tomorrow. That's not your job." As he stepped closer, Danny punched Matt in the arm and said, "Hey man, let's get cleaned up and go check out that new bar near the arena. How about it?"

"Nah. You go ahead. I'm going to finish up here."

Despite Danny's refusal to leave, Matt resumed working. After he raised the sledge hammer up to his shoulder, he brought it back down with all the power he could muster. Mortar and bricks busted apart in pieces with fragments sailing through the air.

"MATT!"

Matt stopped. He hooked his thumb over the waistband of his jeans while his other hand rested atop the wooden handle of his tool. "What is it, Danny?"

"You never told me about Stiles's woman. What did she think of it?"

"Of what?"

"Duh—her office space, dude."

"I guess she liked it. You'd have to ask her."

"I hear she's hot. Pearson said she's got an incredible body. He said he got a boner just watching her walk. Makes me wish I'd been around at the time."

Matt gave him a hard stare. "I thought you were going to the bar, Danny. I'm trying to work."

"What's eating you, man? You've had a burr up your ass all afternoon. What gives?"

"It's just been one of those days. Go on, Danny. Maybe I'll catch up with you later."

"Sure, bro. See ya."

Danny kicked a rock with his boot and then walked away. He heard Matt mumble something inaudible as he slung the sledge hammer onto the ground. Danny turned when Matt called out to him.

"Danny, don't go. Come back here."

Danny walked over and said, "You changed your mind?"

Matt kicked a hole into the ground with the heel of his work boot. He locked eyes with Danny before he spoke. "This has to stay between us, Danny. No one can know."

"Sure. How long have we been friends? Have I ever let you down?"

"I mean *no one*. Got it?"

"Sure. Spill it."

"You remember I told you about the girl I met my first night in Charlotte? Before the interview with Stiles."

"Hell, yeah. 'Course, I remember."

"Stiles's fiancé. That's the girl I was with. Camille Carson."

"Are you serious?" When Matt nodded, Danny chuckled and threw his head back. "Oh, shit!"

CHAPTER TWENTY ONE

Matt found out the hard way that a mixture of broken heart and 80-proof whiskey is a cocktail for disaster. Not only did he feel like hell, he had a bruised jaw from an altercation with some dude over a stupid bar stool. *Don't ask*, he decided to reply if anyone wanted to know what had happened. Why had he let Danny talk him into going to a bar in the first place, he wondered the next morning.

At the time, he thought maybe it would take the sting out of Camille's surprise visit. Over shots that kept on coming, he had recounted for Danny his encounter with her at the jobsite. Danny already knew the complete low-down of their first meeting. Matt had told him as soon as he returned to Savannah after his job interview. Once he knew all the juicy details, including Camille's sleepover in Matt's hotel room, Danny had insisted that he would be crazy not to take the job in Charlotte and even crazier if he didn't show up for their planned rendezvous the following Friday. However, when she stood him up, Matt packed up his gear that very night and drove back to Savannah, straight for Danny's place where he drank beer for breakfast. Just like the message on the orange T-shirt he gave to Camille. He thought about that after he sobered up.

He got wasted then and wasted again last night. When would he learn? Now his head throbbed, and his mouth felt like cotton. Coffee didn't help. As he was filling out paperwork in his office trailer, he heard a knock on the door. Maybe if he ignored it, the person would go away. The incessant pounding continued until he dragged himself out of his chair. He cracked the door only wide enough to see one of his workers, a man named Pepe, looking up at him from the bottom step. Behind him was a short Hispanic woman with a round face and rounder body. Her eyes were cast down, not meeting his gaze.

"Mr. Boss, sorry to bother you," Pepe said. "Need to talk."

Matt held the door wide and stepped aside. "Sure. Come in."

Pepe spoke to the woman in Spanish as he took her hand and helped her inside. He pointed to a folding chair and offered his assistance as she eased down in the seat. Again, Pepe apologized for the sudden intrusion. Matt waved him off and pulled up a chair for Pepe. Then, he rolled over his own desk chair and sat down facing them.

As if he remembered his manners, Pepe said to Matt, "Oh, this is Manny's mother, Senora Sanchez."

Matt nodded at her and said, "*Buenos dias.*" He turned back to Pepe and asked, "Who is Manny?"

"Manny. Good man. He worked here before you come. He was foreman before me. Senora Sanchez is worried. Manny...he missing long time. Five weeks....more. He worked late for Mr. Jay one night and he not come home. No one see him. No call. Nothing. Senora say Mr. Jay to pay him $1,000 for extra work. She not see money, not see Manny. She need help. Find her son. Mr. Jay not return phone calls. Please...you, help."

"Pepe, I don't know anything about this. If he's owed money, I'll check into it. I'll call the office today, but I don't know what I can do to help in finding him. Has Mrs. Sanchez called the police?"

"No. She don't call. Manny come here....no Green Card. Police call Immigration."

"I don't think so. She needs to report it. Does she want me to call?"

Pepe spoke to her in Spanish. She shook her head adamantly. Matt was not prepared for the barrage of tears that followed. Although Matt knew enough Spanish to get by, she spouted out words so fast he could not comprehend. He reached for a tissue from his desk and handed it to her. She blew her nose and continued her monologue while Pepe reached over to pat her hand.

"What is she saying?" Matt asked.

Pepe scratched his cheek and paused before he spoke. "She say she afraid if police find Manny they send him back. He here over fifteen years. He save money for his little sister surgery. That why...that reason he do extra work for Mr. Jay. He have no family in Mexico. She say if he go back, not good. Last year, her uncle go back. He work here for twenty-five years! Still, he sent back. Drug cartel kill him! Put in grave with other bodies. She scared that happen to Manny. He a good man, Mr. Boss. He work hard for family. Manny smart boy....speak better English than me. Something happened to him. He not leave his family like this. Never."

"What does she want me to do?"

"She want you to talk with Mr. Jay. Find out. What happened?"

"Okay. I'll do that. How do I get back in touch with her?"

"Just find me. I tell her what you find."

Matt's heart ached for the poor woman who just wanted to know what had happened to her son. He saw the desperation in her eyes, the dark circles beneath them that told him she had not slept in a long time. He knew there was no way he could refuse to help.

"I'll let you know what I find out," he said as he stood up. Pepe and Mrs. Sanchez got up to leave. He led them to the door where they almost collided with Danny as he entered.

"Excuse me," Danny said as he stepped aside to allow them room to pass. He looked at Matt and extended his hands out as a question. "What was that about?"

"Ever hear the guys talk about someone missing? A man named Manny?"

"Yeah. Sure. He was the foreman. He disappeared. Still missing, I hear."

"That was his mother. I promised to help. What's the name of Jay's assistant? The one that gave us the employment forms when we came to work."

"Oh, yeah. Her." Danny snapped his fingers as he tried to recall. He picked up the carafe from the coffee maker and held it over his mug. "The pretty girl. I think it started with an A.

Ashley, maybe. No, that's not it." He filled his cup and turned back to Matt. "Amber. That's it!"

"Well, I'll start with Amber. Jay was to pay Manny $1,000 for extra work. Maybe she knows something."

Danny let out a low whistle. "One grand? For what? Man, that must have been something special for that kind of money."

"Special or illegal."

After he blew across the surface of his cup, Danny laughed. "I can see the wheels already spinning in your head."

§

Matt once took a college course about the behavior patterns of homo sapiens. According to the instructor, they had remained unchanged over thousands of years. The one thing that fascinated Matt was the lecture on the body language and unconscious signals of a liar. Since then, he considered himself skilled at detecting when someone was lying to him. That is why he thought a face-to-face meeting with Amber and Jay was important. He might learn something about the disappearance of Manny Sanchez and the payment of one grand, or he would find out nothing. Either way, he would know if they were being truthful or not.

He left the construction site earlier than usual in order to swing by the company headquarters. First, he would confront Amber, then Jay. He figured Jay was still at the office. He had received an email from him right before he left the construction trailer.

Danny was right about Amber. She was pretty. On his entrance, she greeted him with a big smile that showed dimples. He was glad he took the time to wash up and brush dirt from his jeans before he left the trailer, but wished he had thought to shave that morning. His hangover had shot down that idea as soon as he rolled out of bed.

At Amber's desk, he said a quick howdy and then got right to the point. "Amber, do you know anything about some extra work that Jay asked Manny Sanchez to do?"

"No. I thought Jay had cancelled any overtime."

"Yeah. Well, you handle the time reports, don't you? You didn't see anything for Manny that warranted additional pay?"

"No. Why?"

He started to give specifics, but decided not to divulge what he knew until he was clear about what *she* knew. "Just checking. Do you know how I can reach Sanchez?"

Her brows knitted. She licked her lips. Her silent stare lingered long enough to make him wish he'd found another approach. "Wouldn't you know the answer to that?" she said. "You're his supervisor, aren't you?"

"Actually, he's missing. In fact, I've never met him. His mother came by this morning. She hasn't seen him in weeks, and he hasn't been at work for awhile."

"That's strange. Come to think of it, I haven't seen a time card for him lately."

"Maybe Jay knows something. May I see him?"

"I guess. Let me ring his office and let him know you're here."

Matt's wait went on longer than ten minutes. He hung around Amber's desk and drew her into small chitchat while she logged out of her computer and gathered her belongings before heading home. At last, Jay came up front. He cordially invited Matt into his office in a way that seemed to say, *How nice that you dropped by.* His mood changed with Matt's first question.

"Who told you that I owed Manny one grand? Why would I pay him that kind of money?" Jay asked.

"His mother said you hired him for some extra work."

"No. That's not true. I don't know where she got that idea."

"Then, do you know where Manny is? He hasn't been at work."

For a few seconds Jay was distracted by a few short beeps of his cell phone. He received a text that he did not bother to answer. His gaze went back to Matt. "No, I have no idea where he is. You know these guys. They come and go. If they think there's some kind of heat on them, they take off."

"I don't think that's the case. Someone should call the police. Report him missing."

The color left Jay's face. He cleared his throat before he spoke. "That is for his family to handle. Stay out of it."

Taken aback by his brusque remark, Matt said, "Okay. I just think it needs to come to someone's attention."

Jay shot up from his chair, suggesting he was done talking. Although he had more questions, Matt allowed Jay to escort him to the door. It didn't sit well with him when Jay faced him and put a hand on his shoulder. It was done in a condescending matter, and it made Matt want to slap the hand off.

"Leave everything to me," Jay said. "I'll contact Mrs. Sanchez personally and offer any assistance. Thanks for dropping by, Matt."

On his way to his car, Matt was surprised to find Amber leaning up against her parked car in the space beside his. With arms crossed, she shot him a dimpled smile.

"Well?" she asked.

"Well what?"

"Did you find out about the extra pay? I hope I didn't miss something. Jay would be on my case."

"Jay said it wasn't true. There was no extra time or extra pay. Amber, I'm just going to say this straight up. He lied to me, and I want to know why. Can you throw any light on the mystery?"

While she thought about his question, she removed the elastic band from her ponytail and raked her fingers through her hair. It cascaded down onto her shoulders. She brought her index finger to her lips and said, "I'll have to think on that."

"Maybe you can think about it over a drink. I know I look like hell in my work clothes, but maybe we could grab a beer at a place where I might fit in. Whaddya say? Care to join me?"

"Only if you let me follow you. I don't want to leave my car parked here. Jay will get nosey about it. He doesn't know I have a life outside the office. I wouldn't want to disappoint him."

"Then we'll keep it our little secret." He gave her a wink and a smile.

CHAPTER TWENTY TWO

If you keep buying someone drinks, they usually open up. At least, that had been Matt's experience, but with Amber it didn't seem to ring true. For a petite woman, she handled her liquor well, never even got a buzz. Jay's personal confidante divulged no secrets, giving Matt no insight into the Sanchez matter.

His gut told him that Mrs. Sanchez hadn't lied about the promised money, but he felt for sure that Jay had. After he walked Amber to her car and saw her off, he stood in the parking lot of Ed's Tavern and called Pepe. He told him he had nothing to report and urged him to take Manny's mother to the police to report her son missing.

When he got resistance, he conceded. "Okay, okay. I will get assurances from the police that they will not deport him if he's found. Pepe, if I get that, will you take Mrs. Sanchez to see the police?"

"Yes, yes. She worried. Every day that go by, she more upset."

Fifteen minutes later, Matt called him back. Yes, he had the word of the person he spoke with in Missing Persons. They would not turn him over to Immigration officials unless he had done something illegal. An hour later, Pepe called back to tell him they had made an official report. Every law enforcement official in the county would now be on the lookout.

Just as Matt started to end the call, Pepe said, "Wait, wait. Something you should know. Mr. Jay call Senora Sanchez. Her daughter Maria answer phone. He say to tell her mother he give one thousand dollar cash to her, end of week. He not say it for Manny's work. He say help for family. Strange he say that."

Hush money? But Matt didn't put the question to Pepe. Instead, he said, "Tell Mrs. Sanchez I hope Manny is found safe."

§

Camille stood at Jay's side on the portico of Emerson and Jennifer Kirsch's home and waited for the door to be answered. Jay couldn't take his eyes off Camille in a short strapless sundress. He said she looked so sexy and enticing that he might have to make love to her long before they returned home. She rolled her eyes and elbowed him for saying such a thing.

In awe, she stared up at the white columns of the Greek revival home. For an interior designer, the house earned the same reverence a priest would afford the Sistine Chapel. Because of Jay's friendship with the Kirsch family, she hoped that one day she would be given the opportunity to add her own creative touches to the massive interior with its high ceilings, arched doorways, and custom crafted woodwork. Jay told her that Jennifer liked to decorate almost as often as she changed hairstyles.

Camille's appreciative smile for the house was misinterpreted by Jay, or so she thought when she noted his salacious gaze. He palmed her ass and buried his face into her neck. His kisses ceased when Emerson opened the door wide.

"You better save that for later, my friend," Emerson said with hearty laughter. He stretched forward to plant his own kiss on Camille's cheek. "Hello, sweetheart. Come in, come in. You are a vision of beauty as always." He turned to Jay and said, "How's your father?"

"Good. Thanks for asking."

"I should call him." Emerson had been partners with John Stiles for over twenty years and although their relationship had soured, he remained a mentor to his son.

"After he gets over the shock of hearing from you, I think he'd be glad you called."

"Can't stay disconnected for forever, right?" Emerson said. "Come on in, you two. Party's just getting started."

With his hand on her back, Jay ushered Camille through the doorway. A small group mingled near the spiral staircase where a server offered hors d'oeuvres to guests from a silver tray. In the midst of chatter, Camille recognized the girlish laughter of

Jennifer Kirsch. She spotted her between two petite women who made the blonde beauty look even taller than her five-nine height.

In a sleeveless jersey top with matching pants, Jennifer excused herself in order to make her way over to the arriving guests. She extended a slender hand to Camille. "So nice to see you. Glad you and Jay could make it." For Jay, she stretched up on tiptoes to kiss his cheek, then wiped away her lipstick print. Her voice purred, "Hello, darling. Is it true? You proposed to Camille?"

Jay smiled. He reached for Camille's hand and held it flat over his palm in front of Jennifer. "Of course it's true. See?"

Jennifer placed her hand under Jay's to examine the ring on Camille's finger. "Wow, it's beautiful. Congratulations. When Emerson told me, I was speechless. I thought no woman could settle you down, Jay."

"I couldn't let this one get away," he said, draping his arm around Camille.

"I'll have Emerson offer a toast in your honor. Why don't you two head out to the terrace? Jay, tell the bartender to fix one of his yummy margaritas for Camille. She'll love it. Emerson and I will be along shortly. We're still greeting our guests."

Jay and Camille made their way through the foyer following the sounds of a live band, coming from the back terrace. Someone called Jay's name. He turned to see his sales director headed toward them. With hurried steps, Ernie's drink sloshed around, but somehow managed to stay in his glass.

"Hey, Jay. Hi, Camille. Glad I caught you before you went out." Ernie paused to smile at Camille. "Wow. You look so nice, sweetie. You don't mind if I borrow Jay for a minute, do ya?" He tapped Jay on the chest and said in his boisterous voice, "You gotta go downstairs and see what Em has installed. He's got a TV screen that comes down from the ceiling. State of the art, man. Got special features like you wouldn't believe. You gotta see it. I think we could use something like that in our conference room. C'mon and I'll show you what I'm talkin' about."

Jay turned to Camille. "Honey, do you mind? Let me find out what Ernie is so pumped up about, and then I'll join you outside."

"Sure. Go ahead. I'll be fine."

As she stepped onto the brick terrace, Camille spoke briefly to a few people she recognized as business associates of Jay. A steel drum band played island music on the opposite side of the pool. While she enjoyed the tinny percussions, she tapped her hand at her side. She saw Matt Garrison before he saw her.

Damn! What is he doing here?

When he had her in his sights, he stopped in his tracks. He'd just gotten two drinks from the bar that he held suspended in each hand as he stared back at her. In order to deliver the extra drink to the person waiting for it, he had to walk by Camille. There was no other passage.

As he approached, she said, "I didn't know you would be here."

"It was a surprise to me too, but here I am. Where is your fiancé?"

"Inside." She focused on the drinks he held. "You came with someone?"

"Yes."

"Well, does she have a name?"

"Yes."

"And it is?"

"Amber."

She swallowed, almost choking. "The only Amber I know is Jay's assistant."

"That would be the one."

"Really?" From across the pool, she saw Amber watching them. "What happened to your jaw? Looks like you've been in a fight."

"Maybe."

"Look, Matt, I don't want us to have any hard feelings. Can we be friends?"

His eyes locked with hers. "I don't think so."

"Why?"

"Because we were going to be *more* than friends. At least, that was the impression I got." He broke eye contact and took a sip of his drink. "I better go. Amber is waiting for her drink."

Indifferent to Amber's stare, Camille grabbed his arm before he got away. "Look, Matt, we're going to be crossing paths. So, unless we're on friendly terms, it's going to be awkward for both of us."

"You are the fiancé of my boss and a future tenant of a building I'm working on. That is the extent of our relationship. I can be polite and professional if you can."

"Sure."

"Tell me something, Camille. That morning we were together—It was just a tease, wasn't it? I mean, you told me to blow off the job interview, stay with you, but....hell, I don't get it. I mean, you go from saying you're going to break up with the guy to becoming engaged to him. Who does that?"

"You don't know me. If you did, it'd make sense to you." His response was a blank stare. Camille flitted her eyes away to take in the threat from across the pool. "You better go before your date starts to show her claws. And you can tell her that I don't know what I did to make her dislike me, but I apologize for whatever it was."

"I'm not your messenger." He started to walk away, but stopped. "Camille." She looked up, hopeful that he had changed his mind about being friends. Even in his annoyance, his brown eyes stayed soft. They made her weak enough to want to come into his arms, beg for his forgiveness, but she couldn't and wouldn't. She had to remind herself that her heart belonged to Jay.

She licked her lips, fought back feelings she had no business having. "What, Matt? You wanted to say something."

"Nothing. Forget it." Her eyes stayed on him until he said, "You look nice."

"Thanks. You better go. Amber is waiting."

§

Jay stared at Emerson's television screen and couldn't believe what the news reporter was saying. With a microphone up to her mouth, she stood along a highway in the adjoining county to give her report.

She started out by saying, "About an hour ago, police received a tip about skeletal remains found in the wooded area behind me. It was discovered about fifty feet off Highway 115." The reporter did a sweeping motion with her hand to indicate an area secured by police yellow tape. "As you can see, this is an isolated stretch of highway between Davidson and Mooresville and it is extremely dense with trees. I spoke with Sheriff Tom Jackson of Iredell County a few minutes ago and he said the remains will be transported to the coroner's office to determine the identity of the individual. The remains were found by two brothers, Josh and Joseph Carter, who were walking through the woods in search of their dog. They spotted what they thought was a pile of trash thrown into the woods, but upon closer examination they realized it was clothing and then, they discovered a skull and other human bones. We do know that the coroner has been called to the scene and is en route. It is not yet clear if the death was a result of foul play or natural causes. We will have an update for you at eleven. Back to you, Robin."

Jay feared it could be Manny. He was glad Ernie was too wrapped up playing with all the buttons on the remote control to pay any attention to the story. "Ernie, I'm going outside to join Camille. You're right about the set-up here. It could work for us. I'll give it some thought."

As though the house had been deprived of oxygen, Jay gasped for breaths, his forehead beaded with sweat. He blotted it with his handkerchief. Instead of making his way to Camille, he walked out the front door where he almost collided with a couple.

"Sorry," he said.

The man clasped Jay's hand. "Jay. John Taylor. We played golf together with Emerson back in March."

"Oh, yes. I remember."

"Are you okay? You don't look so good?"

"I'm fine. Just came outside for some fresh air."

Jay did not stick around for small talk. He sauntered down the front steps and drew his cell phone from his pocket. While he waited for the call to go through, he walked down the circular driveway and out to the street where houses as grand as Emerson's lined both sides.

"C'mon. C'mon," he said, tapping his hand at his side.

No answer. He dialed again. Still, no answer. He dialed once more. The call was picked up on the fifth try.

He heard Streaker's growl. "Your timing stinks, Goldie. I'm in the middle of something. Call ya later. Bye."

"Shit!" Jay yelled when the phone went silent. He re-dialed the number.

After four rings, Streaker picked up and said, "Can't this wait? I'm with someone right now."

"No, it can't. Are you watching the news?"

"Are you crazy? I don't watch the news, the weather, or the Dow report! I like *fucking*, which was what I was about to do until you called. Now the lady is not in the mood. Thanks, Goldie." Jay heard a door squeak and then close. "What the hell do you want, anyway?"

"They found a body in the woods. I think it's near Morris's lake house. It might be Manny."

"Or it could be someone else. Bodies are found all the time, Goldie. Go back to whatever you were doing while I try to get back inside Katie's pants. My window of opportunity is closing fast."

"See what you can find out, Streaker. You've got contacts. I need to know if it's him. Please."

Jay heard a soft muttering that sounded like cursing, then a long audible exhale. "Okay, okay, I'll see what I can do. Don't call me. I'll call you. Got it?"

"I need to know as soon as possible."

"You need to grow some patience. If the body is unidentified, it might take a while. If it's Manny, then he was killed that first night, five weeks ago. That's a lot of time. In the woods, out in the open, exposed to the weather, with critters and maggots eating on a corpse. Shit, there may not be enough left to know who it is. My guess is they won't have dental records to make a match, and DNA takes a while."

"Well, we know now he didn't live long enough to go to the authorities."

"That's right, Jay. Turn a man's death into a positive spin. 'Atta boy."

CHAPTER TWENTY THREE

With his arm around Amber's waist, Matt waited with other guests for some big announcement from the guest of honor. He didn't know Emerson Kirsch and he couldn't care less what the man had to say. In fact, he preferred to split and put some distance between himself and Camille. They had ended up in the same vicinity at the buffet table and then again at the bar although neither acknowledged the other.

In front of the band, Emerson stood with his shot glass suspended in mid-air. After a series of shushes, all chatter was suspended while they anticipated his words.

He began with, "Everyone raise your glass. I know, you guys thought this was just my backyard barbeque I do every year and you're right. But tonight we have something to celebrate. I think everyone here knows Jay Stiles." Emerson scanned the crowd. "Jay, where are you, buddy? Ah, there you are." He drew attention to Jay, grinning big while his arm was draped over Camille's shoulder. Emerson continued, "I've known Jay since he was a tall scrawny teenager driving his dad's golf cart like a maniac. Over the years, he has become like a son to me. When John Stiles retired, he left his company in the capable hands of his son Jay. I've taken Jay under my wing. Unfortunately for him, over the years I've dished out plenty of unsolicited advice. Sometimes he listened and sometimes he didn't. But you all know me. Some of it was just pure bullshit." There was laughter. Emerson shrugged and smiled sheepishly. "And, my friends, that's a lead-in to what I'm about to say. If he had asked me, I would have advised him not to ever let the beautiful woman at his side get away. But Jay is a smart man. He figured that out on his own. So now I have the pleasure to announce his engagement to Camille Carson. They make a lovely couple, don't they? Let's toast to their future, to their happiness—"

Emerson was still yakking when Matt set his glass on a tray and leaned over to whisper in Amber's ear. "Let's get out of here."

Before she could respond, he grabbed her hand and led her through the crowd. Inside the house, he snatched up her purse and ushered her out the front door. She struggled to keep up with his brisk steps.

At his car, he paused with his hand on the passenger door handle. Instead of opening the door for Amber, he turned to face her. "What am I doing?" After a pause, he added, "Sorry. That was rude. You should be there to celebrate your boss's engagement. Now it looks bad that I whisked you away like that. C'mon, I'll take you back."

She smiled and placed her hand on his arm. "No. You did me a favor. Thanks."

His brows knitted. "What?"

"I would have felt like I was christening the Titanic with full knowledge of its demise."

She laughed when he seemed befuddled. "I would have felt like a phony, Matt. Congratulating the happy couple when I know it's a train wreck about to happen." She smiled. "I'll make you a deal. I'll explain myself if you explain why you lied to me about your little chitchat with Camille. Let's go to my place. I hear wine can be a great truth serum."

Beats the heck out of being here.

When they arrived at her apartment, Amber left Matt in the kitchen with a corkscrew and a bottle of Sauvignon Blanc while she went into the bedroom to change from her mini-skirt into shorts and a tank top. After he filled two wineglasses, she led him by the hand into the living room and pulled him down onto the sofa. With one leg up on the cushion, she turned to face him. She clinked her glass against his.

"To us. To friendship. To office romance. To whatever the hell we are to each other because I'm not sure of our official status."

Amber spit out her sardonic words so fast it left Matt stunned. She did the toast solo while he stared back at her. Over the rim of her glass, her eyes locked into his. She took another sip and then set her glass down hard on the coffee table.

"I'm confused," he said softly.

"Are you? Me too. I know you are new to the company, new to Charlotte, but somehow you know Camille Carson. How? I'm not a fool, Matt. I saw her put her claws on your arm to keep you from walking away. Your little discussion had enough heat for me to feel across the pool."

He downed half of his wine in one gulp, a delay tactic. "Yes, we knew each other briefly. One night. Camille is history. I didn't sleep with her if that's what you think."

"Is that the truth?"

He broke eye contact, then stared down at the carpet. Technically, it was true. "Yes," he replied softly.

"Okay, then. Now that we've got that out in the open, I'll explain why I didn't want to stay for their little celebration." She smiled at him and paused, which piqued his interest. Finally, she said, "I set it up. The engagement. That was my doing." She laughed and took another sip. "Crazy, huh?"

"What are you talking about?"

"You see, Camille and Jay had a big fight. She was going to break up with him. By accident, she sent an email to me and it explained the whole thing. It was supposed to go to someone named Alex, but I guess she mistakenly clicked on my name. Anyway, I got this email saying that she met some guy in a bar and they really hit it off. He was from out of town and they made arrangements to meet in a few days at the same bar where they met." She reached over for her glass to finish off the wine. "I showed the email to Jay. Maybe I shouldn't have. I mean, why should I care? I guess it was out of loyalty. Anyway, I helped him devise a plan to keep her from meeting with this guy."

"How?"

"We got her out of town."

Matt diverted his eyes down. He felt a tightness in his jaw and a sick feeling in his stomach. He drank the last of his wine and shot up to retrieve the bottle from the kitchen counter.

When he came back, he refilled both their glasses and turned to her. "How did you get her out of town?"

"We had her picked up by limo, driven to the airport and flown to a surprise location where Jay had a romantic weekend planned. She resisted at first. She thought the pilot would bring her right back. All she wanted was to meet with Jay and break up, but he had other plans."

"What plans?"

"I told Jay if he wanted to make sure the other guy was out of the picture, he needed to ask her to marry him. A ring would claim her as his. Anyway, I told him to propose and to clench the deal, he needed to give her the one thing she always wanted."

"What's that?"

"You'd have to know her. She's always wanted a state-of-the-art office. I think it was a psychological need or something. To prove she was successful, I guess. When I was around her, that's all she ever talked about. Her dream. I guess it's because of her humble beginnings. Jay told me she grew up poor and I think she's always had a need to prove that she made it and overcome the odds."

After Amber took a sip of wine, she said, "I feel bad for having any involvement in Jay's plan, but I felt sorry for him. After he read that email, he was so upset. I know he loves her like crazy, but I shouldn't have gotten involved. He sucked me in like it was part of my job." She frowned. "If she only knew the real Jay Stiles."

"Who is the real Jay Stiles?"

Amber's mouth twisted in a sly grin. "He's a lying, conniving snake."

"I've seen signs of that myself."

"When you questioned him about Manny's extra pay." A statement, not a question. Amber added, "I wouldn't be surprised if he knows something about his disappearance."

"Amber, do you know any more about it than what you told me?"

"No, Matt. I was honest with you. I don't know anything, but like you, I have a feeling Jay is hiding something. Let's not talk about him anymore. Let's talk about something more pleasant." She kissed him on the lips lightly. "Or we don't have to talk at all."

Matt turned his glass up and emptied it. He stared out into space to keep his eyes from locking into hers. He tried not to be affected by her hand rubbing his thigh. His mind was spinning like a top.

Jay.

Camille.

Her words: *I had every intention of meeting you that night.*

Further explanation: *Things happened that were out of my control.*

"Matt, are you okay? What are you thinking?"

Amber's words jarred him back. He turned to her and smiled. "Nothing. I was just wondering about something...if I'd stayed in Savannah....not moved here."

"Well, I'm glad you did. Shall I show you how glad?"

Again, she stretched forward to kiss him. As before, her lips merely brushed his. But then she got up on her knees and straddled his lap. Her arms wrapped around his neck. His face got buried between her breasts. He put his hand on her back to brace her as he leaned forward to let his empty glass slip from his hand onto the carpet. He figured it wasn't wine that he wanted after all.

CHAPTER TWENTY FOUR

Upon awakening, Matt stared up at the ceiling, his head cradled in the palms of his hands. Above was an overhead light and fan. In his apartment, he didn't have either. His head hurt and his mind was a fog. He turned his head sideways to find Amber asleep on her side. Memories of last night kicked in. Her place. Her bed. Their clothes on the floor.

When she stirred, he felt her bare back rub up against his arm. With his fingers pushed into his eye sockets, he cursed. In one night, he had complicated his life. *Damn!*

When he slid over to the edge of the mattress and sat up, Amber rolled onto her back. If he was careful, he could get dressed and leave before she ever woke up. However, her eyes opened just as he pulled on his pants and zipped up. She smiled at him. He looked down to see her chestnut hair fanned out across her pillow. Dark eyes stayed on him in a tease, almost coaxing him back into bed.

She sat up and pulled over his pillow, hugged it against her chest. "You're not leaving, are you?"

He eased down onto the mattress and placed his hand on her knee. "Yeah. I better go."

"It's Sunday. I'll fix breakfast. Do you like pancakes?"

"Amber, I have to go."

Matt stood up. Because her silent stare made him uncomfortable, he busied himself by picking up her clothing from the floor and running his hand over them to smooth out any wrinkles.

"Matt, do you think last night was a mistake?"

"No, of course not."

"Then why am I picking up signals of regret?"

Matt sat down facing her. His bent knee, up on the mattress, bumped against her leg. While his hand stroked her cheek, he said, "It's just that it's not fair to you. Look, last night was great. I mean it. It's just that I'm—well, I'm not ready for a relationship, that's all. I may not even stay in Charlotte. I meant what I said last night. It might have been a mistake for me to come here."

"Am I a mistake, Matt?"

A light kiss to her lips was meant to take away the hurt in her eyes, but it had no effect. Her body stiffened. He placed his hands on her shoulders when he spoke. "Amber, I'm messed up. I don't know what I want."

"You're in love with Camille Carson, aren't you?"

He shot up from the bed, grabbed his car keys from the bedside table. "I gotta go."

Before he even got near the door, he heard Amber call to him. "I'm right, aren't I? You're in love with Camille."

"No, you're wrong. I'm over her."

Amber wrapped the bed sheet around her torso and followed Matt into the living room. He got down on his knees to look under the sofa. "Have you seen my shoes? Where in the hell did I leave them?"

"I know I'm right, Matt. I see it in your eyes. It's Camille."

He stood up and scratched his head. "I took them off when we were on the sofa. Or did I take them off before that?" He bent over and looked under the coffee table. "Damn. I gotta have my shoes."

"That's why you wanted to leave when Emerson made that announcement. You couldn't stand to hear that she was engaged to someone else."

"No!" Matt showed her his back, headed for the kitchen, still in search of his shoes.

"For one minute forget about your damn shoes!" While she kept the bed sheet in place with one hand, she used the other to grab his arm. He twisted around to face her. "The email that Camille sent." She made her voice softer, almost a whisper. "It was you, Matt. You said you had one night with her. It's starting to make sense to me now."

God, he felt awful. His head pounded. His scramble to leave caused a wave of dizziness. He drank too much, that was it.

Finally, he slumped down into a chair at the kitchen table. He allowed himself only a minute to recover before he stood up. Keeping his eyes fixed on the window over the sink, he said, "I better go."

"I'll get your shoes." She walked over to open the closet door and reached down for them. "I'm a neat freak. So what?" She attempted a smile. Her hand stroked his arm. "Matt, you don't have to go."

"Yeah, I do." He slipped into his loafers. As his eyes met hers, he said, "Amber, about what you know or *think* you know, I'd appreciate it if you—"

"Wouldn't tell anyone? It's crazy to be hung up on her now that she's engaged to Jay. No offense, but you're pathetic, Matt."

"Yeah, I'm pathetic, that's for sure. Promise not to say anything, okay?"

"Sure. No one would believe me anyway."

He put his hands on her shoulders and kissed her forehead. "Thanks. Sometimes life gets complicated."

"Sometimes we find ways to make it complicated."

§

Jay was humiliated. Never in his life had the unthinkable happened. Camille was sweet, even understanding in fact, but still—. They were one of the last couples to leave the Kirsch's party. As usual, they left a trail of clothes all the way to Camille's bedroom. There was plenty of kissing, groping, exploring each other's bodies, but that was it. He could not get an erection. Finally, he rolled over to the far side of the bed.

Of course, he couldn't explain to Camille that his mind was on other things, like the body found in the woods that might or might not be Manny. All night, he tossed and turned, but could never fall asleep. At first light, he kissed her goodbye with a soft kiss that landed on her cheek while she remained asleep.

Until he heard back from Streaker, Jay could find no peace. He called Emerson and cancelled their golf game and then begged off of a dinner party with Camille and some of her friends. Alexandria would be in attendance and he hated to miss out on her unabashed flirtation, but today he wasn't in the mood.

Jay couldn't wait any longer. He drove over to Streaker's apartment on a side of town he tried to avoid. Although it was considered safe, it was full of artsy people. Even Camille's neighbor, Tyler, came from the neighborhood. But he knew Streaker liked it because of the bars and the women he called "free spirits." With a bit of apprehension, Jay parked his Porsche out front and hoped that it was in the same condition when he returned. Hell, they might strip off some parts for some crazy psychedelic sculpture or something. Damn hippies.

Streaker answered the door without a shirt, a cigarette dangled from his lips. He greeted Jay with a blank stare, but backed up so he could enter. "Didn't I say I would call?"

"Well, you didn't, and I need to know." Jay walked over to the sofa and sat down.

"I just got in. Shit. Wipe my ass, Goldie. I'm the one taking all the risk."

"Did you find out anything, Streaker?"

"Yeah. I went to see my former partner from the force. Had to wait until the coast was clear." Jay looked confused. "Never mind. It's a long story. Anyway, when a certain someone headed out of town, we met and I got her to tell me what she knew."

"Get to it. Have they identified the body?"

"Yeah. Sorta." Streaker ground his cigarette out on a dirty plate and sat down in the recliner across from Jay.

"What does that mean?"

"There was no body, Jay. Only skeletal remains. The coroner determined that the person was probably Hispanic based on hair analysis. He also could tell that it was a male in his twenties. So, it could be Manny. They found scraps of clothing that they showed to Manny's mom. She swears they belonged to him. They're sending DNA samples to Raleigh for testing to make it a slam dunk, but they're going on the assumption that it's him."

"Damn!" Jay raked his fingers through his hair. He stood up and paced, wearing a path in front of Streaker.

"Don't beat yourself up, Goldie. You didn't do it."

"I gave him the money! He was carrying the money, Streaker! One thousand dollars. I paid him in advance because I didn't want to show up at the jobsite and pay him there. Someone might get suspicious."

"I guess that explains why they found a portion of his pants with the pocket turned inside out. They think it was robbery. Probably got jumped soon after he left the truck....after we wrecked." Streaker paused to light another cigarette. He studied Jay who had stopped pacing and turned his back to him. "Goldie, you're not going to fall to pieces on me, are you?" Jay shook his head and ran his hand over his face. Streaker added, "Shit. If I knew you didn't have the stomach for this, I'd never have—"

"I'm okay," Jay said, "This is screwed up, that's all. What if they put the pieces together? Your wreck. Manny in the vehicle. Where he was employed. It all comes back to me. They'll come around again. Ask questions. Shit! Maybe I should leave town."

"Yeah, Goldie. Take off. No explanation. That'll clear your name. Won't look suspicious at'all." He paused to exhale a puff. "Are you out of your fucking mind? Keep your usual routine. They have to have hard evidence. They've got nothing! Stay calm. Don't crap all over the place 'cause I'm not gonna clean up your mess. Not anymore, Goldie. I told you before, this is all on you. If you think about going to the cops or leaving town, then I'm paying your little girlfriend a visit. That's not a threat. That's a promise."

"Maybe it would be better if we go to the police before they come to us. If we have the same story with a different spin to what really happened then maybe—"

"Shut the fuck up!" Streaker went into the kitchen and came back with two shot glasses and a bottle of Jack Daniel's whiskey. He filled both and held them in the palm of his hand. "You don't get it, Goldie. This is not the same as when your daddy got you off for smoking pot, or driving drunk, or speeding. *No one*, not even your old man, can get you out of this jam. You'd be looking at murder charges for sure. The best you could do would be to get ten to fifteen behind bars, and that's with leniency.

"Here, drink this so you can calm down. You know what? You're not leaving my sight, not until you pull yourself together. Even if it takes days. I don't trust you, man. Drink up. You might be here awhile."

CHAPTER TWENTY FIVE

Camille sat in her parked car and dreaded having a face-to-face meeting with Matt, even if it was strictly business. Maybe she'd get lucky and he wouldn't be around. She'd leave a note taped to the unfinished doorway of her office space.

She wanted Jay to deal with a change to her floor plan, but he said he was tied up and asked her to handle it. It was why she was at the site of her new office on her own.

Inside the 100-year-old building, a thin layer of debris coated the wood flooring. A shaft of light from a window showed dust particles floating in the air. She feared that her navy pencil skirt and white sleeveless top would need a trip to the cleaners after walking through the mess. When she glanced down, she saw that her high heels were already covered in grime.

She observed construction workers standing on scaffolding as they filled in mortar between gaps on a brick wall. Others nailed two-by-fours as they framed and sectioned off the interior. As she strolled through, she felt their eyes on her. The noise of their work bounced off the stark interior. Their back-and forth-banter in English and Spanish seemed to be directed at her. She ignored their stares, their words. Halfway to her designated office space, she almost jumped out of her skin when she heard a scream. Spinning around, she saw workers circled around a man who hobbled around on one foot. In pain, he squeezed his eyes shut while others tried to figure out how to help. While Camille looked on, powerless to do anything, the sour smell of sweat reached her nose. She felt hot breath on her neck. A gruff voice from behind said, "Now that's a nice piece of ass."

She turned just as Matt grabbed the burly guy by the throat and pinned him against the wall. Finally, Matt released his grip and pushed the man aside. "Get back to work, Pearson."

As if nothing had happened, Camille pivoted on one foot and sauntered off toward her office space. Studying the walls, ceiling, and flooring, she saw that the space still had a long way to go before it was completed. After her thorough inspection, she came to the conclusion that the changes she desired were feasible and would actually save on labor and materials. Matt should be happy with that, she reasoned. She did not know that he stood behind her until she felt his hand on her shoulder. When she turned around, he clamped his hand around her wrist and pulled her away.

"What do you think you're doing?" she asked.

"Come with me."

"Where are you taking me?"

"Outside."

The minute they stepped out, the sunlight streamed into her eyes with the intensity of a spotlight. Through blinks, she zoomed in on Matt, his annoyance apparent by his scowl.

"Are you trying to get me in trouble?" He flung his hard hat to the ground. "What if OSHA had come in and seen you in the building without a hard hat and in your high heels? You know the rules, Camille."

"You hurt me!" She rubbed her wrist.

"Why are you here?"

"I wanted to tell you that I don't want that interior wall like I saw on the plans. Can we go back inside so I can show you?"

He reached down for his hard hat and then tucked it under his arm. "Let's go in my office and you can show me what you're talking about—on the plans."

He extended his arm and let her lead the way. On the top step leading inside the trailer, she paused when she almost lost her balance. Although there was a railing, she braced herself by putting her hand on his shoulder. While she bent over to slide her shoe's sling-back strap onto her heel, her breast brushed up against his arm. As if unaffected, he stayed silent and turned the door-knob.

A burst of cool air hit them as soon as they walked inside. The air conditioning unit rattled from the back end of the trailer. Matt walked around his desk and rolled out the floor plans on top of the chaos already there. He stepped back so she could have a better look.

"So, show me," he said.

She looked down at the plans and pointed. A section of hair swept over her cheek. She hooked it behind her ear and said, "I want to do away with this wall. I'll have my cabinet guy come in to build a worktable. It's going to be huge. It'll have storage space and little cubby holes for fabric swatches. I'll need this to be one big open space, not partitioned off. That wall is not load bearing, so I don't see any problem just eliminating it."

His blank stare made her uncomfortable enough that she resorted to her habit of twisting her hair around her finger. It always happened when she felt uneasy, or challenged.

Finally he spoke, "First of all, I can't do that just because you want me to. There has to be a change order and that has to come from Jay. And secondly, I don't know if I like the idea of *your guy* coming in here during the construction phase of my project."

"This is not *your* project. It's Jay's, in case you've forgotten. And for your information, Jay told me to come here and tell you about the change. As far as *my guy* is concerned, he has to build the worktable before you put in the doorway because it's too big. It wouldn't fit through otherwise."

With hands on his hips, he said, "Your monster worktable creates a separate change order because it affects the amount of flooring and I've already ordered the materials. Maple."

"Maple? No way. I told Jay I want bamboo."

"Well, Jay told me maple, so you've got a communication problem with your fiancé."

With her arms crossed under her breasts, she glared at him. When she noted that he lowered his eyes to take in the view, she changed her stance, brought her hands to her hips.

"So, what does this mean, Garrison? Do I have to tell Jay how rude and uncooperative you are?"

"Those are Jay's rules, not mine. Any changes must go through him. He has to sign the change order. There are no exceptions." He paused to scratch his cheek.

"Well, I am going to talk to Jay about all of this." Camille bumped against him as she started toward the door. Before she could get away, he put his hand on her arm.

He held her gaze for an extended time before he spoke. His voice softened when he said, "Camille, how much do you know about Jay's business?"

"What do you mean?"

"I mean, do you know everything he's involved in?"

"No. We don't talk much about business. Why would you ask that?"

"Are you sure you know him well enough to marry him?"

"I know enough to know how much he loves me."

"What if he's not totally honest with you?"

"Are you implying he's a crook just because he has a lot of money?"

"It'd be a shame if you got hurt."

"I won't!" she snapped. "I'm a big girl. I know what I'm doing."

"Fine!"

"Look, Matt, why can't we just be civil to one another? I don't want the sparks to fly every time we meet."

"Neither do I." He held the door open which she took as her cue to leave. When she stepped forward, closer to him, he looked at her and said, "Have your carpenter come by with the dimensions for the table. Then I'll submit the change orders for you. When they're approved, you can come back with that guy and we'll go over the details just to make sure we're all on the same page. And, Camille, when you do drop by, get a hard hat and leave the high heels at home. It would also help if you dressed more conservatively. You're too much of a distraction. Hell, you're a safety hazard. The guy screaming in pain? He was watching you sashay through the building and hit the nail gun trigger by mistake. Now somebody has to take him to the ER."

She gave him a sardonic smile. "Sorry I'm such a pain in the ass, Matt."

"The foot."

"What?"

"Today you were a pain in the foot."

§

There's a bomb inside my head ready to explode, Jay thought when he stepped outside Streaker's apartment on Monday morning. He hated himself for getting so stinking drunk that he couldn't drive home. He had crashed on Streaker's sofa that smelled disgustingly of stale cigarettes and spilled liquor.

Known for his dapper appearance, Jay knew he now looked like hell, the same way he felt. His plan was to go home where he could shower, shave, and change clothes. Feel like a human being again. Thank God he had nothing major on his calendar for the day. Maybe he'd just close his office door and tell Amber he wanted no interruptions, he decided.

His head started to clear on his way to his car, but when he got there he couldn't believe his eyes. A bad dream. No, a nightmare. Along one side of his Porsche someone had taken a sharp instrument, a knife or a key, and scratched the silver paint from one end of the car to the other. The marking was deep, done with force. All he could do was stare, but it didn't make it go away. Not an illusion; it was real. In the distance, he heard a car roar to life, then the motor revved up. Tires screeched. He looked up to see a metallic gold Cadillac shoot out of the parking lot like a rocket. Memory kicked in. It was the same car that had tried to engage him in a game of road rage when he and Camille drove back into town from their trip to the coast.

He marched back to the apartment, pounding on the door because Streaker locked it behind him. In worse shape than Jay, Streaker stuck his head through the opening and peered at him with bloodshot eyes. "What the hell, Goldie?"

"Do you know anyone who owns a gold Cadillac?"

"Not personally. Why?"

"A guy in a gold Cadillac just keyed my car! Come look!"

"I'll take your word for it." He shot a look of annoyance. "Tough shit. Now leave me in peace."

Streaker tried to shut the door, but Jay pushed it open. "You set him up to do this, didn't you? You got this guy to harass me, to keep me from talking. You son of a bitch!"

Before Jay knew what was happening, Streaker had him in a chokehold. He dragged him inside and slammed him against the wall. Pinned there and unable to move, Jay felt Streaker's body flush against his. He felt his hot breath, his hand tightening on his throat so that he struggled to breathe.

"Let me explain something to you, Goldie. I operate alone, don't need no muscle to keep you in line. I think I've made it crystal clear what would happen if you fuck up. Now get outta here." He released his grip. Jay slumped and brought his hands to his neck. When he started to walk away, he heard Streaker mutter, "You're killing me, Goldie. You're killing me."

Jay got in his car and drove off. At a stoplight, he glanced over at an Exxon station and spotted the driver of the Cadillac pumping gas. When the light changed, Jay pulled into a McDonalds's parking lot and waited. Soon the gold car cruised by and Jay followed at a distance. When it turned into a strip shopping center and parked in front of a Wal-mart, Jay took the next entrance and parked two rows back. Soon the driver stepped out of the car. Built like a NFL lineman, he walked with a bit of a swagger, more like a pimp than an athlete, Jay thought. Although the man wore sunglasses, Jay felt his eyes on him. Just in case he was burned, Jay sunk low in his seat. The black man proceeded toward the store. When he walked through the automatic door opening, Jay decided it was time to teach the dude a lesson.

No one messes with Jay Stiles.

Jay opened his glove compartment and got out the hunting knife he kept under the owner's manual. Then, he eased out of his car and looked around. Through the glint of the sun's reflection on windshields and chrome, he saw no one when he walked over to the gold car. He turned his back to the vehicle and eased down in order to puncture the tire with the knife. He had to use force, but the blade went in. Air leaking out made a hissing sound. He went around to the opposite side and did the same thing, but before he could get to the two front tires, he saw the man coming out. Quickly, Jay crouched down and duck-walked back to his car. Once inside, he closed the door, careful not to make a sound. He didn't look back when he drove away.

CHAPTER TWENTY SIX

Jay and Camille dined at an upscale restaurant within walking distance of Jay's townhome. Out of habit, she regarded her surroundings, disapproving of the heavy baroque decor that made it look dark and heavy. The focal point of the entrance was a humongous chandelier with strands of glass beads and globes that she thought overwhelmed the space. Although management failed to impress her with interior design, she loved their delectable dishes prepared by a popular chef schooled at some of the best restaurants in Paris.

Jay raised his brow and set down his fork when Camille announced she would like to voice a complaint about one of his employees. Cutting to the chase, she told him about Matt's insolent behavior that morning. While she ranted about how she had been treated, Jay's grin grew broader.

"I'm not kidding, Jay. He was downright rude."

"Okay, honey. I'll have a talk with him. Maybe I'll take him out for coffee in the morning. I can't have my project manager treating my girlfriend like that, now can I?"

"I just asked for one little change. It's not like I asked for the moon." She paused to sip her wine and then added, "Now that I've got that off my chest, you said you had something to discuss with me."

He pushed his plate aside and cleared his throat. "Move in with me."

"Jay, not that again. Why are you bringing it up? I told you I like having my own place."

"I don't think it's safe where you live. My place is gated. We have security."

"Well, I have Tyler. He's my security."

"Tyler is a joke. He would fall over in a strong wind."

"Don't let his skinny ass fool you. He's trained in martial arts. Have you seen his biceps? He's a cabinet maker. Very muscular. I feel sorry for the poor fool who decides to cross him."

"Look, Camille, it's just silly. I stay over at your place half the time so what's the big deal?"

"No, Jay. There's no reason discussing this. I've made up my mind."

"But your safety, honey. You'll be protected if someone—"

"Does this have something to do with your car being keyed?" When he refused to respond, she went on, "Does someone want to harm us? Are you in some kind of trouble, Jay? You got rid of those thugs that were after your father, right?"

"There's no threat, sweetie. It would just give me peace of mind, that's all."

"I can take care of myself. This subject is closed—finis. Now please cut off a small piece of your shrimp scampi. It looks yummy. You can try my crab cake."

§

The following afternoon, Camille got a call from Jay. He said he had coffee with Matt and everything was straightened out. In fact, Jay said Tyler was at work on the worktable already. Jay had called him personally to tell him to start. Surprised that things were moving so fast, she headed over to the jobsite to see for herself.

Once she arrived, she climbed the steps that led inside the trailer. She found the door unlocked and walked in. She was greeted by someone other than Matt. A tall slender man with a mop of sandy blond hair and blue eyes introduced himself as Danny. She remembered a conversation with Jay in which he said Matt played hardball and wanted his buddy Danny to be hired as well.

"I'm looking for Matt," she said to him.

"He'll be back in a sec. Went to pick up some supplies. Have a seat."

Danny bumped up the air conditioning. He wiped away the sweat that had beaded on his forehead. "Man, it's hot," he said. "Are you the interior designer that's taking the front corner?"

"Yes, that's right."

"Thought so. I wasn't around when you were here. Heard about it though."

I bet you did. She wondered if the worker with the nail stapled through his boot was okay. She had caused a distraction, so it was her fault. However, it would have been Matt's butt on the line if a safety inspector had happened to make an appearance at that particular moment.

Danny presented her with a cup of cold water and then sat behind Matt's desk. He pretended to study a piece of paper, but she felt his attention was on her.

"Thanks for the water, Danny. It's so hot outside and my throat feels parched."

He displayed a boyish grin, but said nothing. She assumed he was just shy. Finally, the awkwardness melted away when Matt entered with a crumpled piece of paper and a clear plastic bag of screws and other whatnots. He tossed them down on his desk and smiled over at Camille.

She stood up and set her empty cup on the corner of the desk. "Hi, Matt. I thought I would drop by and check out Tyler's progress on my worktable. I assume he came by this morning to measure before he picked up supplies."

"Yes, he's started on the work. At least, I saw him carrying in some two-by-fours awhile ago."

"Great. If you'll just get me a hard hat, I'll get out of your way and go see."

"Mind if I tag along?"

"No, that's fine."

To Danny, he said, "Make another call to see if the sheet rock's coming in today. I'd like to start on that tomorrow."

Danny nodded and pulled his cell phone from his jeans pocket. Matt held the door open for Camille and followed her out. They walked under a cloudy sky which prompted Camille to say, "We're supposed to get heavy rain, maybe flooding, tomorrow. Good thing all your work is inside."

"Yeah, good thing."

Until she entered the building, she held her hard hat at her waist with both hands wrapped around it like it was a mixing bowl. Although she thought her straight-leg jeans were more conservative and less distracting than her heels and skirt, she sensed Matt's eyes on her butt as she led the way.

"Matt, there's something I forgot to mention." He looked on with interest, but said nothing. "I told Tyler to include an electrical receptacle on the end of the worktable. I need you to have your electrician run the wiring to the center of the room. Is that okay?"

He nodded. "No problem. I'll take care of it."

"Good." She studied his smile and said, "So, you and Jay had a little chat about how I'm to be treated."

"Does it show?"

"Yes. This is the nice Matt Garrison that I met in the bar. I've missed that guy."

Again, he smiled. "Piss me off and the old Matt will resurface."

"Have you decided to forgive me?"

"I'm working on it."

Together they stepped inside the building where the noise level was enough to make Camille place her hands over her ears. At last, the whine of a circular saw came to an abrupt halt.

Camille was pleased to find Tyler busy at work. Already, he had the base of the table in place. Not wanting to be in the way, Camille spoke only a few minutes with Tyler to make sure that he completely understood her specs. He had only a hand-drawn sketch and her verbal instructions to go on. Satisfied, Camille told him goodbye. Matt walked her out.

At her car, he said, "So, when is the wedding?"

She studied his face. The nice Matt stared back at her and waited for her answer. "We haven't set a date yet."

He scratched his chin with his index finger. She noticed he did that a lot, and it seemed to be tied in to his comfort level.

His eyes seemed to gaze at her with tenderness, even hinting at forgiveness. Yet, she wasn't sure.

"It's good that you haven't set a date," he said. She arched a brow that prompted him to add, "I mean you need more time to get to know the man you're going to marry."

"I think I know all I need to know."

"No you don't."

"What's that supposed to mean?"

"Never mind." When they reached her car, he held the door for her as if anxious to see her off. Once seated behind the steering wheel, she shot him a hard stare. He cleared his throat and did the chin-scratching thing again. "What I said was rude. Sorry."

"No, it was honest. I've noticed that about you, Matt. You never have much to say, but when you do speak, it's candid."

Camille hit the button to roll up her window. It ended any further conversation. She watched him walk away with his hands in his pockets, his head down. But a car engine that refused to start forced her to call out to him before he got too far out of sight.

Once he came back, she got out of the car. "It won't start, Matt. I've been having problems with it lately. Do you mind seeing what you can do?"

Matt climbed in behind the wheel to turn the ignition. After several attempts, the motor roared to life. He got out and said, "Did you hear the clicking sound when you turn the key? I think it's the alternator. You need to take it in for repairs or else you're going to be stranded somewhere."

"I think you're right. I should take it in and get it looked at. Thanks, Matt."

"No problem."

§

Streaker looked forward to seeing Samantha. For her, he went home to shower, shave, put on a clean shirt and pants, even slapped on a little aftershave. Who was he kidding? She'd never be his. She'd never leave her no-good, absentee husband. She told him so. They played a game of flirtation, recreational sex, and nothing more. He would settle for that. Had to, because what other choice did he have? As he sat in the back booth of O'Malley's, a small diner where they had shared many good meals, he checked his watch. She was late which made him drum his fingers on the table-top in nervous anticipation.

At last, Samantha entered and acknowledged him with a smile. A man followed her in. When Streaker recognized the man, he swore under his breath. Samantha slid into the booth across the table from Streaker. The man took a seat beside her.

"You didn't tell me you were bringing in the trash with you, Sam," Streaker said.

"Good to see you too, Streak," the man said.

"Hello, Mallory. How long has it been? Let's see, I haven't seen your sorry ass since you threw me under the bus. Five years now, wouldn't you say?"

Mallory was a tall wiry guy. Although he had not one hair on his head, he sported a thick black mustache with matching bushy eyebrows. He looked no happier to see Streaker than Streaker was to see him. Mallory gave Samantha a knowing look as if to say, *I told you so.*

"Streaker, be nice," she said. "He's here because I asked him to come. Mallory has some information that you need to hear."

"I ain't interested in hearing anything that shithead has to say. He gave me up to Internal Affairs, Sam. And I thought we were so tight. Thought we had each other's back."

Mallory's eyes went wide. "I had to, Streak. There was no need for both of us to take the fall. Hell, I didn't do anything wrong. You're the one who stole the evidence, screwed the case for the DA."

"Fuck you, Mallory."

"Boys, let's play nice," Samantha said. "Streaker, you need to hear this. It's about Slick. Tell him, Mal."

"I'm not saying anything until you feed me. I talk when you treat me to the steak and fries you promised. A draft beer too."

Streaker chuckled. "My God! He's had the same training as the K-9 dogs. They don't perform without a treat either. Did you pick him up at the kennel, Sam? Have you had all your shots, Mal?"

Mallory was true to his word. Once he finished his dinner, he pushed his plate aside and cleared his throat to begin. "Streaker, Sam asked me to tell you what I know about Slick. I'm still in the drug unit, but I don't do undercover. I got this from Murray—You don't know him. New guy. He actually looks more scummy undercover than you did. Anyway, Sam told me about the problem you're having with Slick. Slick is a blast from your past, dude. You just don't know it."

There was silence when the server came over to gather their empty dishes. With appreciation, Streaker observed her backside in tight black pants and then turned his attention to Mallory.

"What are you talking about, Mal?" Streaker said. "The name just popped into my head. I made it up. Had to say something or those guys weren't going to let me have anything for pain. They said it would cloud my judgment, so, I just blurted out the first name I could think of. I was desperate to get outta there, man."

"Nope. Your subconscious brought it to the surface. Think, Streak. You know the name."

"I don't have time for games, Mallory. Just spit it out."

"Remember when you shot and killed Big Donny? Right before you took two hits in the back."

"Yeah, it was kinda of a significant day, Mal. But what's he got to do with it?"

"Slick is his cousin. We saw it in the official report for the DA. I guess you forgot. Big Donny's cousin was running a drug operation in Atlanta. Remember when we were tracking Big Donny's movements and he left town one weekend? He was in Georgia with his cuz, Slick. Now Slick is in Charlotte running a bigger operation. And when you fingered him for something he didn't do, well, he connected the dots and realized you were the cop who whacked his kin. Now you have to pay. He's just messing with you now, but eventually he'll get his revenge. In case it hasn't sunk in yet, I'll spell it out for you—He's going to kill you."

Streaker got quiet, letting the information sink in. When he saw the worry in Sam's eyes, he shrugged it off. "Now that I know, I'll be extra careful."

"Streaker, please leave town. Please," Sam said.

"I'll be okay, sweetie. I've been in tighter spots before."

"You should listen to her, Streak. She's right. Slick is not going to let it go."

Suddenly Streaker needed a smoke, but they didn't allow smoking in O'Malley's. He leaned forward to rest his folded arms on the table. His eyes shifted from Mallory to Samantha. He read them like a book. Samantha was sick with worry; Mallory felt redeemed for his earlier betrayal.

"Thanks for telling me this, guys. You're right, I'm probably screwed, but I won't go down without a fight. Like I've said, I've been in tighter spots. I'm not licked yet. Sam, don't look at me like that. I'll be okay, sweetie. I didn't get the name Streaker for nothin'. Most people think I got it 'cause I must've run outside without my clothes." He tried to laugh at that, but the joke fell flat. "I got the name 'cause I'm fast, like a streak of lightning. My daddy gave me that name when I'd run away before he could give me a beating."

He cast his eyes down, made sure he didn't see the pity on Samantha's face. "Thanks for coming, Mallory. I appreciate the heads up. Now if you don't mind, I think I'll drive Samantha home."

More than a cigarette, he wanted to hold her in his arms. He wanted to kiss away her worry, his fright. He'd beat this.

No sir, Wayne Streaker Johnson was not done for yet. Not by a long shot.

CHAPTER TWENTY SEVEN

It was almost five before Matt finished up his paperwork and stepped out of the trailer. As he looked out at the street, he saw Camille leaning up against her car. The wind caught a section of her hair and lifted it to cover her eyes. She used her long slender fingers to rake it away to reveal an alluring gaze directed at him. He had to swallow down his desire for her. He gave her a half-smile that he hoped did not give him away.

"What are you doing here?" he asked.

"Matt, do you have time to go for a ride with me?" His response was a blank stare, which prompted her to add, "My car again—it's making a mysterious noise. Comes and goes. Don't know what it is and just thought maybe you might be able to tell."

With hands in his pockets, he nodded. "Okay. Do you want me to drive or be the passenger?"

"I'll drive, just hop in."

They rode in silence, listening for the phantom-noise. He meant to keep his attention on the view out the window, but his gaze repeatedly veered over to her. Her short skirt covered only the top portion of her thigh, and he found himself fixated on the movement of her foot as it went from the gas pedal to the brake and back.

Finally, he said, "What kind of noise is it?"

"Like something rattling around. Wouldn't you know it? I bring you along, and it quits." She paused and then said, "Matt, I'm worried that—"

"Are you afraid your car will break down and leave you stranded somewhere?"

"No, no, it's not that."

"Then what? What are you afraid of, Camille?"

She turned her head to stare out the driver's side window. "Nothing. Never mind." When she pulled into the makeshift lot at the back of the warehouse project, she looked over at a black Mustang with tinted windows. "Is that your car?"

"Yep, that's mine. Guess everyone has left."

She parked next to his vehicle. Because Matt insisted, she kept the motor running on her Jeep Cherokee while he checked under the hood. Finally, he slammed it shut and walked around to the driver's side. As he wiped his hands with a handkerchief, he said, "Sorry, Camille, I don't see anything. It'd help if we could hear the noise."

She got out and said, "I'm sorry to take up your time."

"No problem. When you take it in for the alternator problem, they might detect the other thing." He cleared his throat and added, "Well, I guess I better head out."

"Yes. I should let you go. Thanks." As he started to walk away, she called to him. He turned around with a puzzled look.

"Matt, there is no strange noise."

He walked up to her with suspicious eyes. "Come again?"

"There is no noise. I just wanted an excuse to talk to you."

"Camille, all you had to do is—"

"Matt, I've been thinking about what you said earlier."

"Don't pay any attention to me, Camille. I shouldn't have said anything."

"No, I'm glad you did. Something's wrong. Something bad. Jay is hiding something from me, and I'm scared."

She bit down on her lower lip, keeping her gaze fixed on him. He saw the worry in her eyes and when they pooled with tears, he pulled her into his arms. He felt her hands pressed flat against his chest. She might have been comforted by their closeness, but he felt anything but comfort. Her touch was like a key that had been turned to ignite feelings he had tried hard to suppress. With his chin resting on her head, he picked up a sweet scent from her hair. The intoxicating fragrance was enough to send him over the edge and his hands moving from her waist to her hips where they stayed.

His fingers pushed her closer so that he could whisper in her ear. "What are you afraid of, Camille?"

With her forehead against his chest, she shook her head. "I'm not sure. Just hold me. Just for a minute."

"I've got you."

Finally, he pulled back and lifted her chin with his finger. He kissed her lightly and ran the back of his hand over her cheek. "Let's not do this here. Maybe we could go somewhere. Your place?"

"I can't. Jay is waiting for me."

He dropped his arms to his side and stepped back. Nothing could kill a tender moment like the mention of Jay Stiles.

He refused to look at her when she said, "Matt, I need time. Jay is not the kind of guy you just walk out on. It's complicated. I'm tied to him financially. He's paying part of my rent and of course, there's the office project."

"He's dangerous, Camille. You need to stay away from him."

"No, you're wrong. He's mixed up in something, but he's no threat. He's very good to me, very tender."

"Spare me the details."

"Don't be angry with me, Matt."

"You need to leave him, Camille, and don't use money as an excuse. I can help with that. You said that you're scared."

"It's not so simple, Matt. I can't just—"

He cut her off, saying, "What is so difficult about leaving him? Jeez, I don't get it. Is the sex that great?"

She gave him a hard stare. "You don't understand. Most of my clients are acquaintances of Jay's. I didn't get them on my own. He could ruin me professionally. Everything is at stake. My job. My apartment. I need to find a way to leave him on good terms. He has some photos of me that I sent. He could put them on the Internet. It would be a problem—embarrassing."

His hard stare magnified the tension between them. Finally, he said, "I better go. Goodnight, Camille. Have a nice evening with Jay."

"Matt, wait!"

But Matt didn't stop or look back. He climbed into his car and started the engine. A quick glance in his review mirror showed her standing by her car with her arms crossed. He sensed her stare as he drove off.

§

While Camille stole a few minutes with Matt that ended badly, Jay waited for her at the Cristina Opera House. It was an Italian restaurant in the Dilworth area of Charlotte where grand old homes were renovated and transformed into upscale restaurants, retail shops, and businesses. He was already seated in the main dining room when she arrived. A wine steward brought over a bottle of Cabernet Sauvignon when she approached. Jay stood up to greet her and gave her a quick peck on the cheek. He held out the chair for her across from his. Once he was back in his seat, he glanced at his Rolex with a twist of his wrist.

"Where were you?"

"I'm not that late, Jay."

"Where were you?" he repeated in a harsh tone.

"Traffic was heavy." She looked away, afraid he might discover her lie.

After their food arrived, she was in the middle of telling him about a big order she had placed for her new client when she realized he wasn't listening. She set her fork down.

"Jay, is something wrong?"

"You'd never cheat on me, would you, baby?"

"What? You think I'm cheating on you?"

"Only a whore would do that, right?" While his eyes stayed on her, he picked up the bottle of wine by its neck and brought it to his lips. In one swallow, he chugged the remainder of its contents.

"Jay, what are you doing? Why are you saying this?"

"If you did, I'd know," he said. "I would know."

A vision of Matt holding her earlier popped into her head. "Have you been spying on me?"

"Maybe I should."

"What brought this on?"

He shrugged and then brought his elbows up on the table, pushing his plate aside. "You're a beautiful woman, Camille. Any man would want you. Maybe someone right under my nose. They might speak to you in a very polite manner, but what they really want is to fuck you. If they had the chance, they'd do it despite the fact that you're engaged to me. Betrayal. The worst kind." He slapped his hand over hers. His eyes narrowed. "I'd kill anyone who did that to me. They'd deserve it too."

"Jay, you're scaring me."

"Good. No one will come between us. Ever. Are we clear?"

She stared back at his cold eyes.

"Answer me, damn it! Are we clear?"

"Yes."

After dinner, Jay ordered a scotch on the rocks. His dessert, he said. Camille sipped coffee while he sat across from her and used his cell phone to text back and forth to some person he refused to name. After he paid for dinner, he tapped the linen tablecloth with his knuckles. "Well, shall we go, Sunshine?"

"Jay, maybe I should drive your car. You've had a lot to drink. We can pick up mine tomorrow."

He laughed boisterously. A couple at the next table looked on with interest. With slurred speech, Jay said, "There's no way I'm letting you get behind the wheel of my Porsche. I'm fine. I'll follow you back to your place. We need to get you out of those clothes. Can't stay dressed up all day, now can we?"

"Can you keep your voice down? Please, Jay. I have a better idea. I'll drive you home in my car and you can get *your* car tomorrow. I think you need to sleep it off."

He clamped his hand around her wrist and pulled her out of the restaurant, extending a cordial goodnight to the host as they left. He pushed her roughly toward her car. "Get in, Camille. Like I said, I'm fine. I'll follow you over."

"No. Jay, go back to your townhouse. It's closer. You're drunk, and I'm going home."

He smiled and shook his head. "I don't think so, baby. Change of plans." He grabbed her around the waist and steered her toward the Porsche. She squirmed in his hold, but he tightened his grip. After he held the passenger door opened, he said, "Get in. You're right, my place is closer."

CHAPTER TWENTY EIGHT

Just for fun, Streaker kept tabs on Camille as a way to mess with Jay. As long as Jay thought he might harm his dream girl, Streaker could keep him in line. It was as much of a surprise to Streaker as it was to Jay when he watched her do the kissy-face with another man in the construction site parking lot. From the 20X lens mounted on his Canon camera, he got a close-up view of the whole thing. The kiss itself was nothing much, short and sweet, but it was the way the dude held her in his arms that got really interesting. His hands slid from her waist to rest comfortably on her hips until he pulled away. He whispered something to her and whatever she said back to him must have pissed him off because the dude dropped his arms to his side and stepped back. Then, he said something to piss her off because she looked like she wanted to slap his face. The magnification of the lens showed the frustration on his face. Streaker was certain of one thing. The guy was not going to get past first base with the beautiful, enticing princess. But to keep Jay on his toes, Streaker decided to embellish a few details. He promised to give Jay a souvenir of what he had witnessed. A dozen photos of their secret rendezvous.

§

All the way to his poker game, Streaker snickered about his phone call to Jay while he had waited for Camille to show up at the restaurant. Streaker had given him the courtesy of a heads up that she might be late arriving, then he laughed while Jay spewed a volley of curse words. It was fun just to hear Jay's jealousy bubble up and almost explode like popping the cork on a bottle of champagne. What fun!

When Streaker arrived at the loading dock of the steel fabrication shop, he put all thoughts about Jay out of his mind. The guys were waiting for him to start their game. The reason

Streaker agreed to come was to have a chance to win back his losses from their last game. They saved a seat for him across from Harlan, the on-again-off-again husband of Katie, a former client of his, who hired Streaker to catch her philandering husband in action. Although Streaker offered proof, she refused to divorce Harlan. She was only willing to kick him out of the house. She'd call Streaker whenever Harlan showed up to threaten her, sometimes even roughing her up. The night Jay called him about the news of a body discovered in the woods, Streaker was with Katie, comforting her from another altercation with Harlan and hoping to stay the night. Unfortunately, after Jay's call, Katie was no longer in the mood and asked Streaker to leave. Damn Stiles was ruining his love life, he grumbled.

Streaker still owed Harlan money after his loss in a game weeks ago. Streaker knew the guy cheated and suspected that he had a rigged deck slipped to him by his busty girlfriend/server who Streaker liked to call "Harlan's bimbo of the month." He had observed a little dip she did right at Harlan's side. Once she walked away, Harlan had adjusted his seat, both hands out of view. It was his turn to deal and voila! The switch took place. Of course, Streaker had no actual proof that he switched decks. He just had a hunch. And since there was bad blood between them, he didn't confront the man who carried a Bowie knife at all times. Besides, Streaker was banging the man's wife. The man had incentive for inflicting pain.

On this particular night, Streaker studied Harlan's movements and those of his gal-pal. Just like he thought, it went down the same as last time. Without Harlan being aware, Streaker managed to distract all the players at the table to do his own switcheroo, this time with a legit deck. Harlan had his co-conspirator cut the deck and then he dealt out the cards. Over the next few hands, Harlan tried to hide his shock over the cards he held. Streaker took joy in his predicament. He noted that when Harlan did have a fairly decent hand, he bit down on his lower lip. Other times, his lips puckered in a circle. On the final round, Streaker, oozing with counterfeit confidence, raised his bid. Harlan took the bait and folded. Streaker threw down his cards: three eights that certainly didn't beat Harlan's three Jacks. The guys around the table all laughed, hard enough to bust a gut, but Harlan saw no humor. Streaker put his arms around his winnings and scraped the pile of cash to the edge of the table.

Harlan jumped up, knocked his chair over backwards, and then flipped the table upside down. When it crashed on the concrete floor, a silence held tight. Harlan drew his knife. The overhead light picked up the shine of its wide blade. Streaker figured it was sharpened to precision, designed to draw blood quick and penetrate deep. He was determined not to find out.

Streaker leapfrogged over the upended table and lunged for Harlan, pinning him against the wall. With all his might, Streaker squeezed and twisted the man's wrist as his hand had a tight grip on the knife. Their faces reddened, under the strain of their physical powers stretched to the brink. Sweat beaded up on Harlan's forehead. He huffed and puffed, but refused to surrender. But when his strength gave out and Streaker managed to bring his arm down, Harlan was forced to drop the knife. Then, Streaker punched him in the gut, causing Harlan to let out a grunt, but Streaker wouldn't allow him to bend over in agony. Instead, he took all of his winnings and stuffed them down the front of Harlan's pants. With one hand to the man's throat, Streaker pushed Harlan's head into the brick wall.

"We're even, Harlan. Nobody owes nobody nothing. And if you ever lay a hand on Katie or even come near her again, I will hunt you down and kill you. Got that?" He waited until the man nodded before he released his hold. "Good. I'm glad we had this little talk. My grandma always said good communication is important. Goodnight, gentlemen."

All eyes were on Streaker as he walked away. He knew no one would follow him out. They'd be quiet and subdued for awhile, but then they'd sit back down and start another game.

§

Streaker lit a cigarette and turned down the alley that had haunted him since that fateful night when he lay at death's doorstep. It was the area he did undercover work with Samantha when they were both assigned to the special task force. Once he reached the back entrance of the rundown hotel where they ran a sting operation, he stopped to reflect on the night he got shot. Like then, it was a moonless night. However, the streetlight allowed enough illumination for him to search for the pockmarked bricks where the bullets ended up. In all, there were more than a dozen shots fired. Two meant for Samantha ended up in him when he pushed her aside and got shot in the back. But before he went down, he took out notorious pimp and drug dealer Big Donny when he returned fire. The roly-poly black man died instantly from a shot to the chest. The EMT that attended to Streaker said he was lucky. One bullet missed his spine by inches. The other nicked his liver. He required six pints of blood during emergency surgery. Of course, to hear Sam tell it, he was on his deathbed. She told him she owed him her life. He figured that was why she put up with all his crap.

Once he had been a decorated cop, considered a hero, but he had lost his way. Recovered from his injuries and back on the job, he signed up for the heavy stuff: a special task force intent on ridding an area of the city of narcotics. Of course, he had to walk the walk and talk the talk. His rugged looks fit the part. He even had dreadlocks, which he boasted as a feat that not many white boys could pull off.

In his opinion, some of the dealers and users were regular folks that just lost their way. They wanted money, but lacked the education and resources to make it. The mean streets were the path they chose. He befriended them, partied with them, shared smokes with them, but in the end he betrayed them. They never suspected he was a cop or that he was wearing a wire. Only after a bust did they learn the truth. He'd get cleaned up and testify against them in court. He made sure he wasn't around when they were sentenced, didn't want to feel their stares when they were led away in handcuffs.

Finally, he had enough. When the cops shot and killed an unarmed sixteen-year-old kid on his first buy, Streaker was more than mad; he was livid. After that, he didn't give a shit. He let the life seduce him into making bad choices. Marijuana, pain meds, and booze got him through the days. Hook-ups with a hot woman in a warm bed got him through the nights. He still felt ashamed that Samantha found him in the sad state he was in, stoned out of his mind in a back alley not far from where he stood now. She had found out what he had suspected. Internal Affairs was building a case against him, but she managed to keep them at bay until she got him cleaned up. She reminded the captain of his heroic act that saved her life. Thanks to her he was allowed to walk away from it all. The police, the drugs, the lifestyle. He felt he owed it to her to stay out of trouble, but damn, that was just too hard. Hell, it was unrealistic.

§

Camille was a liar and a whore. Jay never imagined he would think that, but after Streaker's call, he knew she had lied to him about why she was late coming to the restaurant and lied again about being faithful. Of course being the asshole that Streaker was, he could have exaggerated the way Garrison pulled her into his arms and laid a big fat kiss on her lips. To hear Streaker tell it, the dude had his hands all over her. He'd have taken her somewhere and fucked her, but Camille said something that changed the mood. Streaker said he saw the whole thing, the two of them wedged in between their cars in the back lot of the jobsite like two animals in heat. He had laughed about it as he told Jay she was two-timing him with one of his employees.

"Who's the boss now? Huh, Goldie?" Streaker had teased. "Did the dude know when you hired him, he'd get some extra fringe benefits? Hmm, I think I'll come work for you. Get me some of that."

The more that dumbass talked and laughed, the madder Jay got. In his rage, he spit out a string of obscenities and hung up on him.

On the drive to his townhouse, Jay replayed the whole conversation in his head. Camille sat in the passenger seat quiet as a mouse. She looked worried that he was going to wreck, so he thought he'd mess with her a little. He swerved a little to the right and then back to the left and acted like he wasn't watching the road. Her whole body went rigid. He turned his head away so she couldn't see his big smile.

He pressed the code to get into the gated parking garage and hit the accelerator until tires squealed. At his assigned space, he came to an abrupt halt, causing her head to jerk forward then back. He laughed at that despite her cold stare. They took the elevator up to his floor. She pulled away from him and stood in the back corner until the door opened.

After he unlocked his door and followed Camille inside, he inspected his living quarters. He nodded his approval at the maid's cleaning earlier in the day. The place was spotless, nothing out of order. Throughout the townhouse were touches of Camille's creative style. She chose a contemporary decor for him with lots of glass, black lacquer and chrome. He loved the abstract painting in bold, bright hues that hung over the fireplace. And of course, he adored the nude painting of her that hung in his bedroom. *Thank you, Tyler.*

As soon as he set his keys in the ceramic bowl on the credenza, he pulled her into his arms. It was no surprise to him that she wiggled out of his hold. She brushed past him to plop down on the L-shaped sofa with its multitude of pillows. She grabbed one and hugged it to her chest.

"What now, Jay?"

"I'll fix us another drink, babe."

"You've had enough."

"And you haven't had nearly enough. It'll loosen you up." He started toward the bar. "Make yourself at home, honey. Take your shoes off, put your feet up."

Camille got up and stood behind him as he reached for a bottle of scotch. As she attempted to take the bottle from him, he raised it up high out of her reach, then brought it down to his glass, almost chipping the rim. He poured sloppily, letting the liquor spill onto the bar. With shot glasses in each hand, he turned to find her eyes on him. Her pouty lips were a complete turn-on. When he handed her a glass, he planted a rough kiss on her lips. She took two steps back and glared at him.

He chuckled and tapped his glass against hers. "Cheers, baby. To us."

She set the glass down on the bar with a look of disgust. In response, Jay shrugged. With lips set tight, she said, "Jay, why are you acting like this?"

"I don't know what you're talking about, sweetie." He grabbed her wrist. "Let's go sit down."

"No, I'll stand. I want to know why you have been acting so strange. You're hiding something from me and I want to know what it is."

"Baby, you're imagining things."

"No, I'm not. A man who worked for you was found dead." She paused, then continued, "Yeah, I watch the news. I think his name was Emanuel Sanchez. They said he worked for Stiles Enterprises, yet you've never mentioned anything to me about him being missing or his body being found. I'm sure the police probably questioned you. And that other guy? The contractor. They still haven't found his body. He did work for you. I know because I tried to hire him for a remodeling project for a client of mine, but he refused to take it when I mentioned my relationship with you."

"You never told me that."

"Why should I? That guy—Morris—he told me that you two were in the middle of a dispute over money, and he didn't feel comfortable working with me. Although he said I was probably a nice lady, he thought he'd pass."

"Why didn't you tell me?"

"I didn't think it mattered. But since you haven't mentioned anything about this tragedy to me, I think it's odd. You lied to me about your father being in financial trouble with some scary thugs, didn't you? *You* are the one who owed money and it was to Morris."

"No, you're wrong."

"Then, I'll just call good ol' Dad and see how things are. Maybe he came to your rescue, not the other way around." She pulled her cell phone out of her jacket pocket and began dialing until Jay snatched it out of her hand.

"No need to bother my father." *Bitch! Who the hell does she think she is?*

"So, I was right. Don't you see? Too many things happening that you can't explain," she said. "Your behavior at the restaurant—so bizarre. I don't know what's going on with you, Jay."

He set his glass down and glared at her. "Are you accusing me of something, Camille?"

"No. I-I just don't know what to think."

"Baby, didn't I change like I said I would? Haven't we spent more time together?"

"Yes, but—"

"Then, what's your problem? You're being ridiculous. I hardly knew Manny Sanchez. Didn't even hire him. I have no idea how he ended up dead. And as far as Nick Morris is concerned, we did have a dispute, but I paid him in full. I have the proof. Can I help it if he killed himself? Nothing to do with me, baby."

"I don't want any secrets between us."

"The same goes for you, baby. No lies, no secrets, and no betrayals."

With his hands holding her wrists, he walked her backwards. He liked that her eyes widened with fear. She licked her lips and swallowed hard. When he pinned her against the wall, he felt the pounding in her chest.

"Let me go, Jay. Let me go."

Instead, he brought his mouth over hers and bit her lower lip. She groaned and squirmed, but he wouldn't let her escape. He had her right where he wanted her, flat against the wall with his body pressed against hers. His hand found its way under her skirt. He took a fistful of her flimsy silk panties, then yanked hard enough that they came off in his hand. She tried to jerk her knee up, but he stepped back before it brought unbearable pain to his groin.

Bitch! "Okay, baby, we can play rough if that's what you want."

"Let me go!" she screamed.

"No, baby. You're mine. That ring on your finger says so. Don't fight me when I want it, understand?"

But she fought him all the way to the bedroom. He underestimated her strength. Carrying heavy bolts of fabric and wall covering books must have given her the same benefit as lifting weights, he surmised. Still, he managed to overpower her. Once he had her on her back, he brought both her arms up over her head and held them together with one hand while he worked to pull her legs apart. She cried the entire time he was inside her. When he was done, he rolled off and watched her rapid retreat with her clothes in hand. Five minutes later, he heard the front door slam shut. He figured she called a cab on her cell and waited outside for it to show up. He didn't give a damn. Let her go. She'd be back and he'd be inside her again in no time.

By morning, Jay's head started to clear. He was thankful that he did not have a hangover. He found that a cold shower got him recharged and ready to face the day. While he stood under the shower head, he ruminated over Streaker's call. What the P.I. told him did not make sense. The dude was jerking his chain, just trying to get him riled up. He knew there was no way Camille would kiss Matt Garrison. She hated the man. After all, she had recently complained to him about how rude Matt had been to her and begged Jay to reprimand him. In fact, she tried to avoid going to see him in the first place and wanted Jay to handle it. When he told her he was up to his neck in work, she had agreed to go to Matt directly and discuss the changes she wanted. The fireworks had started immediately. Jay had been amused by her annoyance when she told him about their altercation. Yep, there's was no way the two of them got cozy behind his back. Besides, she barely knew the guy.

Streaker was a piece of work. Why would he tell him such a bold face lie? he wondered. Jealousy? Maybe it was because he'd never have a woman as hot as Camille. Still, he seemed specific with details. Like how did he know Garrison drove a black Mustang unless he actually saw it?

Jay had a plan. He'd find out the truth. Oh, yeah, he'd get to the bottom of it. Sooner rather than later.

CHAPTER TWENTY NINE

Jay had a busy day. It started with a meeting with the property management director, general contractor, and maintenance supervisor over a condo project that had been completed six months earlier. Although all but three units were sold and management had been turned over to another company, the project still had a grip on Jay and his valuable time. He spent a good portion of his day dealing with the litany of grievances and pointing fingers at others to blame. The Home Owner's Association accused him of taking shortcuts during construction to lower costs and increase his profit. Well, screw them, he grumbled. Didn't they understand how business worked?

It was four o'clock before he got around to popping in on Matt at the jobsite. He found him inside the trailer up to his eyeballs in paperwork. Finally, he took his stare off the computer screen to look up at Jay. Unlike the last project manager, Matt didn't jump to attention whenever he walked into a room. The dude was a little too laid back for Jay's liking, but he had to admit Matt did a good job overseeing the renovation of the facility.

It was actually a good thing that Matt had trouble tearing himself away from his work because it gave Jay a chance to spot something he might have missed. On the edge of the desk, he saw a paper cup with a lipstick print. Camille's shade of pink. Of course, he knew it only meant that she had been there.

When Matt looked up, he seemed to be fixated on Jay's face. Then, Jay remembered the scratch on his chin put there by Camille's sharp nails when she fought him. He hadn't noticed it himself until he dabbed on shaving gel and felt the sting.

Jay stepped closer to the desk and said, "Got a minute, Matt? Let's walk around the job site. I want to see how it's going."

Matt grabbed two hard hats and followed him out. They walked along the makeshift walkway of boards and then entered a side door. Inside, all overhead lights had been turned off. Matt searched for the light switch on a wall to the right and flicked it on. In the shell of brick walls and new sheet rock, the sound of their footsteps bounced off the empty space.

With hands in his pockets, Jay ambled along the outer perimeter. He concentrated on the restored brick wall where mortar had been filled in, and then looked up at an overhead beam. His eyes were still fixed on the object when he said to Matt, "So, did you make peace with Camille?"

"Yes."

Jay thought he saw Matt wince at his question. *Good.* Before it was over, he'd make him pee in his pants.

"Glad to know you two kissed and made up."

Matt ignored the remark and said, "Jay, let me show you a crack over here. I think you should take a look at it."

As they strolled side by side to the far wall, Jay said, "Camille is to be treated like any other tenant. With respect. In a professional manner. That's the point I was trying to make with you the other morning."

"I get it." Matt shined a flashlight beam on the back wall and pointed where the circular light landed. "See that crack? I think it's just a shrinkage crack—so does Danny. But if you want, I can get an engineer to give an opinion. That overhead beam could create enough stress to cause it, but I doubt it."

"When was the last time Camille was over here?"

"Yesterday. She checked on Tyler's work."

"Oh, yes, good ol' Tyler. The cabinet maker and part-time Picasso. He painted Camille in the nude. Crazy, huh? I have the painting in my bedroom. It gives me a hard-on every time I look at it." Jay chuckled as he studied Matt's reaction. Another blank stare.

"About the crack," Matt said, "Do you want me to consult with an engineer?"

"There's no threat, is there?"

"What?"

"The crack. Isn't that what we're talking about?" Jay ran his left hand over the small split that ran from floor to ceiling in the brick wall. "I agree with your assessment. It looks like a shrinkage crack. That can be easily patched." Jay walked away with Matt at his side. He turned to him and said, "So, Matt, what is your assessment of your relationship with Camille?" Matt gave him a silent stare. "C'mon, it's a simple question. Are you friends or foes?"

"Like you said, Jay, she is a tenant and I will treat her that way. Actually I think it's best that she deal with Danny if she has issues with her office space."

"Funny, that's exactly what I was thinking. Can he be trusted?"

"What do you mean?"

Jay smiled. "I mean, he won't be trying to make a move on my fiancé, will he? Can't have anyone on my team making a pass at my girl. I'd either have to fire their ass or kill 'em."

"You don't have to worry about Danny," Matt said. "About the crack, we'll patch it. Shouldn't be too noticeable."

"Good. Well, I've seen all I want to see here. Keep me abreast of any new developments."

Jay removed his hard hat and pushed it into Matt's muscled abs. To his disappointment, Matt didn't even grunt from the force. The dude was a rock inside and out. He couldn't crack him no matter how hard he tried. *Damn!*

§

After Jay left, Matt met Danny at a bar on Tryon Street near Fifth. It was a popular place to mingle over a cool brew after work. Most of the crowd came from the banking sector, guys in white starched shirts with loosened ties and ladies in high heels and pencil skirts. However, Danny and Matt did not feel out of place in their jeans and knit shirts. They kept extra clothes in the trailer for such occasions. A little soap, water, and deodorant and they were good to go.

Danny had to yell over the music when he repeated what Matt had just told him. As he planted his elbow on the bar, he said, "You kissed her? Where?"

"On the lips."

Danny frowned. "You know what I mean, dude. Where did the insanity take place?"

"The back lot at the job site."

"You can't mess with the boss's girl. I think it's in the employee handbook."

"Relax, Danny. It won't happen again. We're done."

"Yeah, I've heard that before."

"No, I mean it. I think she and Jay deserve each other. She knows he's a douche bag, yet she thinks she has to stay with him."

"So, you're over her?" Matt took a sip of beer and nodded. "Good," Danny said and clamped his hand on Matt's shoulder. "Time to move on, bro. What about Amber? Maybe you two could get back together."

"Nah, I don't think so. I'm going to take some time off from women for awhile. Maybe enter a monastery."

"Now that's clear thinking." Danny tapped his bottle against Matt's.

Matt drank the last of his beer and signaled to the bartender for another. "Between you and me, Danny, I think Jay had something to do with Manny's death. I hope the cops find out before Camille does something stupid like marry him. When the two detectives came around, I told them what Manny's mom told Pepe—that Jay was going to pay him a thousand bucks."

"What did the cops say?"

Matt waited until the bartender set his beer on the counter and walked away. He turned to Danny and said, "They said Pepe told them he made it up. There was no pay-out. He lied to me."

"That doesn't make sense. Why would he lie to you?"

"I don't think he did. I think he lied to the police."

"Damn, that's messed up. Something strange is going on."

Matt took a sip of beer and wiped the foam from his lips with the back of his hand. "Yeah. I wish I could get Camille away from this craziness, but she's in denial."

"Dude, didn't you just tell me you were through with her?"

"I am," Matt said with a slight nod. "I still want her to be safe. What's wrong with that?"

Danny chuckled. "And you say *she's* in denial."

CHAPTER THIRTY

Camille should have been back at her cramped office finding the perfect shade of carpet to go with the fabric for Mrs. Larsen's new duvet cover. The carpet rep had dropped off samples of the new line that were supposed to be more durable, more stain resistant, and a better grade. Instead of dealing with business, she sat at a table in the main dining room at The Terrace View with her friend Alex, letting Mike, aka Alfredo, pour them a second glass of Chardonnay.

"Quit looking at me like I've lost my mind," Camille said to her friend. "I'm breaking up with Jay and that's that."

"Why?"

"You want specifics? Okay, I'll give you specifics. For one, he raped me. And he may be involved in something illegal or at least unethical. I don't know what's going on."

"You have lost your mind."

As Camille swirled the wine in her glass, she watched rain pound against the window in white sheets. For a brief moment, she thought about her umbrella lying on the floor in her car and then she turned to hear what Alex was saying.

"My God, you've lost your mind." Alex's repeated comment hurt. Camille expected more understanding from her friend.

"You don't believe me. Why am I not surprised? You think the man walks on water. Sure, at one time, I did too. He's changed, Alex. He went over to the dark side."

"He raped you? Come on, Camille."

"I wasn't in the mood, so he forced himself on me."

"I did the bondage role-playing thing one time. It was kind of exciting I thought."

"You're no help. Forget it, Alex."

"Sweetie, no man is perfect. I do think you're wrong about Jay. I've never seen anyone who works as hard as Jay. He's what? Not yet forty and already so successful. My husbands were

170

all bums. They lived off my money." She smiled at the waiter as he approached. "Alfredo, be a sweetie, and bring us a dessert to share. Surprise us. I don't care what it is. My friend needs cheering up."

"Certainly, Alexandria. I will bring over my favorite. The pastry chef made it fresh this morning."

"Thanks, dear. One dessert. Two forks."

As he walked off, he shot Alex a flirtatious wink. She said, "Isn't he a yummy morsel? I could have *him* for dessert."

"Is it my imagination or does he develop a European accent when he talks to you?"

While they shared laughter over Camille's remark, her cell phone rang. The more Camille listened to the caller, the more anger showed on her face. Once the call ended, she banged her phone down on the table.

"Sorry, Alex. Gotta go. You'll have to eat my share of the dessert. I have to kill someone."

§

A call from Tyler spouting a tirade of grievances laced with obscenities and crazy talk that sounded like he was quitting on her custom worktable sent Camille speeding to the jobsite. She had made a vow to avoid the place, and Matt specifically, but now she *had* to make an appearance. Her fury made her drive faster than the wet conditions allowed, and she almost hydroplaned close to downtown. She couldn't wait to confront Matt. In fact, she wanted to chew him up and spit him out in little pieces.

While she walked toward the warehouse holding an umbrella over her head, she spotted Danny leaning against the doorframe just far enough inside to dodge the rain. He was sipping from a can of Coke when she walked up to him. He became the first target of her rage.

"Where is he?" He gave her a perplexed stare. "Don't just stand there, Danny. Answer me, damn it!"

"Now hold on, Camille."

"You son of a bitch! Where is he?"

He jerked his chin to indicate that Matt was somewhere inside. She stormed in and left a trail of water from her closed umbrella. She found him near the back of the building where scaffolding was being taken down. He didn't notice her until she flung her umbrella aside onto the concrete floor.

With legs spread apart and hands on her hips, she yelled, "Did you think I wouldn't hear about it? Did you think you could get away with it?"

He walked over. Workers stopped their work to look on. He stood before her with arms crossed over his chest and said, "I guess you heard from Tyler."

"You bet I did. You fired him? He works for *me*, Garrison, not you."

"He was smoking a joint. High as a kite. Of course I threw him out."

"But he wasn't bothering anyone! Believe it or not, he does his best work when he's high."

"Funny that the two of you left out that little detail in our discussions. I will not tolerate drugs, guns, or unreasonable people on the jobsite. Guess you fit in the last category, so you need to go before I kick *you* out."

"How in the hell am I supposed to get my worktable finished? Tyler said he's not coming back, doesn't like a hostile work environment. What do I do now?"

"That's not my problem. I'm sure you'll think of something. Now if you'll excuse me, I have work to do."

"No, this is *your* problem, Garrison! I'm not going anywhere until you tell me how you're going to get my worktable finished."

"Just leave, Camille. Come back when you've had time to calm down."

"You warned me that the 'bad Matt' might resurface. Guess he's back!"

"Please leave, Camille. You're making a scene. These guys need to work."

"I'm not leaving until this is resolved. That table is crucial."

Matt looked up at the ceiling and let out a long exasperated sigh. "I don't have time for this shit. I've got a deadline I'm trying to meet. So, if you're going to act like a spoiled brat, then that's how I'll treat you."

Before she had any warning, he grabbed her around her hips and threw her across his shoulder like a sack of potatoes. All eyes were on them. She pounded on his back and demanded that he set her down. The tirade of angry words that she slung at him was nothing more than an echo off the bare floors and walls. They had no effect on Matt as he headed for the closest exit.

"Danny," he called out. "Open that door for me."

Danny turned the knob to open it wide, watching with amusement as Matt walked out with his extra load. With her hair dangling over her face, Camille pleaded for Danny's help, but he only grinned back at her and waved goodbye.

Matt stepped out onto the sidewalk into the pounding rainstorm. Sheets of white rain gave him little visibility as he looked both ways for traffic and then proceeded across the street to her car. He set her down on the driver's side. While Camille dug in her purse for her keys, she never broke eye contact. Like a squeegee, her hand wiped water from her face.

"You'll pay for this, Matt. You're making a big mistake!"

Once she was settled behind the steering wheel, she watched Matt stop in the middle of the street. *What in the hell is he doing? Stupid jerk.*

He stared up at a dark angry sky with the rain pounding his face. *Idiot!* Then, he turned on one heel and marched back to her car. As he peered down at her, she gazed up at him with suspicious eyes. Suddenly, he opened her door.

"Scoot over," he said as he tapped her arm with the back of his hand.

"What?"

"You heard me, Camille. Move over."

Because he was already lowering himself down, she had no choice but to swing her legs over the console to make room for him. In a clipped tone she said, "Are you driving me somewhere?"

He adjusted the seat back to allow more leg room. "No. We need to talk."

She anticipated an apology. But one glance into his dark somber eyes told her she was wrong. He wiped away the droplet of water from the edge of his nose and then stared straight ahead.

"I can't do this anymore, Camille." He turned to face her. "I've been offered my old job back. I'm moving back to Savannah."

"When did you decide this?"

"Just now. Seconds ago." She looked stunned, but said nothing. "They called me yesterday, and I told them I'd think about it. It's for the best. I'll give Jay two week's notice, and then I'm gone. In the meantime, if you need anything—any assistance at all—then see Danny."

"Why are you doing this?"

"I can't be around you."

"This is crazy! We're not kids. We don't have to kick sand at each other in the sand box. We're adults, Matt. We can be civil to one another, don't you think?" She paused, then added, "Matt, don't do this."

"My mind is made up, Camille. I don't want to see you. I don't want to hear from you. Be nice to Danny."

"Matt—"

Calling to him didn't make him stop. She watched as he stepped out into the street. When a car sounded its horn and had to brake, Matt did a mock bow in defiance and let it pass. Its wake from the flooded street splashed up onto his jeans. His next gesture to the passing vehicle was a one-finger salute.

§

It was settled. Matt was leaving. He called Pete Maddox, the owner of the company where he worked in Savannah, and told him he was coming back in two weeks. Maddox was thrilled.

He told Matt that the general contractor that had been like a burr in Matt's ass was now gone. Fired. Nothing had been the same since Matt had left, his boss said. They needed him back immediately, should've never let him leave. Matt listened politely to his humble drone of regrets and then told him he had to hang up, still work to be done on the project in Charlotte. Matt then called his parents and told them he'd stay with them until he could find his own place. His mom was thrilled and anxious to get his old room in tip-top shape. She told him she'd been using it as a sewing room.

Over the weekend, he made a quick trip home to Savannah to drop off some of his things. He and his father had some quality time together working on an old sailboat that they wanted to restore to its original condition. Scraping off barnacles was hard, tedious work, but as long as they worked side by side, the time spent was enjoyable. On Saturday afternoon, Matt's brother Scott drove down from Charleston after managing some personal time off from his hospital shift. The three Garrison men sat in the shade of the garage and drank beer and reminisced about the good old days.

In all, Matt had a good weekend away, but on the drive back his mind turned to Camille. The closer he got to Charlotte, the more he thought of how she had hurt him, how she had stomped on his heart. He could wallow in self-pity, but it wouldn't change a thing. She was not his, no longer in his life. He spent the next week in misery and made everyone around him miserable too. Danny told him to get his head out of his ass, and Matt told Danny to go to hell. Best friends at each other's throats.

With only a few days to go before he left town, Matt was treated to a send-off by Danny and some of the guys at the jobsite. They took a reluctant, not-in-the-mood-to-party Matt to a steakhouse that looked like it came straight out of the old West. It was miles away from town, out in the county where pastures were the norm. There, the steaks were thick and served medium rare, the fries—fat and greasy, and the draft beer poured from a wooden keg. Peanut shells littered the floor. A country band belted out one song after another. The lyrics were about lost love, divorce, or a woman leaving her man. Matt couldn't bear to listen. Since the free-flowing beer kept coming, he kept drinking.

No one noticed that he sat alone in the corner, reflecting on Camille's visit to the jobsite earlier that day. He had caught her talking with Danny and Tyler. Good ol' Tyler was allowed back with the understanding that he not smoke pot. Thanks to him, her worktable was near completion. Matt kept his distance and observed the trio discussing the wood molding around the base. Apparently Camille was satisfied with the work; he saw her nod. She looked up for just a moment, and their eyes met, but he quickly pivoted on one foot and walked away. He knew that her big brown eyes and sexy smile would be his last image of her.

In a drunken state, a tall blonde made her way over to him. She reminded him of a Western version of Camille in denim shorts, boots and a cowboy hat. Whatever Hot Blonde was selling, he wasn't buying. While her hips swayed to the beat of the music, she draped her arms over Matt's shoulders as she faced him. She said, "Well, cowboy, wanna dance?"

Matt looked around. He called out, "Danny? Danny?"

His pal waltzed over with his mug sloshing beer onto the floor. Danny laughed and came up alongside the girl, putting his arm around her bare mid-section.

"She's yours," Matt said to Danny. He removed the girl's arms from his shoulders. She fell back against Danny. "I gotta go. I'm catching a ride back with Pepe. Have fun and thanks for the party."

"You can't go! This is for you, man!"

"I know and you guys stay and enjoy. I've gotta get out of here. Get some fresh air."

"Ah, you're no fun," the girl said with slurred words.

Matt's gaze moved from the drunken girl to Danny. To his friend, he said, "Danny, don't do anything stupid."

"Don't worry, I won't."

"Okay, well, I'm going to find Pepe. See ya tomorrow. You know it's a work day."

"I know, I know. I'll be there."

Matt walked out with Pepe, pleased to finally have some face-to-face time alone with the foreman who had avoided him for days. When Matt insisted on riding back with him, Pepe complied with a reluctant nod.

After they turned onto the unlit highway that coursed through the countryside, Matt said, "Pepe, why did you tell the police there was no money coming to Manny?"

Pepe's eyes got big, but they stayed fixed on the road straight ahead. He shook his head in defiance. "No money, Mister Boss. It was a mistake. Manny's mama was wrong about that."

"Did Jay pay you to stay quiet? Did he pay the senora not to tell the police?"

"No money. I tell the truth, Mister Boss."

Matt could tell from a quick observation of Pepe's body language that he was not being truthful, but he let it go. They rode the rest of the way back to Charlotte in silence.

CHAPTER THIRTY ONE

Things were looking up, Jay thought as he drove toward his office. The dark cloud that lingered over his head had dissipated. His future looked bright. He'd sold the industrial land that had dogged him for two years, the last three units of the condo project were sold, his cash crunch was over, and his fears concerning the deaths of Manny and Morris had subsided. There was nothing concrete that would point a finger at him. But what really lifted his spirits were thoughts of Camille. She was the brightest sparkle in his life, the envy of every man. The little episode when he had gotten drunk and forced himself on her was just a lesson to let her know he was in charge, not her. If she did have a secret rendezvous with Matt, then it didn't happen the way Streaker described it. He never provided any proof, no photos, as promised. Besides, Jay was sure Camille got the message and would think twice before she ever cheated on him. He decided to give her a little break, let her stew for awhile. She'd soon realize how much she missed him. How she couldn't live without him.

The ring of his cell phone jolted him from his thoughts. Matt Garrison. What in the hell does he want, he wondered.

The first words out of Matt's mouth confirmed a problem. "We have a leak. The back lot is filled with standing water. It's a damn mess."

"Can't you shut it off?"

"I shut off the valve to the property, but that's not it. It's the water department's main valve and they have to do that."

"Shit!"

"Just thought you'd want to know. We've got that big delivery today and there's no way we can get a truck back there to unload."

"How in the hell did this happen?"

"Apparently a truck ran over the pipe—the new one put in parallel to the side street. Danny saw two concrete trucks back there. One tried to get out of the way of the other and we think he backed over the pipe and crushed it."

"Shit!"

"Nothing we can do until the city shows up. They can cut off the main valve, dig up the pipe, and then replace it. This is definitely a setback."

"I'm coming over," Jay said and hung up. He made a U-turn and headed for the jobsite.   Fifteen minutes later, Jay saw that the back lot looked like a muddy swimming hole. Because the water department truck had double-parked, drivers were forced to maneuver around it and honked in protest as they got by. Matt's crew was hard at work, getting materials out of harm's way. At least, the water was shut off. With his boots coated in mud, Matt plodded over to meet Jay who stood precariously on higher ground to protect his black dress shoes.

Matt wiped his forehead with the end of his T-shirt. "I think the worst is over. We've got it under control now. I cancelled the delivery of the materials, just in time too."

"Good. I want that pipe replaced today."

"They're sending a second crew to do the dig, but they said it might be awhile before they can come."

"Oh, yeah? We'll see about that." Jay dialed a number from his list of contacts. While he waited for the call to be picked up, he said, "I know people at the water department. This guy will speed up the process."

Jay demanded action, not in one hour or two, but A-SAP! After some cajoling, he got what he wanted: a promise of a crew on the site within twenty minutes.

With a smug smile, Jay said to Matt, "It helps to know people in high places. Well, I need to head over to the office. Got a meeting. I'll be back later."

"Maybe by the time you get back, the problem will be resolved."

Two hours passed before Jay returned. As he exited the Porsche, he stepped into mud and cursed. He was even more pissed when he inspected the insult to his car. The runoff of water into the street coated the tires with muck, but at least it blended well with the hideous scratch along the driver's side.

Jay dodged low places filled with standing water and made his way over to Matt. "I see the water department has sent a crew to dig. How in the hell are they going to get that broken pipe out? It weighs a ton."

"They've made a call for equipment. It should be here soon. There's still some digging to do before they get to that point."

"The sooner the better," Jay said. "I want to stay on schedule, damn it."

"Yeah, me too, but we've both been in construction long enough to know it doesn't always work that way." Matt put his hands on his hips and looked at Jay. "While we're waiting, there's something I want to discuss with you. It might be better if we talk in the trailer."

"Let's do it right here."

Matt shrugged. "Okay. Did you get a call from Camille this afternoon?"

"No. Why? What's this about?"

"Nothing. I just thought she would call you."

"Spill it, Matt. What's going on?"

"She's been dealing with Danny like we agreed, but he was gone this morning. She needed something, but I never returned her call. I've been busy with all that's going on. Just thought maybe she discussed it with you—whatever it is she needs. I'm not intentionally avoiding her, but it would be better if—."

Jay had a sardonic smile when he said, "What is it with you two? General animosity or a lover's quarrel?"

Matt's brows knitted. "Excuse me?"

"Cut the act, Garrison. I've heard talk. Are you fucking my girl? Just be honest."

"I don't know where you're getting your information, but it's wrong."

"I'd better be because I wouldn't stand for you crossing a line. Know what I mean? You'd never work again, at least not in this state."

"I'm glad you brought that up, Jay, because you remember tomorrow is my last day, right? I'll square some things with Danny, make sure he's got all the bases covered, and then I'm gone."

"You told me you'd work a notice."

"I did. It's been two weeks. Time for me to go."

Jay ran his hand over his face and exhaled a deep breath. He shook his head. "I don't need this. Not now. What will it take to make you change your mind?"

"My mind's made up. I'm leaving."

"If it's about money, I can give you—"

Jay paused mid-sentence when he noted a flurry of activity in the area where the digging took place. Two men who had been standing at ground level jumped down into the hole with the two workers. All eyes were fixed on an object, as if trying to make sense of what lay at their feet. At a frantic pace, they all began to dig.

Jay turned to Matt. "What's going on?"

"I have no idea." Matt watched two guys hop out of the ditch and sprint over to speak with Pepe. When Matt saw Pepe waving his arms frantically at him, he said to Jay, "I guess we're about to find out."

Pepe sprinted over. He took a second or two to catch his breath before he spoke. "Mister Boss," he said to Matt and then looked at Jay. "Mr. Jay, there's a body down there. In a garbage bag. We open. See dead man."

CHAPTER THIRTY TWO

It was as Pepe described: a heavy-duty garbage bag torn open at the top to reveal a head. Maggots had worked their way inside the nose and mouth cavity. The smell was horrific. Matt covered his nose and mouth with both hands as he stepped back. He was glad he had been too busy dealing with the flooding issue to take time for lunch. It wouldn't have stayed down. Workers had abandoned their work inside the building and now surrounded the ditch to see for themselves.

Matt yelled out, "Everyone move back. Don't touch anything. Wait for the police."

They stared at him with haunted eyes. When he gestured by waving his arms in the air, they shuffled backwards, mumbling among themselves.

Five minutes passed before two police cars arrived. The patrolman from one car went to his trunk and brought out yellow police tape. The other walked over and waved everyone further back. He ran his hand through his thickness of red hair and walked up to Matt.

"Did you call it in?"

"Yes," Matt answered, "but I'm not the one who discovered the body. The four men over there did. They work for the Water Department and were digging to replace a broken pipe."

The officer gave a tilt of his chin in Jay's direction. "Who is he?"

"Jay Stiles. He owns the property."

"And what is your name? You work here?"

"Yes, I'm the project manager. Matt Garrison. I just took over this job recently, so I don't know how much help I can be."

"Homicide is on their way, so we'll sit tight." He drew out a small notebook from his pocket. "Now I need to get some names written down. We'll need everyone to stay behind the

182

tape. Until the detectives says differently, no one can leave. Everyone needs to stay put."

"Some of these guys are undocumented," Matt said. "I'm surprised they haven't taken off."

"We're not here to round up people. We're here to investigate how a body got put in that hole."

§

Four detectives showed up in two unmarked dark sedans with lights flashing. They made a quick survey of the area, the body, and the crowd standing around. One walked away with his cell phone to his ear. Two patrolmen strolled over and got in a huddle with the detectives. The red-headed patrolman shared his notes with the lead detective, a broad shouldered man with serious muscle as if he lifted weights when he wasn't solving crimes.

Muscled-guy locked eyes with Matt and headed his way. He extended his hand out to shake Matt's. "Sergeant Jody Brick here," he said. He looked at his own notes that he had copied from the patrolman. "You are Matt Garrison, right? Tell me this. When was the pipe put in?"

"It was before I came to work here. Not sure, but I have some paperwork that will tell us. Do you think the body was put in then? Before the pipe was covered?"

Brick shrugged. "Maybe."

Every time Matt looked out at the street, he saw another police vehicle added to the mix. The medical examiner climbed out of a van with a canvas bag slung over his shoulder. The crowd parted so he could make his way to the body. With one knee on the ground, he waited until a crime scene investigator finished taking photographs of the body. Then the medical examiner signaled for the body to be lifted out of the hole. Two young officers grabbed hold of each end of the plastic bag and hoisted the corpse up onto the ground.

After the ME slipped on latex gloves, he used a knife to rip open the bag. With the help of an officer, he turned the body sideways enough to pull a wallet from the back pocket. He tossed it up to Brick. Also in gloves, the sergeant pried it opened. He held up a driver's license and credit cards that he pulled out. In another pocket, the ME found a cell phone.

Matt saw the recognition on the faces of the detectives as they viewed the items. The identity of the body stirred a flurry of activity. Brick walked away, made an urgent call, and tapped his hand on his side as he waited. His partner squatted next to the ME, and together they turned the body enough to view the backside. The ME put a pen light to the back of the head. Matt could not hear his remarks, but he assumed the exposed, decaying cavity was a result of a gunshot wound.

Fifteen minutes later, another unmarked car pulled up. It came to an abrupt halt over the curb and onto the sidewalk. A burly man with more hair in his moustache than on top of his head hopped out from the passenger side. The driver displayed the same sense of urgency. They sought out Brick and scrambled over as soon as they spotted him. The three men formed a tight huddle, keeping their voices down. The mustached cop looked out at the crowd and sought a specific target. His eyes locked on Jay who returned a blank stare. Jay inched backwards and then pivoted on one foot. He walked toward his car, but before he got too far, someone called out to him.

"Sir, you can't leave! No one can leave yet until we have statements."

Jay stopped. The detective stroked his moustache as he walked up to him and held out the driver's license that was taken from the body.

"Hi, Mr. Stiles. Remember me? Detective Jake Axelrod. I questioned you recently about the disappearance of Nick Morris." He looked over at the body. "That's him. We found him on your property."

"Believe me, I have no idea how he got there."

§

Matt watched as crime scene investigators combed the area for any evidence and helped the ME prepare the body for transport. The detectives allowed his crew to set out sandbags to keep the water away from the building. The men worked at a frenzied pace. On edge because of the police presence, they kept their heads down, focused on their work.

Carrying his toolbox, Tyler walked up to Matt and asked if he could leave. "The cops won't mind, will they? I've got to pick up Camille at the car dealership. She's having work done on her car."

"Finally," Matt muttered. "Tell you what, Tyler, I'll pick her up. I owe her an apology. You can head on home."

"Sure. Fine by me." He took a scrap of paper from his pocket. "Here's the address."

Matt got stuck in traffic, but at last he arrived at the dealership. He found the service department on the left side of the building and spotted Camille before she saw him. Unobserved, he studied her in her short tight skirt with arms crossed, looking out at the street and probably wondering what was taking Tyler so long. When she turned her head, her eyes locked with his. He smiled and waved. Her response was of surprise. With her mouth gaped open, she walked over to his car that he kept running.

She peered through the open car window and said, "What are you doing here?"

"Get in, Camille."

"Where's Tyler?"

"I asked him if I could pick you up."

"Why?"

"Hop in." When she did not move, he leaned over and opened the passenger door. "Camille, something has happened. Just get in."

He waited until he turned onto the main highway and into the flow of traffic before he looked over at her. With her legs crossed, her skirt rode up to mid-thigh. Her right foot made tight circles in strappy high heels. She didn't have to say a word to let him know that her anger at him was still raw. Her lips were set tight. She kept her gaze on the view outside the passenger window, which in his opinion wasn't worth the effort.

Despite her silent treatment, he said to her, "A body was found on the jobsite this afternoon. It's Nick Morris. A business acquaintance of Jay's. Before you say anything, hear me out. Camille, you should rethink your decision to marry Jay. You're in way over your head. You should trust your instincts." He paused, waited for a response, but got none. "I'm telling you, Jay's a dangerous guy. He might have been involved in Morris's death. I don't want you to get hurt." Again, he got silence in return. "I'm leaving for Savannah tomorrow, so it's no skin off my nose. But I wouldn't feel right if I didn't say something."

Her fixed gaze on the side window and her silence irritated the hell out of him. He mumbled more for his own benefit than hers, "Of course, you're so smart, no one can tell you anything. Maybe it's all his money that's made you so blind."

He wasn't prepared for her explosion of tears that streamed down her cheeks. Matt gulped and said, "Hey, hey. I didn't mean to upset you." She continued to cry, her face buried in her hands. He scratched his brow with his thumb and rolled his shoulders back. Finally, he said, "Please, Camille. I'm sorry. I take back what I said. I can't stand the crying, so please."

She lifted her chin and wiped at her tears. "Why do you hate me so much?"

"Hate you? Is that what you think? Hell, I don't hate you! I love you."

Oh, shit.

"What did you say?"

"I think you heard me."

He kept his eyes on the road ahead.

"Why didn't you just tell me that? You've been acting like you hate me."

"Well, I don't."

"This changes everything!"

"It changes nothing."

"When did it occur to you that you were falling in love with me?"

"What difference does it make?"

"I need to know." He stayed silent. "Please, Matt."

"The first morning we were together. At the hotel. There! Now you know. Never happened to me before. I mean, like that. So quick. Never thought it was possible, but it changed things for me. I can't explain it."

"If only you had called me, told me. If only I had known!"

After avoiding eye contact, he stole a glance and then scratched his cheek. "You'll have to tell me where to go. I don't know where you live."

"Take a right at the next light. Then, it's a straight shot." She pressed a tissue to her cheeks to soak up the last of her tears. "Matt, I'm not going to marry Jay. I haven't told him yet. I'm moving out of the apartment. He helps with the rent and I can't afford it on my own. And I'm not moving my office into the warehouse." When he said nothing, she added, "Did you hear me, Matt? I'm not marrying Jay. I'm in love with someone else."

"Really?"

"Dummy, it's you."

"Is this it?" He pointed to the apartment complex on their right. "Which unit?"

"Just park beside Tyler's van." He was thankful for her silence, but when he put the car in park, she reached over and placed her hand over his. "Matt, I know you heard me. I know we've been going at each other, but I think it was because we couldn't show our true feelings. Now we can. We can start fresh."

He shook his head. "It's too late, Camille. If you want to know the truth, I've been working hard to get over you. I've made some progress, but—"

She cut him off. "Well, I'm not going to beg." She opened the car door. "If you change your mind, you know where to find me. Thanks for the ride."

He watched the swing of her hips as she walked away. He kept his eyes fixed on her until she slipped inside the apartment. It hurt that she didn't look back. His knee rubbed against his keychain as it dangled from the ignition switch as if beckoning him to crank up the engine and get the hell out of there. He couldn't. He pounded his fist on the steering wheel and cursed. Afraid to leave, but more afraid to stay.

CHAPTER THIRTY THREE

Detective Axelrod led Jay to an interview room at police headquarters. He gestured to a cheap padded chair next to a wooden table, one of its ends flush against the concrete wall. Jay's eyes took in the cold surroundings. He plopped down into his seat and leaned forward, elbows up on the table.

Across from Jay, Axelrod pulled out a matching chair and tossed a legal pad onto the table. "I want you to get comfortable, Mr. Stiles. We'll get you something to drink soon, but first let me ask you some questions. Tell me a little about your relationship with Nick Morris."

Jay gave a nervous laugh. "It was a business relationship."

"Let's see, the last time we talked you said you met Morris about six years ago. He did some work for you then?"

"Yes. He did a complete upgrade on a house I bought in Dilworth. I got it at a bargain and after a total renovation, I sold it for double what I paid for it."

"So you flip houses?"

"What do you think, Detective? You've been to my company. The house thing was just a little sideline. You know I do upscale condos and commercial buildings. Morris did the last condo project for me. New construction. He did the upgrades. Granite counter tops, custom cabinetry, built-in bookshelves, that kind of stuff."

"My wife is dying to have granite countertops. I bet the condos are very nice."

"Yes, they start at four hundred grand. I sold the last penthouse for around two mill."

"Two million? Wow! Well, that's out of my range."

"I'm sure."

Axelrod pulled his chair in closer and scribbled on his legal pad. "Let's talk about the check you wrote out to Morris. What was the amount?"

Jay glanced at his watch. "You know the amount, Detective. Three hundred thousand and to answer your next question, I still have no idea what happened to it. I'm just wondering if he had it on him when you found the body."

"No, we didn't find it. We searched his office, and it wasn't there either. Strange. You'd think a person would put a check that size in a safe place."

"Maybe he had it on him, and the person who killed him took it."

"Now, that's an interesting theory. You might be on to something there."

Jay scoffed at the remark, raising his brow. "Detective, I can't do all your work for you. Surely, you thought of that possibility."

"Yep, I did think about that. You know, if we can eliminate you as a suspect, we can get on with the real work, Mr. Stiles."

Detective Axelrod kept the pressure on for two hours, going over Jay's alibi, his ownership of a handgun, and his last conversation with Morris. Around and around in circles, they went. The detective focused on any discrepancies, any contradictions, any holes in his story. Finally, he rubbed his moustache and stared up at the ceiling tiles.

Axelrod repeated a question he had put to Jay in different variations. "Do you have any idea how Morris's body ended up on your work site?"

"I don't have a clue."

"I'll have to be honest with you, Jay. It looks bad that the two of you did business together, you owed him money, and he ends up buried on your property."

"I don't know what to tell you, Detective. I wish I knew."

Axelrod stood up and dragged his chair back against the wall. "Let's take a little break. I'll be right back. "

§

Axelrod walked across the hall to the surveillance room where detectives were glued to the monitor, all eyes on Jay as he sat alone.

Detective Hutchinson pointed to the screen when Jay leaned forward and drummed his fingers on the table. He said, "He's starting to look a little worried."

"Just like I said, Hutch. He thinks I don't know shit. Thinks he's got more smarts than all of us combined. I want to dance with him a little longer. See if anything surfaces."

"He's an arrogant son of a bitch." Unlike Axelrod, Detective Hutchinson had a full head of dark hair. He ran his fingers through its thickness and rested his hand on the nape of his neck. "I don't know, Axe. We've got nothing to tie him to the crime. The bullet taken from the skull is a .45, and according to our records, Stiles owns a .38. There's nothing about a .45."

"Could be it's not registered. I'll ask him." Axelrod turned to Sergeant Brick who caught only the last few minutes of the interview. "You saw what was on the bottom of the victim's shoes, didn't you, Brick?" He nodded. "Small pieces of gravel. They look like they were wet when he was put in the bag. It rained the night before he was reported missing. You can tell by the heels that he was dragged a distance. The work site has red mud, larger grade of gravel rocks. So, he was killed somewhere else. Maybe at his office." Axelrod turned back to Hutch. "Remember we saw a gravel lot in the back? His administrative assistant said he always parked back there. Hidden from the street. It was dark with a busted pole light. He might have been plugged when he left his office that night. Last call to his cell at 5:10."

Hutchison, tired of staring at the monitor, ran his hand over his eyes. He leaned far back in his swivel chair to looked up at Axelrod. "I can't see this guy doing the kill. I think he hired someone to do it for him. We'll know more when the autopsy is done, but when the ME examined the body on site, he said the shot was fired from a distance."

"Well, there's no way Stiles could do a single head shot unless it was close range," Brick said. "My hunch is he wasn't even there. Look, guys, he was the one who wanted that pipe dug up. He made the call to the water department according to Garrison and told them to get over quick. Why would he do that if he knew the body was there? Doesn't make sense."

"Brick's right," Hutch said. "No way. He hires someone to do his dirty work. Doesn't know where the body was disposed. Well, Axe, how d'ya wanna play it? It's your call."

"I think he was there when it went down," Axelrod said. "I don't buy the alibi. He keeps wanting to show me the receipts from the bars without me asking for them. Brick, check it out. See if they have surveillance for that night."

The detectives stared at the door when they heard a knock. A head popped through the opening. Long chestnut hair swung forward and landed on a narrow shoulder as the female officer stood sideways, one hand on the doorknob. Her greenish eyes landed on Axelrod.

"Hey, A-Rod," she said. "The ME called. He's getting ready to start the preliminary autopsy. Thought you'd want to be present."

"Why didn't he call me himself?"

"He did. You didn't answer."

Axelrod look down at his cell phone attached to his belt. "Hell, I turned it off. Madge, you mind calling him back? Tell him to give me about fifteen minutes."

After she left, Hutch looked at Axelrod and grinned. "A-Rod? When did she start calling you A-Rod?"

"Now isn't that special," Brick chimed in and winked.

Axelrod rolled his eyes while the two men chuckled. "Crap! I never should have told her I played baseball in my younger, slimmer days." He shrugged. "My coach said I could be the next Rodriguez. I just opted for the glamorous life of a cop instead of a career in baseball. All that fame and money? Who needs it?" As he got up to leave, he shot them a wry grin.

When Axelrod entered the interview room, Jay lifted his head off the table and pushed his palms in his eye sockets. "You're back," he said.

"Yeah."

"Let me give a better explanation about the three hundred grand I paid to Morris. When he went missing, I stopped payment on the original check and mailed a replacement. You can check with his secretary if you need proof. I make a lot of money, Detective. I wouldn't kill someone over three hundred grand."

"Believe me, men kill for a lot less."

CHAPTER THIRTY FOUR

Matt took his keys out of the car ignition and exhaled a deep breath. At Camille's door, he knocked once, then twice. When she opened the door, her smile was an open invitation into her arms, into her heart. He pulled her close, gave her a crushing kiss, and walked her backwards into the apartment. He kicked the door closed with his foot.

Now that he faced her, he couldn't get his mouth to work, but his hands did just fine expressing his passion. One found its way inside her blouse, tugging it down off her shoulder. His palm kneaded her breast, causing her to let out a soft moan. Her breaths matched his, quickened by arousal and expanding her chest in and out. When she tilted her head back, he kissed her neck, splayed his hands over her buttocks. Her knee slipped between his thighs, but he stepped back. Her bewildered gaze begged for an explanation.

"I have to shower first, Camille. I'm grimy and sweaty and I won't touch you like this."

"It's okay. I don't mind."

"I do."

Conceding with a nod, she grabbed his hand and led him to the bathroom. "Towels are under the sink. Please hurry."

"You better believe I will."

§

For over four hours, detectives came and went from the interview room. Jay was tired of their shit. He told them everything he felt comfortable saying without implicating himself or Streaker. What more could he add? He knew they couldn't hold him because they didn't have enough to charge him. Who did they think they were dealing with anyway? He thought of shutting down the interrogation and asking for a lawyer, but then he speculated that seeking representation would make him look guilty. Besides, he reasoned that he was doing just fine on his own going up against Detective Axelrod.

The guy has shit for brains. Streaker was right. They've got nothing. No forensics, no eye witness, no motive.

He watched the door as it clicked open. With the same legal pad, Axelrod walked in and sank heavily into a chair. His blank expression gave Jay no hint of his next move, his next asinine question.

He began by saying, "Well, Mr. Stiles, the best thing you can do for yourself is to man up and take some responsibility. I'm here to help you. Once this goes to the prosecutor, it's out of my hands. I know you're holding back. Maybe you're protecting someone." His long pause seemed deliberate, allowing Jay a chance to respond. Jay opted for silence. Axelrod continued, "Do yourself a favor and get it off your chest. You're not the only guy who has sat in that chair, wanting to make some sense out of a wrong. It's like a cancer that just festers and eats you up, man. Know what? You'll feel better when you let it go."

Jay shifted in his chair and cleared his throat. He ran his fingers through his hair and stared up at the ceiling. Finally, he looked directly at Axelrod. "I have nothing else to say, Detective. Unless you're going to charge me, I'm free to walk out. Am I right?"

"Yep. You're free to go."

§

Downcast, Axelrod, hands in pockets, slouched as he walked over to Hutchinson's work area. Hutch swiveled around in his chair, his back to his computer monitor. "Axe, we'll still get him. It's just a matter of time."

"I know. I just wish we had more. The DA said there's not enough probable cause to issue a search warrant and he's right. The ME got zilch in trace evidence from the body, just the bullet that we can't tie to Stiles. Basically, we've got nothing. His alibi seems to check out, at least, with the second bar. I'm still not convinced he was at Lulu's, but they don't have video. I know this guy's up to his neck in this, I just can't prove it."

A figure appeared in the doorway. Madge leaned against the doorframe and smiled. "Hey, A-Rod, you're gonna want to hear this." She stepped aside and allowed two homicide detectives to walk in. "These guys have something to tell you."

Detective Rob Smith crossed his arms over his chest and spread his legs wide. He exchanged a glance with his partner as if they had jointly scored a touchdown and wanted to do a victory dance. Axelrod looked from one to the other with curiosity and waited to hear what had gotten the guys so jacked up.

Finally, Smith said, "The guy you just cut loose? That's Jay Stiles, right? He owns Stiles Enterprises over on Morehead?"

"Yeah, so?"

"Our victim worked for him. We think the two murders might be connected. The project manager at Stiles's construction site said he was told that Stiles paid our vic one grand for some extra work. The family denies it, but hey, could be true. Maybe it was a cash payment to help cover up the case you're investigating—Morris, is it? The guy missing from the lake and then dug up."

"Damn, this is getting interesting," Axelrod said. "Tell me more. Make me smile."

"Our vic was Emanuel Sanchez, found dead in Iredell County. He'd been missing for awhile. We couldn't figure out how he ended up over in another county, but we think he was a passenger in a truck that wrecked on Highway 115. The deputy said that when the driver gained consciousness, he asked where his passenger was. He told him he didn't have a passenger. The deputy thought he was confused 'cause the dude was out cold when they found him. Could've been doped up. They found pills and alcohol. They took him to the hospital and then straight to jail. He's out on bail, got a court date coming up."

"What's the guy's name?"

"Wayne Johnson," the other detective offered. "You know him."

"The name sounds vaguely familiar," Axelrod said. "Who is he?"

"A former cop. From vice. Looks like a cowboy."

Axelrod's brows knitted. He rubbed his chin. "Streaker?"

"Yeah, that's him. That's the guy."

"He's a private investigator now," Axelrod told them. "Hell, yeah, I can see him involved in this. Worked for Stiles? Maybe. Where's his truck? We need to process it."

"It was totaled in the wreck, towed to that wrecker service off the interstate. By now, it's probably been hauled away to the junk yard unless they're waiting for the insurance adjuster to see it."

"You mean it could be squashed down to the size of a soup can?"

"Could be," Smith said. "Let's hope not. I'll make some calls."

"Thanks. I'll see if I can find Streaker. Since his truck is gone, do you know what he's driving now?"

"No, but if he bought a new vehicle, DMV will have a record. Same license plate, maybe."

"Madge, can you check that out? I'm going to check on the kind of gun he carries." Axelrod walked over to Hutchinson's chair. "Wanna bet it's a .45?"

The partners did a high five and laughed.

CHAPTER THIRTY FIVE

Once the water was running, Camille gave Matt adequate time to shower before she slipped in behind him. With his eyes closed and his head under the full spray, he was unaware of her presence, which delighted her. She wrapped her arms around his waist, pressed her breasts into his back, and anticipated his reaction.

She kissed his back and said, "I hope you don't mind."

He turned around. "Do I look like I mind?"

She looked down at his erection and smiled. "Turn around again."

"Why? I like the view," he said, letting his eyes take in his first sight of her fully naked.

"You'll see."

Once he faced the wall, she pressed tighter against his backside, putting herself completely under the shower flow. Her hair became drenched and flattened against her head. Her hands glided across his wet skin to rest on his chest. After a few seconds, she bent her knees so that her hands could stroke his thighs. Then, they work their way inward, her fingertips touching his erection. She took his shaft in her hand, massaged it in her palm. Matt uttered a moan that spoke to his pleasure. His head turned sideways, so that she saw his smile. Pressing even tighter against his buttocks, she refused to allow him to turn around. She was glad that he permitted her busy hands to work their magic, but when his arousal built in leaps and bounds, he turned abruptly and hoisted her up in his arms. He had the strength to keep her that way for as long as needed, but she took away some of the strain by wrapping her legs around his waist and her arms around his neck. His lips crushed against hers. Camille noted his rapid breaths, his heart racing. He left a trail of kisses from her neck to her chest. Some kisses were light, but most were open-mouth and wet with enough passion to leave marks, the burn of his whiskers on her soft skin.

He lifted her higher so that his mouth covered her breast. His tongue flicked and circled her nipple, sucked it hard, then harder, sending her to the moon and back. She closed her eyes and arched her back, forming a bow away from him. It brought her thighs up, tighter against him. Her most sensual area, deep inside her, was wet, although it had nothing to do with the water. Somehow, Matt managed to brace her against the wall, freeing one hand so that he could stroke her and push her legs apart, making ready for what was to come next.

When he thrust his penis inside her, Camille opened her eyes wide, not expecting it so suddenly. The feel of him inside her made her moan in ecstasy. His hands braced her back, keeping her upright while his thrust went deep, then deeper. He increased the momentum by making each stroke quicker, and penetrating deeper. Her breaths became choppy, an audible gasp with each thrust. She opened her eyes to see his shut tightly and his jaw clenched just as he reached his climax. He growled as he emptied himself into her. Camille came as well and dug her fingers into his back, leaving red marks. Due to the acoustics of the shower walls, the sounds coming from her were thunderous, something between a scream and a moan, but making clear the pleasure she felt. When her orgasms ceased, she slumped forward in his arms, feeling the might of his strength.

They clung to one another, prolonging the inevitable separation. At last, Matt set her down, kissed her forehead, and reached over her head for a towel. He wrapped it around her so that it covered her shoulders and nothing else. He pulled her into his arms.

"Let's get you dried off," he said.

With his hands on both ends of the towel, he pulled it back and forth across her back, kissing her breasts as the motion pushed her forward. Placing her fingertips on his shoulders, she smiled down at him and enjoyed the special treatment. He then took the towel and ran it over her legs, soaking up droplets of water. After he wiped the back of her calves dry, he brought the towel up and rubbed it between her upper thighs, causing a renewed arousal for them both.

She laughed and backed away. "Oh, no you don't."

"I didn't fantasize our first time being in the shower. I thought it would be in bed," he said.

"The second time will be, but first, let's take some time to cool off."

"Now that you're mine, I don't want to let you out of my hold, Camille."

She took the towel from him and ran it over his body. She knew that she could easily get down on her knees, take him in her mouth, and again initiate another round of hot and heavy sex, but at the moment, she wanted only to feel him close, his body against hers. She tossed the towel aside and turned on her heel. He followed the very naked Camille into her bedroom. With one swift motion, she yanked the covers back and spread across the bed. On her side, she patted the space beside her.

"Lay down next to me, Matt. Hold me for awhile. Or you can hold me forever, if you like."

He took her up on the invitation, springing from his feet. He landed softly at her side and gathered her into his arms. He massaged her back with nimble fingers and then stroked her breasts. She placed her hand over his and stopped him.

"Just hold me for now, then you can fulfill your fantasy about the bed thing."

He smiled and kissed her forehead. "I love you so much, Camille." His hand went under her hips and pulled her closer. With his lips against her ear, he said softly, "It was killing me how much I loved you. Loving you from a distance and not being able to do a damn thing about it was making me crazy. That's why I decided to leave."

"I love you too, Matt. I wished I had realized it sooner. My priorities got out of whack. Money can't buy happiness. Being with the one you love is—"

He put his finger over her lips to hush her. "I'll never be able to give you what Jay can."

"No. You give me so much more."

Like a little bit of heaven, she found comfort in his strong arms that held her until the room grew dark. She thought that Matt had gone to sleep until he got up on one elbow and stared into her eyes with renewed longing.

"It's time," he whispered.

She knew what he meant when he ran his hand over her nakedness. He palmed her breasts and stared down at them as if enthralled by their feel in his hand. He lowered his head until he had one in his mouth, sucking for a long time before he gave equal time to the other breast. His hand stroked her tummy, then moved lower, squeezing her pubic area and then spreading her legs apart. By the time he stretched out over her, she was wet and ready for him. He groaned as he penetrated her, waiting for a few seconds before he went deeper. Then, he pulled out and turned her onto her stomach. He pushed her legs apart and entered her again. As each thrust went deeper, she moaned with her face buried in the pillow. He climaxed before she could reach orgasm. He fell limp over her, but lifted himself up and turned her over onto her back. He pushed his middle finger inside her and rubbed his thumb across the outer area. He made wet kisses, involving his tongue and sometimes his teeth, all along her groin. She begged him that she couldn't take anymore, but the stimulations kept coming. She closed her eyes and surrendered to the pleasure of his touch, his love. The erotic combination of fingers, lips, tongue, teeth made her come in one big burst like a busted damn. She screamed in ecstasy and dug her nails into his back.

Camille was so spent from the experience, she could not move, but finally, she rolled off the bed and switched on a lamp. For a moment, she felt dizzy with the awareness of what she had just experienced. She felt her swollen lips, and on different parts of her body she saw whisker burns and red marks as evidence of the intensity of their lovemaking. She slipped on his borrowed orange T-shirt that she had failed to return. Matt lifted his head off the pillow to give her a lust-filled stare.

Later, they drifted into the kitchen and made omelets while music played from the I-pod on the counter. While they ate and drank wine, they made small talk, teased one another, and shared laughter. Not until they cleaned up the dishes did they face up to what had happened at the jobsite that afternoon.

In emotional agony, Camille placed her palms on her throat and said, "I knew Jay had secrets. I can't believe he might have killed Nick Morris and also had some involvement in Sanchez's death. I confronted him with questions, but he swore to me everything was fine."

Matt stroked her cheek. "Where I come from, murder is not fine."

§

Camille had almost drifted off to sleep with Matt's arm draped over her when she heard a knock at the door. She gasped and sat up in bed. As he rubbed sleep from his eyes, Matt propped up on one elbow.

"It's him!" She touched Matt's arm, and then added, "Jay. He's here."

"You sure? He should still be with the police."

She got up and peeped out through the blinds. "It's him. I see his car. He can't get in— I've changed the locks. Matt, I have to go to the door."

As she started to move, he grabbed her arm. "No. Stay here. He'll go away."

"You don't know him like I do. He won't give up."

"Camille—"

"I'll get rid of him, Matt. Please. Hide in the closet, just in case."

Matt swung his legs off the bed and pulled on his pants. "If he touches you, I'm coming out."

§

Camille peered at Jay through a small opening in the door. Jay used the forced of his hand to open it wide and gain entry. He walked into the center of the room and pivoted around to face her. His dark look and the absence of his tie and jacket gave him an unsettling presence. When he tried to come close, she backed away.

She folded her arms over her chest. "What do you want, Jay?"

He scowled at her orange T-shirt, showing his disapproval. For him, she had always worn sexy, silky attire. Secretly, she was glad the casual attire bothered him.

"You changed the locks? Why?"

"For my safety," she said. "Why are you here?"

"I need you, baby. I need you so bad."

When he reached out for her, she ducked under his arm. "Please leave."

"Camille, I need you. My world is falling apart."

"Stay away, Jay. I know what you did."

"You know what?"

"That you killed a man. Nick Morris. You killed him! His body was found buried on the job site. I heard."

"No, baby. I didn't, I swear. I'm being framed."

"Yeah, right. You should just take responsibility for what you did."

"Okay, I admit I was going to do it, but I couldn't. Morris was going to make lots of trouble for me. I had to stop him. I *did* confront Morris at gunpoint, but I didn't pull the trigger. I didn't do it. Baby, you've gotta believe me."

"You're lying."

"Streaker did it. He did it to save me. Self-defense."

"Come on, Jay."

"No, no, baby. It's the truth. I couldn't do it. I held the gun up, but my hand was shaking so bad. Morris started yelling at me, daring me to pull the trigger. Then, he knocked the gun out of my hand and came after me. Remember those marks on my neck? Morris tried to choke me. He almost crushed my windpipe! I was down on my knees, trying to get his hands off me, and I heard a blast. I looked up to see Streaker coming over. He shot Morris in the back of the head. One shot, that's all."

"Why didn't you call the police?"

"I held the man at gunpoint, that's why. I would've been charged with attempted murder. I can't tell the police what happened because Streaker will find out. He's been threatening me. Got this big black dude harassing me. You remember that gold Cadillac, don't you? That's Streaker's guy. It has to be. Don't you see what he did? He buried the body on my property to frame me."

Her hands were shaking by now. His words confirmed that Matt was right. He had tried to warn her, but she wouldn't listen. She felt sick to her stomach, almost dizzy. Her voice trembled when she said, "Jay, you need to tell the police all this, not me. There's no way out for you unless you're truthful."

"And I told you I can't! Because of Streaker! If I go to the police, he'll come for *you*, then he'll kill *me*!"

"I want you to leave right now. You can't stay here."

Again Jay walked toward her and tried to gather her in his arms. She took two steps back.

"What's wrong? Why won't you let me touch you?"

"Jay, get out! Don't you get it? It's over. I can't marry you. Actually, I want you out of my life. So, just leave."

Before she had time to react, he grabbed her wrist and pulled her in close. "No, I won't lose you, too, Camille. We're going away, you and me. Go pack some clothes. It's the only way to keep us both safe. We'll start over somewhere. I have money—we'll be okay."

She wrestled to get free. "Let go of my arm! Stop it, Jay! I won't go anywhere with you. You're a liar and a killer! Let me go!"

"Camille, if I lose you, I've lost everything. I love you!"

"I don't love you, Jay."

He released his hold. "Don't break my heart, baby. Please don't do this." Again, he tried to gather her in his arms, but she crossed the room, putting as much distance as she could between them. "Camille, you act like you're scared of me. C'mon now." He walked toward her, his hands extended out.

"Stop right there! Keep away from me!"

In surrender, he dropped his hands to his side. Tears pooled in his eyes. If she wasn't so scared, she thought she would have a twinge of pity for him.

"If you don't leave right now, I'm calling the police."

"You wouldn't do that."

"Try me."

Worry crept into his eyes, hanging doggedly as his stare lingered on her. She knew he understood that her threat was more than empty words.

"Okay, okay. I'll leave." Jay dropped his head down, placed his hand on the nape of his neck, a habit of his she had seen many times whenever he became pensive. With eyes closed, he said softly, "I have nothing. Everything important to me has been stripped away. My life is over. It's okay if they come for me."

"Who are you talking about? The police?"

His odd stare at nothing there and his peculiar laughter sent a shiver down her spine. He said, "Police. Streaker. The black man in the gold car. It doesn't matter. I have nothing to live for."

"Jay, what are you going to do?"

"Do you really care?"

From the top drawer of a small desk, she retrieved the engagement ring. As she held it out for him, she said, "Here, take it."

"No. You keep it to remember me by."

"Jay, what are you going to do?"

"Bye, Camille. Have a nice life."

The intensity of his crystal blue eyes sent a chill down her spine.

CHAPTER THIRTY SIX

While Streaker lay on his stomach across her bed, Samantha straddled him. She massaged his bare shoulders with some therapeutic lotion that her husband had given her for her birthday. It smelled of mint and eucalyptus. He groaned as she moved her hands around in tight circles. She traced his scars left by gunshots with her index finger.

"This is just wrong," she said.

With his face buried in the softness of a pillow, he mumbled, "What's that?"

"You being here. Sleeping on Larry's side of the bed, screwing his wife, driving around in his truck."

When he flipped over on his back, she almost fell off the bed. "Baby, you said yourself he's probably doing some chick while he's on the road. Why all of a sudden you get all righteous on me?"

Up on her knees, she piled her copper hair on top of her head and then released it so that it fell like a curtain on a stage. He stood up to dig a pack of cigarettes from his jeans pocket. He frowned when he realized it had been crushed by her weight. He walked over to get a lighter from the top of her dresser.

"You can't smoke in here!" she yelled. "I've told you, Larry will smell it. He has a nose like a bloodhound."

"You let me smoke in the kitchen."

"Not in here, Streak. The smell will linger in the mattress, the drapes."

"Great! I'm going outside."

He brushed past her before she could object, the screen door banging behind him as he stepped outside. Although he heard the same door creak open a few minutes later, he did not turn to acknowledge her presence.

The flame from the lighter illuminated the hard lines on his face. From behind him, Samantha stretched on tiptoes to kiss his shoulder. After she opened the front of her robe, she pressed her bare breasts against his back. Her arms wrapped around his waist.

"What's bothering you, Streak? Tell me."

"The news you gave me about my pal Stiles."

"I told you, they let him walk. Did he really kill that man they found at the construction site?"

"Yeah, and I'm afraid he won't own up to it. He'll say I did it. You can't trust anybody anymore."

Samantha fanned a plume of smoke away and hugged him tighter. "It'll work out, Streak. You've managed to get out of scrapes before. This is just one more."

"They'll be back for him. Axe is the lead on the investigation. You know his reputation. That's why I gotta do what I gotta do."

"What's that?"

"Make sure Stiles doesn't drag me into his mess."

"What are you going to do, Streak?"

"I need to use Larry's truck again tomorrow. Is that okay? When is he coming back?"

"He won't be back for another three days. It's fine if you drive his truck, but remember you can't smoke in it."

"Shit!"

§

Camille breathed a sigh of relief and went back to the bedroom. On the corner of the bed, Matt waited for her. When she slipped into the opening between his legs, he buried his face between her breasts.

She said simply, "Jay's gone."

Holding up his hand with a minute space between his index finger and thumb, he said, "I came this close to busting out of this room."

"Thank God it didn't come to that."

"Camille, why do you keep a gun in your closet?"

"I don't."

"I saw it when I was hiding."

She backed up so Matt could stand. He went to the closet and pointed to the interior wall. "There's a ledge." Before he reached for it, he paused. "Maybe I shouldn't put my prints on it. I need a cloth and a plastic bag."

Once it was contained in a plastic bag with a zip-lock seal, he held it up for Camille to see. "Do you recognize this?"

"Yes. It's Jay's. He used to keep it in the bedside table at his townhouse. He must have put it there when I was at work. The day he left flowers on my table. Why would he bring it here?" She answered her own question with a gasp. "Oh, no! Do you think he used it on Morris?"

"I don't know, but I'm calling the police. I've got a card from one of them. Sergeant Jody Brick." He lifted her chin to meet her gaze. "Are you okay with me making the call?"

"Yes. Actually, I hope they find him. I'm afraid he's going to get himself killed."

§

On a vacant lot, Jay spent the night inside his car. He couldn't go home. What if the cops decided to bring him in for more questioning? What if they found some trace evidence that would tie him to the murder of Morris? One of his hairs or a thread from his suit. What if Streaker was looking for him?

He hoped that the cowboy stayed away from Camille. He tried to warn her, but she wouldn't listen. Damned if she didn't seem afraid of *him*, the one person who loved her like crazy. Hell, she even cowered when he tried to get close.

Jay adjusted the seat upright and stared out the front windshield. He squinted against the reflection of the sun on the hood of his car. His watch said it was ten. Late. If he was in the office, he'd be meeting with his staff about a pending project, another retail/office mix in a renovated building close to downtown. But he couldn't think about that now.

On the floorboard, he saw one empty bottle of whiskey and another half full. His head pounded. If he got out of the car, he'd either puke or pass out. With eyes closed, he leaned back to let a wave of nausea pass. Where in the hell was he, he wondered. A part of town where people like him never ventured. After he left Camille's apartment, he had a mission: to find the big black dude who keyed his car. If he was correct in his assumption, the guy was a drug dealer, and Jay would be on his turf.

Jay climbed out of the car and grabbed hold of the roof to recover from a wave of dizziness. He lumbered away and stood among crabgrass and dandelions. He bent over, threw up, and then felt better. Back at the car, he found bottled water underneath the front seat. He used it to rinse out his mouth, then poured what was left over his forehead. After wiping his face dry with his sleeve, he plopped down behind the wheel and turned the ignition.

Back on the street, he spotted what looked like a prime location for a junkie needing a fix. He parked between two buildings in an alley. Even at the early hour, he found a bar opened for business. He waltzed past the eyes on him, and then hopped up on a barstool. He ordered a beer from a beefy bartender with a towel thrown over his shoulder. The guy stared at him, didn't move.

Jay said with a chuckle, "I can't figure out if you want to kill me or serve me a drink."

"Let's toss a coin." Finally, the bartender filled a glass with beer on tap. When he set it down, he said, "If you didn't stink of whiskey and dress like a hotshot lawyer, I'd say you were a cop."

Jay chuckled at the absurdity of his remark. "Believe me, I'm not a cop. Actually, I'm hiding from them."

"Oh, yeah?"

"Do you know where I can find a big dude with a shaved head in a gold Cadillac Eldorado? I've got a proposition for him. A money-making proposition."

"You must mean Slick. Yeah, I might know where he is. How much is it worth to you?"

Jay locked eyes with the heavy-lidded dark ones that never seemed to blink. "Oh, I get it. Okay, here's a twenty." He pulled out his wallet and slapped the bill onto the bar.

The bartender scratched his cheek with one fat finger. "My memory is still a little foggy."

"Will another twenty clear your head?"

"Yeah, that'll work." The man tucked the bills inside his shirt pocket underneath the towel. "The apartments down the street, across from the gym. Where his whore stays."

"Thanks." Jay took a sip of beer before he pushed it away and hopped down from the stool. As he headed for the door, all eyes were on him.

At first, he thought he'd wasted forty dollars on bad information. The Cadillac was nowhere to be found. He cruised the street up and down, circled the block three times. Then he heard and felt the bass vibration of hip-hop music. He looked over to his left to see the car beside his. Although Slick couldn't see him because of the tinted windows, Jay had no doubt that the dude recognized his car. After all, it still displayed Slick's handiwork when he keyed it.

Jay whipped the steering wheel to the left, coming inches from hitting Slick's car. He saw the rage on the black man's face. When the Cadillac accelerated faster, Jay switched lanes, and got behind it. He pressed the gas pedal harder and rammed the back bumper, although it had little effect on the much larger car. Jay laughed and switched lanes again, this time cutting in front of the Cadillac. Slick hit the brakes hard. In his rearview mirror, Jay saw him bang his hand against the steering wheel with fury. Jay stayed in front, but slowed to a crawl, and made a right turn at the light. Slick followed, his front bumper only inches away from the Porsche.

In a gravel lot behind a pool hall, Jay parked. The Cadillac rolled to a stop a few feet away. Jay got out and stepped away from his car. He took a long look at blue sky, green trees, even the gravel that crunched under his shoes. His hand was clammy, but it still held a knife securely. He raised his arm, made sure that Slick saw his weapon.

"Hey, asshole," Jay yelled. "I didn't get to take care of your front tires."

Slick bolted from the car and shouted, "You son of a bitch! I'll kill you!"

"Come and get me, motherfucker!"

CHAPTER THIRTY SEVEN

Axelrod figured he got maybe four hours of sleep, tops. His wakeup call came at six, in the form of rock music ringtone on his iPhone. He hit the answer button as fast as he could so it wouldn't awaken his wife. However, she rolled over and rubbed sleep from her eyes. He mumbled a brusque *hello* to the asshole who woke them.

Detective Smith spewed words from his lips like oil gushing from a well. Axelrod told him to slow down and repeat what he just said.

"I said we picked up a suspect on the Sanchez murder. We're almost certain he's the guy who iced him. Last call Sanchez made on his cell phone was to this dude. We've been looking for him for awhile. Dude went underground when he knew we wanted to pick 'im up, but a unit grabbed him about three hours ago. He's got a lawyer and won't admit to the killing."

"You want *me* to interview him?"

"Nah, nah. Here's the thing," Smith said. "He says he's got info about that other murder, and he wants a deal before he'll say anything more. The DA's on her way. We think he's gonna talk about your guy, Nick Morris. We think before he killed Sanchez, Sanchez gave him the skinny on what went down. Could break your case wide open."

By now Smith had Axelrod's full attention. He knocked the covers off and sat up on the side of the bed. "Damn! I hope you're right, Smithy. We need this. He could give us what we need to charge Stiles—and maybe Streaker. When is the DA going to be there?"

"She's on her way as we speak. Gotta strike while the poker's hot. You wanna be there?"

"Damn straight I do. I'm on my way."

Axelrod skipped his morning shower, just splashed cold water on his face, slipped on some clothes, and headed out the door. He'd grab some coffee at the station, he decided. Before he left, he kissed his wife goodbye and made no promises to be home in time for dinner.

§

Matt dragged Camille's suitcase from the hall closet and plopped it down on her bed. As he stood there, she sneaked up behind him and wrapped her arms around his waist. He felt her kiss on his back. He turned around to draw her into his arms. His lips found hers.

"I can't believe I let you talk me into this, Matt."

"I want you to be somewhere safe."

"Are you sure your friends won't mind if I stay with them?"

"Positive. You'll like Brian and Kelly. Nice couple. And you'll like Savannah. Can't wait to show you around the place. Can you be ready to leave in about thirty minutes? We need to stop by my place so I can get the rest of my stuff."

"Matt, I can't go like this! I haven't showered or done my makeup. There's no way I'll be ready that soon. Why don't you just go to your apartment and I'll stay here to put myself together and finish packing. When you get back, we'll hit the road."

He shook his head. "No. I don't want to leave you alone. What if Jay comes back?"

"He won't. Besides it's only for a short time. You'll be back soon, right?"

"Camille, there's no way I'm leaving you alone."

"Look, this way we'll save time. Besides, I won't be alone. Tyler's coming over for coffee, so I can tell him goodbye." She paused when she heard a knock. "Hey, it's him now."

Tyler yawned as he walked in. He didn't bother to comb his hair or put on shoes. His clothes looked like he had slept in them. When Camille walked away and left the two men alone, Tyler's gaze stayed on Matt long enough to make him step back with discomfort.

"Your muscle tone and bone structure are amazing," Tyler said to him. "The perfect male specimen. Would you consider modeling for me? I have this painting in mind and you would—"

"No! Out of the question." Matt scowled and glanced down at his watch. "I gotta go. Look, Tyler, keep an eye Camille until I get back—except when she's in the shower."

Tyler grinned. "You got it, bro."

§

While Tyler made coffee, Camille jumped into the shower. She enjoyed the warmth of the water as much as the luxury of time to reflect on her future with Matt. But her happy thoughts were interrupted by a burst of noise. Her heart raced, fear spread throughout her body, making her shake. She stuck her head outside the shower curtain and strained to listen. She heard shouts, then a loud thud as if a heavy object had collided with a wall. An unfamiliar voice came next. It was deeper than Tyler's. *Oh, God! It's Jay! He's back! Please, God, no!*

CHAPTER THIRTY EIGHT

Axelrod arrived at the station and sat on the corner of his desk with a cup of strong coffee while Detective Smith rattled off his theory of Manny Sanchez's last hours. He explained to Axelrod, "The suspect, Hector Ramos, won't admit to anything yet, but we have a good idea how it went down. We think Sanchez was in the truck that wrecked on Highway 115. Here's the deal—he's illegal, doesn't want to get deported, so he takes off. Leaves the driver alone in the truck. He calls his buddy, Ramos, and tells him to come and pick him up. Sanchez must have told him about the money he had on him—that one grand. Ramos wants a cut. They argue and Ramos kills him either accidentally or on purpose. Anyway, he plunges a knife in his gut. Of course, at this point, it's only speculation, but here's what we think—he dumps the body, takes the loot, and drives back home."

"Damn that's cold."

"Yeah. Some friend, huh?"

They both turned to the doorway when the Assistant DA arrived. Marlene Hart was a no-nonsense prosecutor who favored pants suits over dresses. Like the others in his department, Axelrod respected her. Her solid record at convictions made detectives smile and defense lawyers cringe.

As she and Detective Smith entered the interview room, the suspect looked bored and stared up at ceiling tiles. On the monitor in another room, Axelrod watched as Ramos leaned his wooden chair back against the wall where it balanced precariously. In a new pair of Jordan Flight sneakers, his feet rested on the bottom rung.

"Ramos, sit up straight and listen to Mrs. Hart," Smith said.

Ramos abruptly put his chair in an upright position and tilted his chin up in defiance. It made Axelrod want to burst into the room and grab the arrogant bastard by the throat. They didn't have all day to play games. Even more frustrating was having to watch his lawyer sit at Ramos' side and advised him when to answer and when to keep his trap shut.

"I'm not saying another fucking word until I know what I'm charged with. I've got rights."

The lawyer straightened his tie and leaned forward. "Yes, exactly what is my client looking at?"

"Well, we have enough to charge him with first degree murder. V-CAT found," Hart started to say and then went on to explain for Ramos's benefit, "Our Violent Criminal Apprehension Team found merchandise and receipts that should total up to the amount taken from Sanchez's pockets. New flat screen TV, new Xbox, those nice sneakers your client is wearing. All that new stuff and you don't have a job, Ramos. See how it looks? And then there's the knife used to kill Mr. Sanchez."

The lawyer interjected, "You found *a* knife, not necessarily the murder weapon."

Hart leaned forward to look across the table into the eyes of the lawyer. She licked her lips and said, "Let me update you, Counselor. Sorry, I thought you were told. The knife has your client's prints on it and the victim's blood. We have enough to charge with first degree, but if Mr. Ramos can help us out with the other murder, we might consider a reduced charge, depending on his cooperation and if his story checks out."

Ramos shot back, "I'll still go to prison. What kind of fucking deal is that?"

Axelrod caught the hard stare Smith shot Ramos. The detective gripped the side of the table until his knuckles turned white. Smith spoke with soft measured words. "Perhaps, Mr. Ramos, we should use the plural—two murders. Maybe you were in on the first murder. Did you help Sanchez dispose of the body of Nick Morris?"

"Don't answer that!" the lawyer shouted to Ramos. "Detective, you know better. You're grasping at straws, making idle threats."

Smith leaned back, planted his hands flat on the table surface. "Okay, I retract my question." He looked at Ramos.

"You have two priors—breaking and entering as well as aggravated assault. Not exactly a Boy Scout. Whaddya bet we find your DNA on Sanchez's body, on his clothes. And what do you think the chances are we'll find Sanchez's fingerprints and blood inside the cab of your truck, the one that the crime scene guys are processing as we speak? Suppose your girlfriend has had enough of your bullshit, and she wants to talk with us. We could bring her in. So, here's the deal. We've got you cold. What's it gonna be? Life or fifteen-to-twenty years? Whaddya think? You do the math."

The attorney said, "May I have a moment in private with my client?"

They gave him fifteen minutes. Axelrod, Hart and Smith watched as Ramos stayed defiant, shaking his head to the advice given by his lawyer. At last, however, Ramos hung his head down and nodded. The lawyer waved everyone back into the room.

Once the chairs were scraped back to the table and everyone was seated, the lawyer said, "Go ahead, Hector. Tell them what Sanchez told you."

Ramos sat up straight and folded his arms across his chest. He smiled like a Cheshire cat and made them wait. "Well, first off, the man you asked me about—Jay Stiles—the guy Sanchez worked for—he didn't do it. Another guy shot that man. The cowboy shot him." He shrugged and then continued, "That's what Sanchez called him. One shot to the head from a distance. He said Morris knocked the gun out of that man's hand and then jumped on him. He tried to choke him. Would've killed him too except that cowboy blasted his brains out."

"Do you know what happened to the murder weapon?" Smith asked.

"Manny said the cowboy dude stopped on the middle of a bridge and tossed it. If you want to know what bridge, well, I can't help you there." Ramos locked eyes with the detective and smirked. "Think I could have a cold drink and a cigarette now? My lawyer said I could."

Again, Smith gripped the edge of the table. "Yeah, Ramos, we'll get you that drink and smoke. Then, we'll let the deputy escort you to the nice cell we have waiting for you. There you'll have a long time to think about what you did to your friend Manny."

CHAPTER THIRTY NINE

Matt did not hesitate to run the red light. After all, there were no oncoming cars and no police in sight. He rushed to get back to Camille. Although Tyler was with her, he didn't feel comfortable leaving her even for the hour that he was gone. The sooner they got out of town, the better.

When he arrived back at Camille's apartment, he found the door unlocked. Once inside, he almost tripped over Tyler as he lay in a fetal position on the floor. When he turned Tyler onto his back, he saw blood, lots of blood. There was an open gash in his side. Tyler opened his eyes and moaned.

"Tyler! What happened? Where is she?"

"She's gone. He took her."

Before Matt could question him further, Tyler lost consciousness. Matt stepped around him and rushed to the bedroom. If he got his hands on Jay Stiles, he'd kill him. He found a wet towel on the carpet next to the bed, her phone and purse still on the dresser. The suitcase Matt set out for her was open, left in chaos with clothes spilling out.

With his heart pounding, Matt dialed 911. Seconds later, he called Sergeant Brick. The detective assured him that there was already a BOLO for Jay's car, and now with the urgency to find Camille, every law enforcement officer in the county would be looking. He explained to Matt that police would immediately put a "net" around the entire county. Every major highway, the airport, and even the bus station would be put on alert.

Just as the ambulance left with Tyler, Detective Axelrod drove up. Still shaken and dazed, Matt was unaware of his presence until the detective cleared his throat. "Matt Garrison," he said and offered a handshake. "We met yesterday. Jake Axelrod with CMPD. Can you go over some details with me?"

Axelrod's request was reasonable, hell, necessary of course, but at the moment Matt wanted the detective out searching for Camille, time for talk later. He squeezed his eyes shut and envisioned a scared and panicked Camille. *Oh, God, keep her safe.*

"Tell me what happened here," Axelrod said to him.

Matt started with what he found when he returned to the apartment and then backtracked to Jay's appearance the previous night. Axelrod listened without interrupting, but a phone call put the interview on hold. He shot up from his seat and looked at Matt. To the caller, he said, "I'm en route." then, to Matt, "They found Jay's car. Gotta go."

"Is Camille there?"

He shook his head. "I've gotta go. We'll do this later."

"I'm coming with you."

"No. Stay here. I'll let you know."

Matt walked out with him. "I'm coming."

Axelrod did not have time to argue. He shrugged and gestured to his car. "Get in."

§

Streaker introduced himself as Wayne Johnson when he pulled Camille out of the shower. He forced her to get dressed. He watched with a salacious grin that made her both terrified and nauseous. As her hands trembled, she slipped on a pair of jeans and a knit top. Once she stepped into ballet flats, he poked her side with the barrel of a gun and pushed her forward, stepping over Tyler on the floor, out the front door, and into a truck.

On her back, stuffed on the floorboard between the front seat and the storage space of a Dodge Ram, she looked up at signs over the highway. They were headed west toward Gastonia and Kings Mountain on I-85. Her hands and feet were bound with duct tape. She wondered if the police were searching for her by now. As soon as Matt returned to her apartment, he'd call the police. She wondered if Streaker would kill her first and then go back for Jay, or if he would lure him to wherever they were going. Would she ever see Matt again? Was poor Tyler just wounded or was he dead? Not knowing the answers to her questions made her sick with worry.

"You won't get away with this!" she yelled. "They'll find you. I bet they're looking for me right now. Let me go before it's too late."

Camille repeated her spiel, urging him to set her free. To drown her out, he turned up the volume on the radio.

"Quit your yakking back there! Damn bitch!"

His phone shrieked with a ring tone turned up to full volume. It made her jump. He put the cell on speaker and turned down the radio. "Hey, baby," he said to the caller.

The voice on the other end said, "Streaker, what's going on? They're looking for you. I just heard it over the wire. What did you do? They've got it out that you're armed and dangerous."

"Shit! How did they know? Don't matter no how," he muttered. "Don't you worry, Samantha. I've got it under control."

Camille saw an opportunity she would not let get away. She screamed, "Help! Help! I've been kidnapped! Call police! Help!"

"Shut your damn mouth!" Streaker yelled back.

"Who is that? Where are you, Streak?" Samantha asked.

"Gotta go, baby."

Streaker tossed the phone onto the passenger seat and yelled, "Don't fuck with me, bitch! If you want to live, then don't fuck with me!"

§

The tires of the dark sedan Axelrod drove crunched over gravel in a parking lot adjacent to an abandoned pool hall. He was surprised to find Jay's car in a seedy part of town, miles away from his townhouse or office. With Matt in the passenger seat, he pulled up alongside a police cruiser and told Matt to stay in the car. But his order was ignored.

"Okay, but stay back," Axelrod told him.

A crowd of onlookers gathered since the 911 call was made by a woman who claimed to have seen the whole thing. The first responder, a rookie patrolman assigned to the Metro Division, got her statement and tried his best to secure the crime scene. Axelrod strolled up to the driver's side of the car where another patrolman stood sentry.

The patrolman stepped aside so Axelrod could have a look inside the car. He found Jay, lifeless with his head back, his eyes and mouth open. The once handsome, tanned face of the businessman was now pallid and gray, his lips purple. A gunshot wound coated his torso in blood. Because there was no spatter inside the car, Axelrod knew Jay had been shot elsewhere and then placed behind the wheel.

He backed away from the open door and said, "Where's the person who called it in?"

The patrolman pointed to a tiny black lady with a scarf tied around her head. Her pastel cotton dress hung loosely on her skeletal frame. She kept her bony fingers pressed against her mouth and shook her head back and forth, muttering something incomprehensible. Axelrod walked over to her and introduced himself.

"Ma'am, you saw what happened?"

"Yassir, I did. Sho' did."

"You saw the shooter?"

"Sho' did."

"So, you'd be able to recognize him if I showed you a photograph, right?"

Her only response was a blank stare, but he knew she heard his question. He pulled a photograph of Streaker from his coat pocket and held it up for her. "This picture is dated. The guy is older now. Do you recognize him? Is he the shooter?"

She leaned forward and took a quick peek. "Nah sir, not him."

"Are you sure? Take another look."

"I said no."

"What makes you so sure?"

"Because I knows the man." She lowered her head and mumbled, "Can't say his name though. He find out, I'd be dead before it get dark."

"Please, ma'am. I promise we'll protect you."

"You can't do no such thing." She waved her hand in dismissal, but after a long pause, she said, "Ah, I tells you anyway. It was Slick."

"The drug dealer that works this neighborhood?"

"Yassir, but don't say I be tellin' you dat."

Axelrod nodded a gesture of reassurance that was meaningless if Slick ever went to trial. He turned when Matt brushed past him, headed toward the Porsche. He delayed his next question for the witness while he studied Matt's reaction to the sight of the corpse in the driver's seat. Matt stepped back and covered his face with both hands, uttering some expletive.

When Axelrod went back to questioning the witness, Matt charged over and shouted, "Where is she? Whoever did this to him could have Camille. Do something, Detective!"

"Now hold on. Don't jump to any conclusions. This may have nothing to do with her." Axelrod turned back to the woman. "Ma'am, was there anyone else in the car?"

"Nassir, just that pretty white man."

"Detective!" Axelrod pivoted around in the direction of the voice. A patrolman walked up with a cell phone that he held out for Axelrod to see. "We found this in the bushes over there."

With latex gloves on, the young officer smashed buttons with his thumb and stared at the display. "Sweet! It's not locked. Four missed calls. Two messages. No code required to access voice mail." He pressed speaker and held the phone out so that Axelrod could hear the messages played.

Axelrod played the last message a second time, making sure he caught every word. He looked over at Matt and said, "We've just caught a break. Camille was taken by a guy named Streaker and we know where he has taken her."

CHAPTER FORTY

Samantha carried a burden that weighed her down like a sack of rocks. At least, that was the way she felt. At police headquarters, she walked outside and crossed the street to the Intake Facility where the Sheriff's Office processed anyone arrested. For a few minutes of peace and quiet, she sat out front on a retaining wall and stared out at the plush lawn with its canopy of giant oak trees.

Her thoughts were on Streaker. He had crossed a line, and because he had, he had put her in a tough spot. She had a decision to make and once she did, there would be no turning back. Loyalty or betrayal.

Streaker was his own worst enemy, she thought. He'd gotten caught up in a world of darkness and she'd watched his downward spiral and did nothing to stop it, just looked the other way. But this was different. She didn't know the identity of the woman that had screamed for help, but her conscience would no longer allow her to ignore the danger. She hopped down from the ledge and walked back to police headquarters.

In the homicide unit, Samantha sought out her good friend and occasional lunch buddy, Madge Bartley. Five years ago, they had worked together on a special task force. As the only women on the team, they bonded. Since then, they shared their frustrations and joys on every topic from their jobs to their personal lives. Once over drinks, Samantha revealed her secret to her friend. Not one to mince words, Madge told her that her intimate relationship with Streaker was not only risky, but stupid. She had never backed down from that assessment.

Although she might be setting herself up for another long lecture, Samantha rolled her shoulders back and took a deep breath. She found Madge at her desk doing a search for a suspect on the computer database.

Samantha cleared her throat to get her attention. "Have you got a minute, Madge?"

"No, but I'll make time. What's wrong?"

With eyes cast down, Samantha rolled a computer chair close to Madge and sank down in it like a person beaten down by troubles that never seemed to let up. In a low voice, she told her of her call to Streaker and the sound of a woman screaming in the background. When she finished, she exhaled a long breath.

"Madge, I know your objections to my relationship with Streaker, so save the sermon for another time. Right now, I need your help. Someone has got to stop him."

"Do you know why there's a BOLO for Streaker right now?"

"No, not really. I guess it has something to do with the woman screaming."

"He's a suspect in a murder case, Sam. After what you've just told me, we have no choice but to tell the lead investigator. The woman he grabbed is Camille Carson and they're desperate to find her."

Samantha kept her head down, her hands folded on her lap. "Okay. Who do we need to see?"

"Jake Axelrod."

They soon learned that he was out working the case, so Madge called him on his cell phone. She informed him that Camille had been taken by Streaker, and he was on the move. It was news Axelrod already had, but not about the vehicle Streaker was driving.

Madge told him, "It's a silver 2004 Dodge Ram registered to Samantha's husband, Lawrence Delaney. Don't know the license number." After no response other than static, she said, "A-Rod, did you hear me?"

"Yeah, I heard you, Madge. I'm thinking. We know where he's headed. He left a message for Stiles. He's taking her to the mountains near Bat Cave. We've notified the highway patrol and local police. Does Samantha know anything about a cabin where he's taking her?"

"Hang on." Madge held the phone against her chest and asked Samantha. She went back to her call. "Sam says his family owns the cabin. That's all she knows, but she wants to come. She thinks she can talk him into surrendering."

"I'm getting a team ready to head up there. If she wants to come, then she can hook up with us at the precinct."

After the call, Madge said to Samantha, "I'd go with you if I could, but I'm up to my neck in this other case."

"It's okay, Madge. I'll be fine."

"Call me."

As Samantha walked away she looked back over her shoulder. "Wish me luck."

"I'll do you one better, I'll say a prayer."

§

Matt was so pissed, he wanted to hit something, or somebody. Detective Axelrod refused to let him go along to find Camille. He was dropped off at police headquarters and told a policeman would take him back to his car at Camille's apartment. He was told not to even think of crossing the crime tape at her door. While he waited for some cop to drive him, he paced back and forth. With one hand on the back of his neck, he stared down at the floor. The more he thought about it, the more he justified what he was about to do. He called Danny.

"Don't talk, Danny. Just listen. You gotta pick me up at the police station. Now! I'll explain when you get here. I'll be out front. Hurry!"

Matt waited an agonizing fifteen minutes before Danny's truck pulled up along the curb. He jumped in and waved a forward motion. "Go, go, go! Camille's in trouble. We gotta get to her." Matt stared out the front windshield. "Get around that guy! Jesus, Danny! Don't drive like an old lady. Haul ass, man!"

Once he merged onto I-85, Danny said, "This is insane!"

"Just drive."

"Where are we headed?"

"Bat Cave."

"Sounds like a horror movie."

"It is, and we're in it."

§

Camille could tell that the truck had left asphalt and turned onto a bumpy road with more potholes than she could count. She felt every one as she remained hostage on the floorboard. As Streaker accelerated faster, the tires kicked up gravel. Overhead she could see the lush green of trees bowed over the road like a canopy. She figured they were deep in a forest, miles from any town. The jarring motion of the truck as it bounced along the primitive road ended when they came to an abrupt stop. Streaker killed the engine. Apparently, they had reached their destination. He got out and folded down the front seat.

When she met his gaze, he said, "Okay, darlin', we're here. I'll take the tape off your feet if you promise not to run."

"Where would I go? I don't have a clue where we are."

"This is paradise. My grandpappy's cabin in the woods. I hope you're a nature lover 'cause that's all we've got, sugar." Streaker pulled a knife from his pocket and cut away the tape around her ankles. "That better? Now hop on down and I'll give you a tour of the place. Maybe I'll take you around back and show you where the bodies are buried." Her eyes grew wide with fear. He stroked her cheek and threw back his head in laughter. "I'm just messing with you, darlin'."

As Streaker opened the front door, it gave an ominous groan. Camille found the cabin shrouded in darkness, curtains drawn. It smelled musty and damp. The wood floor spoke to her with each step, an eerie creaking as if beckoning her into an evil chamber of no return.

Streaker pushed her down into a ladder-back chair at the kitchen table. He rummaged through a drawer and found a roll of duct tape, which he used to bind her to the chair. He stepped back to admire his handiwork.

"There. You won't be going anywhere."

"What's the plan?"

"The plan is to get Jay to come up here to rescue you. You know, the knight in shining armor saves the damsel in distress. It's an old story, been around for centuries."

"I've got news for you. Jay and I are no longer together. I broke up with him."

"Did you know if you lie, your nose will grow longer?"

"It's true. He won't be coming."

"That's where you're wrong. He'd walk through fire for you, sweetheart. I've known him a long time. Never seen him so gaga over a woman before. 'Course I can't say I blame him."

"He told me that you killed Morris. He said you shot him in the back of the head."

"Yeah, that's right. To save his sorry ass. Somehow a bullet to the back of the head doesn't look much like self-defense. Know what I mean? Cops won't buy it." Streaker put his hands on his hips and shifted his weight from one foot to the other. "The problem is your boyfriend won't keep his mouth shut. He's been wanting to spill his guts ever since it happened. Thinks he can talk his way out of this mess. I have to get him out of town before he gets picked up again for questioning. That's why I'm forcing him to come here. If I have to hurt someone to convince him to shut his trap, then that's what I gotta do."

CHAPTER FORTY ONE

With his head down and one hand clamped over the nape of his neck, Streaker paced back and forth while Camille watched. She sensed his anxiety building as time went by with no call from Jay. He stopped momentarily to retrieve a cigarette from a half-empty pack that lay on the table. After he lit it, he exhaled a plume of smoke that floated up toward the ceiling and then dissipated.

"I told you. He's not coming," she said. "Jay and I broke up. He doesn't care what you do to me."

He drew deeply on the cigarette and then blew smoke in her face. She squeezed her eyes shut and turned her head sideways.

"You're lying, princess. I've been using you as a threat to keep that boy in line for weeks. He knows I mean business. He's going to fucking show up here. Just you wait, you'll see."

"And if he doesn't, then what?"

He smirked at her, then said, "We'll cross that bridge when we get there. If he doesn't show, then you might be right. I can do whatever I want with you, princess. Should be fun."

His threat and his proximity made her heart pound. He looked pleased that she was frightened, letting out a chuckle before he stepped back. She twisted her hands behind her back to loosen the tape but to no avail.

"I don't understand," she said with a voice that trembled. "Jay told me you're a former cop, so you know the law. So, why did you get mixed up in this?"

"It was just a business deal, if it's any of your damn business. Money. I did it for money, why else? Hell, I didn't even know that guy—Morris. I thought if I didn't help Jay, he'd botch the whole fucking thing, go to prison for life. Now, I've gotta explain some things to him. There's still a chance we'll both get out of this mess."

"I don't think so," she said, shaking her head. "It's over. It's too late. Kidnapping me will only makes things worse."

Streaker lunged forward, eyes wide and full of rage. With hands on the sides of the chair, he tilted it back and put his face inches from hers. She feared the chair would tip over, but he kept a firm grip and used all his strength to keep it upright.

"You shut the fuck up, bitch! I'm tired of your shit, so don't say another word. You hear me? I'll smack you the next time you open your mouth. Understand?" She stared back, frozen in fear. "I said—do you understand me?"

She nodded hard enough to rattle her brain. If she was going to make it through the ordeal, she had to calm down. She clung to the hope that Matt had called the police when he found out she was gone. But would they know it was Streaker who had taken her and where? The place was isolated, maybe miles from civilization.

There was no trail of bread crumbs to mark their way. She hoped Tyler was alive although she wasn't sure. If he was, then maybe he saw something, or heard something, a simple clue for the police. She wondered when help would come, if at all. Would she even be alive when they did show up? She closed her eyes and whispered a prayer.

A thumping sound came from outside. A creak of wooden boards. Footsteps that stopped short. Streaker waved his hand in a downward motion as a signal for Camille to stay quiet. He shuffled sideways and inched closer to the door.

The door burst open with a bang, hitting the wall. Like a huge boulder, a dark figure was silhouetted in the expanse of the doorway, the sunlight behind him. The fear that Camille had shown was now transferred to Streaker. His jaw was clenched tight, a vein on his forehead throbbed.

Indeed Camille had prayed, but she was certain that the man in the doorway was not the answer to her prayers.

§

Detective Axelrod knew Streaker expected Jay at any moment. It was to their advantage that he continue to think that. Since the cell phone had been discovered, Streaker had left one more message for Jay which Axelrod retrieved. This time Streaker sounded insistent that Jay call back. His tone was agitated, stressed.

"Hang on, buddy, we're coming," Axelrod mumbled to himself from the front seat of the unmarked police car.

He let Hutch drive while he gave directions. Samantha sat in the back, pensive as she stared out at the passing scenery. Axelrod took in the same view of a winding brook with clear water rippling over rocks. He reflected on the irony of the peaceful setting that masked the danger up ahead.

The sheriff from Henderson County met them on the outskirts of town on Highway 64. Since Sheriff Branson grew up in the area, he knew exactly where to find the cabin. They followed his lead. In addition, they were joined by a SWAT team in a BearCat, an armored military-style vehicle, and two police cruisers with deputies from Henderson County. In a motorcade fashion, they drove with a sense of urgency, lights flashing, but no siren. Except for SWAT in the BearCat, the group parked off the main road. They planned to hike the rest of the way through the forest and then surround the cabin.

§

It was decided that Samantha, with Axelrod close by, would approach first. When ordered to wear a protective vest, she protested.

"Okay, okay. I'll wear the damn thing. Shit, it will make me look more like the enemy than a friend. It's bad enough that I'm setting him up for what could be an ambush."

"Think of it this way, Sam," Axelrod said. "You're saving that woman's life and maybe his, too."

Together they inched up to the front door. The eerie silence made Samantha swallow hard. She expected to see Streaker peeking out a window. To her surprise, the front door was cracked open, but only enough to show dark walls, no sign of movement. With one hand, she pushed the opening wider, but did not enter.

"Streaker, are you there? Streak. It's me. Samantha. Answer me."

There was no response. She looked over at Axelrod who held his palms out to his side in a gesture of puzzlement. He pointed his index and middle finger at his eyes and then waved his hand to the right. She understood his signal. He would go around to the side window and peek inside. She waited.

When he returned, he said, "Nothing. I see nothing."

"I'm going in," she said.

"I'll cover you."

She gave him a smirk. "He's not going to shoot me."

Axelrod shrugged as she brushed past him. Not knowing what she would find beyond the door put her on edge and on guard. She walked through the living room and headed toward the rear of the house where she found the kitchen. On the counter, she recognized her husband's keychain. Only a day ago, she had handed over his truck keys to Streaker. At the time, she feared he might sneak a smoke inside the cab. She never imagined he would do something far worse.

Beyond the counter she saw a chair knocked to the floor on its side. A woman was taped to it. Her hair, streaked with blood, covered her face. The stillness of the body made Samantha pause with dread. She got down on her knees and pushed back blond locks. With a sigh of relief, she found that the woman was alive. The blood came from a cut on her temple.

When Axelrod came up, Samantha said, "Is this Camille—the woman we're looking for?"

"Yes, has to be," he answered. "She fits the description."

Samantha pressed her lips together and nodded. She said, "Camille, are you okay?"

Camille's eyes open into narrow slits. "Uh-huh. I'm okay."

After he pulled a knife from his pocket, Axelrod squatted down and cut the tape to free her. He said, "Where's Streaker?"

"I don't know," Camille answered in a weak voice.

"Did he do this to you? Your head? Did he do that?"

"No. Another man—big—black. He hit me. They went outside." She pointed to the back door that led onto a deck. "I heard shots."

Axelrod stood up and said, "I'm going out back. Stay with her, Sam."

"No way. I'm coming with you. Gotta find Streaker."

He gave her a stern look, but conceded with a nod. Motioning to a deputy at the front door, he said, "Stay with her, and call EMS. She's hurt."

Axelrod and Samantha walked out onto the deck. At first, they saw nothing out of the ordinary until they looked back at the house and saw blood spatter. A single shot had splintered the rough wood siding. Axelrod used a pocket knife to extract the lodged bullet.

Between his fingers he examined it. "Looks like a twenty-two."

"Streaker carries a small handgun in his boot, a .22 caliber," Samantha said.

"Then I think he shot Slick." Axelrod looked down at a trail of blood that led down the steps. "Probably just a flesh wound. Looks like they went out in the yard."

"Yeah, I can see that, but where are they now?"

Axelrod shrugged. "Beats me. Let's see if we can find out."

As they walked down the deck steps, Samantha pointed to a bloody handprint on the railing. "I hope that belongs to Slick and not Streaker."

CHAPTER FORTY TWO

The deputy helped Camille sit up, but made her stay on the floor until the paramedics arrived. She closed her eyes and replayed flashes of her ordeal, as if she was watching a re-run of a movie.

She remembered the look of horror and surprise on Streaker's face the minute the big black man appeared in the doorway. The man Streaker called Slick stomped into the house like an angry bear, his hands swinging away from his body with each step. One hand held a gun with a long barrel. Shiny and menacing. He brought it up and pointed it right at Streaker.

"Now hold on, Slick," she recalled Streaker saying.

"I'm gonna kill you, asshole," Slick had shouted. "You think you can mess with me? I'll show you what I do to motherfuckers like you. I'm going to put a bullet through your brain, you fucking piece of cop-shit."

At that point, Camille had broken into tears of hysteria. She remembered shaking and pleading with the man. "Please, don't kill us. Please, please. I don't want to die."

"Shut up, bitch! Just keep your trap shut!"

But Camille continued to plead for her life. Approaching her, Slick jabbed the gun under her chin hard enough to make her wince in pain. Again, he shouted at her, "Shut the fuck up!"

"Please, don't do this," she said, squeezing her eyes shut.

He used the back of his hand to smack her across the face, tipping the chair over while she was still taped to it. She felt something sharp stab her head, and when the force knocked the object across the floor, she discovered that it was a garden spade.

"Leave her alone!" Streaker had shouted. When Slick blocked his path, preventing him from coming to her aid, he said, "She's got nothing to do with this."

"She's here, ain't she?" Slick said. "That your whore? All tied up like that." Slick snorted out a snicker. "Whatcha fixin' to do? Some kind of sex bondage game? You're a piece of perverted shit, Streaker, you know that? I kinda like it, though. Can I watch? Then I'll get in on the fun."

"Let's take this outside, Slick. C'mon, man. Away from the girl. Whaddya say?"

Camille pictured in her mind how Streaker had walked backwards toward the door as Slick pointed the gun at him. With his eyes still on the black man, Streaker reached behind his back for the doorknob and turned it slowly. He stepped out, still keeping his eyes on Slick.

Only seconds later, Camille had heard two shots—pow! pow! She had managed to work her way over to see outside the storm door. Streaker held up a gun, smoke coming from its barrel. She committed to memory the sight of Slick stumbling forward and holding his hand over his shoulder, grunting. He fired and hit Streaker in the leg. However, Streaker managed to make it down the steps and into the yard. That was her last sighting of him. She remembered how she had jumped when the shot ripped into Streaker's leg and the look in his eyes as if saying to Slick: *I can't believe you did that!*

For the first time in hours, she felt a sense of relief as if she had cheated death. In the moments after the men stepped outside, she whispered another prayer that help would come soon. Time passed, but she didn't know if it was just minutes or hours, but at last, her prayers were answered.

The deputy held a glass of water to her lips and told her to drink slowly. Her throat was parched, and she thought it was the best water she had ever tasted.

§

When the sheriff walked over next to Samantha, Axelrod said to him, "Any other buildings around here? Any neighbors?"

"There's a shed behind that grove of trees, and there's another cabin a quarter mile down the road. If he's there, he might have taken the old couple hostage. Hope not. They're nice folks."

They split into teams of two and spread out. When the sheriff and Axelrod headed toward the shed, they heard a loud blast. Gunfire! The SWAT team crouched down and fanned out around the property. Two team members hustled over to Axelrod and waved their arms to signal to the right.

"It came from the shed. Straight ahead!"

"Go, go, go!" Axelrod shouted at them. Still in a crouched position, four guys went left and four went right. They surrounded the wooden building and held their positions. An officer kicked the flimsy door open with his boot. Light flooded inside and revealed a body in a supine position in the middle of the shed. It was too still to confirm life. The legs stretched out in front with the toes of Western boots pointed outward. A hand held a gun. The weapon rested on the man's chest in a pool of blood, his finger still on the trigger. A cloud of smoke from the fired weapon floated upward in a beam of sunlight.

Samantha pushed past the others to kneel beside the figure. "Streaker. Oh, Streak." Tears ran down her cheeks. His eyes stayed on her as if no one else mattered. She choked on her words. "Streak, what happened?"

"Hi, baby. Hoped you'd hear my shot." She saw blood spurt and bubble up onto his shirt. It was clear that he would bleed out, but before that happened she needed answers.

"Who, Streak? Who did this?"

"Slick. He got his revenge. You warned me—shudda listened." His breathing was shallow, his voice raspy. He tried to smile. "The girl. She okay?" Samantha nodded. "Good. Never planned to hurt her." After he coughed up blood, he smacked his lips together. "Sam, I've always loved you."

"I know." Her vision was obscured by tears. She brushed them away and reached for his hand. She squeezed it gently and whispered, "Don't leave me, Streak. Please. Try to hang on."

"Sorry, baby. Sorry for everything. Bad choices."

She heard his last gasp for breath. His eyes glazed over. He died looking at her. She put her head down and wept. Her tears splattered onto his blood-soaked shirt as she stayed on her knees at his side. A hand was placed on her shoulder. She brushed it off and continued to cry, folded over his body.

Axelrod pulled her away. "Come on, Sam. It's over. There's nothing you can do for him now."

§

Just as Danny parked his truck along with the others on the highway, he and Matt heard the gunshot. They sprinted up the hill and through the trees as fast as their legs would carry them. Once the cabin was spotted, they didn't stop, but made a mad scramble onto the front porch. Matt was first through the door. He called out to Camille.

He found her on the floor, sitting upright with the help of a deputy. When she heard Matt's voice, she turned in his direction. Although he saw blood on one side of her face, he sighed with relief. He rushed over and got down on his knees to bring her into his arms. The deputy tried to hold him back.

"Careful. She's injured. Paramedics are on their way."

"Camille, are you okay? I was so scared."

"I'm okay. How did you know where to find me?"

"The detective told me. He found Jay's cell phone. Streaker left a message that said he took you here and told Jay to come get you. If it wasn't for the cell phone, we wouldn't know."

"Jay? Where's Jay?"

"Don't worry about him, baby."

"What about Tyler?"

"He's going to make it. Got a stab wound in the side, but he's okay."

"Thank God!" She locked eyes with Matt and said, "We were going to Savannah."

He gave a weak smile. "We'll get there, we'll get there. Don't worry about that."

CHAPTER FORTY THREE

The memorial service for Jay filled the sanctuary and the balcony of the First Presbyterian Church downtown. Despite the disturbing circumstances of his death, friends, business associates, and family mourned his loss. Only his accomplishments and his successes were mentioned. From the last pew, Camille clutched Matt's hand throughout the service. She expressed her sympathies to his mother and father and then asked Matt to take her away.

He took her to Savannah. By the time they arrived, the sunset had painted the sky in hues of peach and red melded with clouds of magenta. They stood on a nearby beach, facing out at the ocean. As they took in the view, Matt wrapped his arms around her and pressed his lips against the back of her head. At the water's edge, the surf lapped over their bare feet.

Matt said, "I want us to make a home here, Camille. You and me. Leave all that mess behind us. Start fresh."

"I want that too, Matt. I can have my business here. It's a charming place. Actually, I'd be happy anywhere with you." She turned around to poke her finger into his chest. With a playful smile, she said, "I'm glad I finally pulled that secret out of you."

"What secret?"

"That you love me."

"Oh, that." He kissed her lightly. "Yes, I love you completely."

"And I love you." She smiled. "I'm glad we got *that* cleared up."

"Just in the nick of time, too. I was going to leave for Savannah and forget you."

"Garrison, I don't think you would've ever forgotten me, do you?"

He smiled and shook his head. "Nope. How could I forget the beautiful blonde I picked up in a bar?"

§

Two days later, Axelrod summoned for Samantha. When she showed up, he rose from his desk chair and put his hand on her shoulder. "I just wanted to know if you're okay."

"I'm okay. No matter what you hear, Axe, Streaker was once a good cop, a good person. He just lost his way." She wiped a tear from her eye.

"Yep, a good person who made bad choices. It happens."

"You know, Streaker did us a favor by putting a bullet in Slick's shoulder. All we had to do was follow the blood trail, and there he was, passed out cold on the ground." She smiled her pleasure. "Now he'll go away for life. Two counts of murder."

"Yeah, one more drug dealer off the street."

"Well, I need to head back. Over in vice, we have a whole shitload of scumbags to get off the streets. You know what we are, Axe? We're street cleaners. We're nothing but street cleaners."

"Yeah. I think you're right." From a corner, he picked up a push broom and pretended to put it to use. It made her laugh through her tears.

THE END.